EXCURSIONS.

BY

HENRY D. THOREAU.

AUTHOR OF "WALDEN," AND "A WEEK ON THE CONCORD AND
MERRIMACK RIVERS."

BOSTON:

TICKNOR AND FIELDS.

1866.

CONTENTS.

Henry David Thoreau (see name pronunciation; July 12, 1817 – May 6, 1862) was an American essayist, poet, philosopher, abolitionist, naturalist, tax resister, development critic, surveyor, and historian. A leading transcendentalist, Thoreau is best known for his book Walden, a reflection upon simple living in natural surroundings, and his essay "Civil Disobedience" (originally published as "Resistance to Civil Government"), an argument for disobedience to an unjust state.

Thoreau's books, articles, essays, journals, and poetry amount to more than 20 volumes. Among his lasting contributions are his writings on natural history and philosophy, in which he anticipated the methods and findings of ecology and environmental history, two sources of modern-day environmentalism. His literary style interweaves close observation of nature, personal experience, pointed rhetoric, symbolic meanings, and historical lore, while displaying a poetic sensibility, philosophical austerity, and Yankee attention to practical detail.He was also deeply interested in the idea of survival in the face of hostile elements, historical change, and natural decay; at the same time he advocated abandoning waste and illusion in order to discover life's true essential needs.He was a lifelong abolitionist, delivering lectures that attacked the Fugitive Slave Law while praising the writings of Wendell Phillips and defending the abolitionist John Brown. Thoreau's philosophy of civil disobedience later influenced the political thoughts and actions of such notable figures as Leo Tolstoy, Mahatma Gandhi, and Martin Luther King Jr.[citation needed]

Thoreau is sometimes referred to as an anarchist. Though "Civil Disobedience" seems to call for improving rather than abolishing government—"I ask for, not at once no government, but at once a better government"the direction of this improvement points toward anarchism: "'That government is best which governs not at all;' and when men are prepared for it, that will be the kind of government which they will have."…

Ralph Waldo Emerson (May 25, 1803 – April 27, 1882) was an American essayist, lecturer, and poet who led the transcendentalist movement of the mid-19th century. He was seen as a champion of individualism and a prescient critic of the countervailing pressures of society, and he disseminated his thoughts through dozens of published essays and more than 1,500 public lectures across the United States.

Emerson gradually moved away from the religious and social beliefs of his contemporaries, formulating and expressing the philosophy of transcendentalism in his 1836 essay "Nature". Following this work, he gave a speech entitled "The American Scholar" in 1837, which Oliver Wendell Holmes Sr. considered to be America's "intellectual Declaration of Independence". Emerson wrote most of his important essays as lectures first and then revised them for print. His first two collections of essays, Essays: First Series (1841) and Essays: Second Series (1844), represent the core of his thinking. They include the well-known essays "Self-Reliance", "The Over-Soul", "Circles", "The Poet" and "Experience". Together with "Nature", these essays made the decade from the mid-1830s to the mid-1840s Emerson's most fertile period.

Emerson wrote on a number of subjects, never espousing fixed philosophical tenets, but developing certain ideas such as individuality, freedom, the ability for mankind to realize almost anything, and the relationship between the soul and the surrounding world. Emerson's "nature" was more philosophical than naturalistic: "Philosophically considered, the universe is composed of Nature and the Soul". Emerson is one of several figures who "took a more pantheist or pandeist approach by rejecting views of God as separate from the world."

He remains among the linchpins of the American romantic movement, and his work has greatly influenced the thinkers, writers and poets that followed him. When asked to sum up his work, he said his central doctrine was "the infinitude of the private man." Emerson is also well known as a mentor and friend of Henry David Thoreau, a fellow transcendentalist.

BIOGRAPHICAL SKETCH.

BY R. W. EMERSON.

HENRY DAVID THOREAU was the last male de scendant of a French ancestor who came to this country from the Isle of Guernsey. His character exhibited occasional traits drawn from this blood in singular com bination with a very strong Saxon genius.

He was born in Concord, Massachusetts, on the 12th of July, 1817. He was graduated at Harvard College in 1837, but without any literary distinction. An icon oclast in literature, he seldom thanked colleges for their service to him, holding them in small esteem, whilst yet his debt to them was important. After leaving the University, he joined his brother in teaching a private school, which he soon renounced. His father was a manufacturer of lead-pencils, and Henry applied him self for a time to this craft, believing he could make a better pencil than was then in use. After completing his experiments, he exhibited his work to chemists and artists in Boston, and having obtained their certificates to its excellence and to its equality with the best Lon don manufacture, he returned home contented. His friends congratulated him that he had now opened his way to fortune. But he replied, that he should never

make another pencil. " Why should I ? I would not do again what I have done once." He resumed his endless walks and miscellaneous studies, making every day some new acquaintance with Nature, though as yet never speaking of zoology or botany, since, though very studious of natural facts, he was incurious of technical and textual science.

At this time, a strong, healthy youth, fresh from col lege, whilst all his companions were choosing their pro fession, or eager to begin some lucrative employment, it was inevitable that his thoughts should be exercised on the same question, and it required rare decision to refuse all the accustomed paths, and keep his solitary freedom at the cost of disappointing the natural expectations of his family and friends: all the more difficult that he had a perfect probity, was exact in securing his own independence, and in holding every man to the like duty. But Thoreau never faltered. He was a born protestant. He declined to give up his large ambition of knowledge and action for any narrow craft or profes sion, aiming at a much more comprehensive calling, the art of living well. If he slighted and defied the opin ions of others, it was only that he was more intent to reconcile his practice with his own belief. Never idle or self-indulgent, he preferred, when he wanted money, earning it by some piece of manual labor agreeable to him, as building a boat or a fence, planting, grafting, surveying, or other short work, to any long engage ments. "With his hardy habits and few wants, his skill in wood-craft, and his powerful arithmetic, he was very competent to live in any part of the world. It would

cost him less time to supply his wants than another. He was therefore secure of his leisure.

A natural skill for mensuration, growing out of his mathematical knowledge, and his habit of ascertaining the measures and distances of objects which interested him, the size of trees, the depth and extent of ponds and rivers, the height of mountains, and the air-line distance of his favorite summits, — this, and his inti mate knowledge of the territory about Concord, made him drift into the profession of land-surveyor. It had the advantage for him that it led him continually into new and secluded grounds, and helped his studies of Nature. His accuracy and skill in this work were» readily appreciated, and he found all the employment ' he wanted.

He could easily solve the problems of the surveyor, j but he was daily beset with graver questions, which he manfully confronted. He interrogated every custom, and wished to settle all his practice on an ideal founda tion. He was a protestant a Fentrance, and few lives contain so many renunciations. He was bred to no profession; he never married ; he lived alone; he never went to church ; he never voted ; lie refused to pay a tax to the State ; he ate no flesh, he drank no wine, he never knew the use of tobacco ; and, though a natural ist, he used neither trap nor gun. He chose, wisely, no doubt, for himself, to be the bachelor of thought and Nature. He had no talent for wealth, and knew how to be poor without the least hint of squalor or inele gance. Perhaps he fell into his way of living without forecasting it much, but approved it with Liter wisdom,

" I am often reminded," he wrote in his journal, " that, if I had bestowed on me the wealth of Croesus, my aims must be still the same, and my means essentially the same." He had no temptations to fight against, — no appetites, no passions, no taste for elegant trifles. A fine house, dress, the manners and talk of highly culti vated people were all thrown away on him. He much preferred a good Indian, and considered these refine ments as impediments to conversation, wishing to meet his companion on the simplest terms. He declined invi tations to dinner-parties, because there each was in every one's way, and he could not meet the individuals to any purpose. " They make their pride," he said, " in mak ing their dinner cost much ; I make my pride in making my dinner cost little." When asked at table what dish he preferred, he answered, " The nearest." He did not like the taste of wine, and never had a vice in his life. He said, — "I have a faint recollection of pleasure derived from smoking dried lily-stems, before I was a man. I had commonly a supply of these. I have never smoked anything more noxious."

He chose to be rich by making his wants few, and supplying them himself. In his travels, he used the railroad only to get over so much country as was unim portant to the present purpose, walking hundreds of miles, avoiding taverns, buying a lodging in farmers' and fishermen's houses, as cheaper, and more agreeable to him, and because there he could better find the men and the information he wanted.

There was somewhat military in his nature not to be subdued, always manly and able, but rarely tender, as

if he did not feel himself except in opposition. He wanted a fallacy to expose, a blunder to pillory, I may say required a little sense of victory, a roll of the drum, to call his powers into full exercise. It cost him noth ing to say No; indeed, he found it much easier than to say Yes. It seemed as if his first instinct on hearing a proposition was to controvert it, so impatient was he of the limitations of our daily thought. This habit, of course, is a little chilling to the social affections ; and though the companion would in the end acquit him of any malice or untruth, yet it mars conversation. Hence, no equal companion stood in affectionate relations with one so pure and guileless. "I love Henry," said one of his friends, u but I cannot like him ; and as for taking his arm, I should as soon think of taking the arm of an elm-tree."

Yet, hermit and stoic as he was, he was really fond of sympathy, and threw himself heartily and childlike into the company of young people whom he loved, and whom he delighted to entertain, as he only could, witli the varied and endless anecdotes of his experiences by field and river. And lie was always ready to lead a huckleberry party or a search for chestnuts or grapes. Talking, one day, of a public discourse, Henry remarked, that whatever succeeded with the audience was bad. I said, u Who would not like to write something which all can read, like ' Robinson Crusoe' ? and w r ho does not see with regret that his page is not solid with a right materialistic treatment, which delights everybody ? Henry objected, of course, and vaunted the better lec tures which reached only a few persons. But, at sup-

per, a young girl, understanding that he was to lecture at the Lyceum, sharply asked him, " whether his lecture would be a nice, interesting story, such as she wished to hear, or whether it was one of those old philosophical things that she did not care about." Henry turned to her, and bethought himself, and, I saw, was trying to believe that he had matter that might fit her and her brother, who were to sit up and go to the lecture, if it was a good one for them.

He was a speaker and actor of the truth, — born such, — and was ever running into dramatic situations from this cause. In any circumstance, it interested all bystanders to know what part Henry would take, and what he would say ; and he did not disappoint expec tation, but used an original judgment on each emer gency. In 1845 he built himself a small framed house on the shores of Walden Pond, and lived there two years alone, a life of labor and study. This action was

' quite native and fit for him. No one who knew him would tax him with affectation. He was more unlike

--his neighbors in his thought than in his action. As soon as he had exhausted the advantages of that solitude, he abandoned it. In 1847, not approving some uses to which the public expenditure was applied, he refused to pay his town tax, and was put in jail. A friend paid the tax for him, and he was released. The like annoy ance was threatened the next year. But, as his friends paid the tax, notwithstanding his protest, I believe he ceased to resist. No opposition or ridicule had any weight with him. He coldly and fully stated his opinion without affecting to believe that it was the opinion of

the company. It was of no consequence, if every one present held the opposite opinion. On one occasion he went to the University Library to procure some books. The librarian refused to lend them. Mr. Thoreau re paired to the President, who stated to him the rules and usages, which permitted the loan of books to resident graduates, to clergymen who were alumni, and to some others resident within a circle of ten miles' radius from the College. Mr. Thoreau explained to the President that the railroad had destroyed the old scale of distances, — that the library was useless, yes, and President and College useless, on the terms of his rules, — that the one benefit he owed to the College was its library, — that, at this moment, not only his want of books was imperative, but he wanted a large number of books, and assured him that he, Thoreau, and not the librarian, was the proper custodian of these. In short, the Presi dent found the petitioner so formidable, and the rules getting to look so ridiculous, that he ended by giving him a privilege which in his hands proved unlimited thereafter.

No truer American existed than Thoreau. His pref erence of his country and condition was genuine, and his aversation from English and European manners and tastes almost reached contempt. He listened im patiently to news or ban mots gleaned from London circles ; and though he tried to be civil, these anecdotes fatigued him. The men were all imitating each other, and on a small mould. Why can they not live as far apart as possible, and each be a man by himself? What he sought was the most energetic nature ; and he wished

to go to Oregon, not to London. "In every part of Great Britain," he wrote in his diary, " are discovered traces of the Romans, their funereal urns, their camps, their roads, their dwellings. But New England, at least, is not based on any Roman ruins. We have not to lay the foundations of our houses on the ashes of a former civilization."

But, idealist as he was, standing for abolition of sla very, abolition of tariffs, almost for abolition of govern ment, it is needless to say he found himself not only un represented in actual politics, but almost equally opposed to every class of reformers. Yet he paid the tribute of his uniform respect to the Anti-Slavery Party. One man, whose personal acquaintance he had formed, he -honored with exceptional regard. Before the first friendly word had been spoken for Captain John Brown, after the arrest, he sent notices to most houses in Concord, that he would speak in a public hall on the condition and character of John Brown, on Sunday evening, and invited all people to come. The Repub lican Committee, the Abolitionist Committee, sent him word that it was premature and not advisable. He replied, — "I did not send to you for advice, but to announce that I am to speak." The hall was filled at an early hour by people of all parties, and his earnest eulogy of the hero was heard by all respectfully, by many with a sympathy that surprised themselves.

It was said of Plotinus that he was ashamed of his body, and 'tis very likely he had good reason for it, — that his body was a bad servant, and he had not skill in dealing with the material world, as happens often to

men of abstract intellect. But Mr. Thoreau was equipped with a most adapted and serviceable body. He was of short stature, firmly built, of light com plexion, with strong, serious blue eyes, and a grave aspect, — his face covered in the late years with a be coming beard. His senses were acute, his frame well-knit and hardy, his hands strong and skilful in the use of tools. And there was a wonderful fitness of body and mind. He could pace sixteen rods more accurately than another man could measure them with rod and chain. He could find his path in the woods at night, he said, better by his feet than his eyes. He could esti mate the measure of a tree veiy well by his eyes ; he could estimate the weight of a calf or a pig, like a dealer. From a box containing a bushel or more of loose pen cils, he could take up with his hands fast enough just a dozen pencils at every grasp. He was a good swimmer, runner, skater, boatman, and would probably outwalk most countrymen in a day's journey. And the relation of body to mind was still finer than we have indicated. He said he wanted every stride his legs made. The length of his walk uniformly made the length of his writing. If shut up in the house, he did not write at all. He had a strong common sense, like that which Rose Flammock, the weaver's daughter, in Scott's romance, commends in her father, as resembling a yardstick, which, whilst it measures dowlas and diaper, can equally well measure tapestry and cloth of gold. He had always a new resource. When I was planting forest-trees, and had procured half a peck of acorns, he said that only a small portion of them would be sound, and .proceeded

to examine them, and select the sound ones. But find ing this took time, he said, " I think, if you put them all into water, the good ones will sink ;" which experiment we tried with success. He could plan a garden, or a house, or a barn ; would have been competent to lead a - " Pacific Exploring Expedition " ; could give judicious counsel in the gravest private or public affairs.

He lived for the day, not cumbered and mortified by his memory. If he brought you yesterday a new propo sition, he would bring you to-day another not less revo lutionary. A very industrious man, and setting, like all highly organized men, a high value on his time, he (Seemed the only man of leisure in town, always ready for any excursion that promised well, or for conversation ,' prolonged into late hours. His trenchant sense was never stopped by his rules of daily prudence, but was always up to the new occasion. He liked and used the simplest food, yet, when some one urged a vegetable diet, Thoreau thought all diets a very small matter, saying that " the man who shoots the buffalo lives better than the man who boards at the Graham House." He said, — " You can sleep near the railroad, and never be dis turbed : Nature knows very well what sounds are worth attending to, and has made up her mind not to hear the railroad-whistle. But things respect the devout mind, and a mental ecstasy was never interrupted." He noted, what repeatedly befell him, that, after receiving from a distance a rare plant, he would presently find the same in his own haunts. And those pieces of luck which happen only to good players happened to him. One day, walking with a stranger, who inquired where In

dian arrow-heads could be found, lie replied, " Every where," and, stooping forward, picked one on the instant from the ground. At Mount Washington, in Tucker-man's Ravine, Thoreau had a bad fall, and sprained his foot. As he was in the act of getting up from his fall, he saw for the first time the leaves of the Arnica mollis.

His robust common sense, armed with stout hands, keen perceptions, and strong will, cannot yet account for the superiority Avhich shone in his simple and hid den life. I must add the cardinal fact, that there was an excellent wisdom in him, proper to a rare class of -men, which showed him the material world as a means and symbol. This discovery, which sometimes yields to poets a certain casual and interrupted light, serving for the ornament of their writing, was in him an un sleeping insight; and whatever faults or obstructions of temperament might cloud it, he was not disobedient to the heavenly vision. In his youth, he said, one day, " The other world is all my art: my pencils will draw no other; my jack-knife will cut nothing else ; I do not use it a.s a means." This was the muse and genius that ruled his opinions, conversation, studies, work, and course of life. This made him a searching judge of men. At first glance he measured his companion, and,N though insensible to some fine traits of culture, could-very well report his weight and calibre. And this, made the impression of genius which his conversation! often gave.

He understood the matter in hand at a glance, and saw the limitations and poverty of those he talked 2

with, so that nothing seemed concealed from such ter rible eyes. I have repeatedly known young men of sensibility converted in a moment to the belief that this was the man they were in search of, the man of men, who could tell them all they should do. His own deal ing with them was never affectionate, but superior, didactic, — scorning their petty ways, — very slowly conceding, or not conceding at all, the promise of his society at their houses, or even at his own.

" Would he not walk with them ? " " He did not know. There was nothing so important to him as his walk ; he had no walks to throw away on company." Visits were offered him from respectful parties, but he declined them. Admiring friends offered to carry him at their own cost to the Yellow-Stone River, — to the West Indies, — to South America. But though nothing could be more grave or considered than his refusals, they remind one in quite new relations of that fop Brum-mel's reply to the gentleman who offered him his car riage in a shower, " But where will you ride, then ? " — and what accusing silences, and what searching and irresistible speeches, battering down all defences, his companions can remember!

Mr. Thoreau dedicated his genius with such entire love to the fields, hills, and waters of his native town, that he made them known and interesting to all reading Americans, and to people over the sea. The river on whose banks he was born and died he knew from its springs to its confluence with the Merrimack. He had made summer and winter observations on it for many years, and at every hour of the day and the night.

The result of the recent survey of the Water Com missioners appointed by the State of Massachusetts he had reached by his private experiments, several years earlier. Every fact which occurs in the bed, on the banks, or in the air over it; the fishes, and their spawn ing and nests, their manners, their food ; the shad-flics which fill the air on a certain evening once a year, and which are snapped at by the fishes so ravenously that many of these die of repletion ; the conical heaps of small stones on the river-shallows, one of which heaps will sometimes overfill a cart, — these heaps the huge nests of small fishes; the birds which frequent the stream, heron, duck, sheldrake, loon, osprey; the snake, musk-rat, otter, woodchuck, and fox, on the banks ; the turtle, frog, hyla, and cricket, which make the banks vocal, — were all known to him, and, as it were, towns men and fellow-creatures ; so that he felt an absurdity or violence in any narrative of one of these by itself apart, and still more of its dimensions on an inch-rule, or in the exhibition of its skeleton, or the specimen of a squirrel or a bird in brandy. He liked to speak of the manners of the river, as itself a lawful creature, yet with exactness, and always to an observed fact. As he knew the river, so the ponds in this region.

One of the weapons he used, more important than microscope or alcohol-receiver to other investigators, was a whim which grew on him by indulgence, yet appeared in gravest statement, namely, of extolling his own town and neighborhood as the most favored centre for natural observation. He remarked that the Flora of Massachusetts embraced almost all the important plants of America, — most of the oaks, most of the willows, the best pines, the ash, the maple, the beech, the nuts. He returned Kane's " Arctic Voyage " to a friend of whom he had borrowed it, with the remark, that " most of the phenomena noted might be observed in Concord." He seemed a little envious of the Pole, for the coincident sunrise and sunset, or five minutes' day after six months: a splendid fact, which Annurs-nuc had never afforded him. He found red snow in one of his walks, and told me that he expected to find yet the Victoria regia in Concord. He was the attor ney of the indigenous plants, and owned to a preference of the weeds to the imported plants, as of the Indian to the civilized man, — and noticed, with pleasure, that the willow bean-poles of his neighbor had grown more than his beans. " See these weeds," he said, " which have been hoed at by a million farmers all spring and summer, and yet have prevailed, and just now come out triumphant over all lanes, pastures, fields, and gar dens, such is their vigor. We have insulted them wdth low names, too, — as Pigweed, Wormwood, Chickweed, Shad-Blossom." He says, "They have brave names, too, — Ambrosia, Stellaria, Amelanchia, Amaranth, etc."

I think his fancy for referring everything to the me ridian of Concord did not grow out of any ignorance or depreciation of other longitudes or latitudes, but was rather a playful expression of his conviction of the indiiferency of all places, and that the best place for each is where he stands. He expressed it once in this wise : — "I think nothing is to be hoped from you, if

this bit of mould under your feet is not sweeter to you to eat than any other in this world, or in any world."

The other weapon with which he conquered all ob stacles in science was patience. He knew how to sit immovable, a part of the rock he rested on, until the bird, the reptile, the fish, which had retired from him, should come back, and resume its habits, nay, moved by curiosity, should come to him and watch him.

It was a pleasure and a privilege to walk with him. He knew the country like a fox or a bird, and passed through it as freely by paths of his own. He knew every track in the snow or on the ground, and what creature had taken this path before him. One must submit abjectly to such a guide, and the reward was great. Under his arm he carried an old music-book to press plants; in his pocket, his diary and pencil, a spy-glass for birds, microscope, jack-knife, and twine-He wore straw hat, stout shoes, strong gray trousers to brave shrub-oaks and smilax, and to climb a tre& for a hawk's or a squirrel's nest. Pie waded into the pool for the water-plants, and his strong legs were no insignificant part of his armor. On the day I speak of he looked for the Menyanthes, detected it across the wide pool, and, on examination of the florets, decided that it had been in flower five days. He drew out of his breast-pocket his diary, and read the names of all the plants that should bloom on this day, whereof he kept account as a banker when his notes fall due. The Cypripedium not due till to-morrow. He thought, that, if waked up from a trance, in this swamp, he could tell by the plants what time of the year it was

within two days. The redstart was flying about, and presently the fine grosbeaks, whose brilliant scarlet makes the rash gazer wipe his eye, and whose fine clear note Thoreau compared to that of a tanager which has got rid of its hoarseness. Presently he heard a note which he called that of the night-warbler, a bird he had never identified, had been in search of twelve years, which always, when he saw it, was in the act of diving down into a tree or bush, and which it was vain to seek ; the only bird that sings indifferently by night and by day. I told him he must beware of finding and booking it, lest life should have nothing more to show him. He said, " What you seek in vain for, half your life, one day you come full upon all the family at din ner. You seek it like a dream, and as soon as you find it you become its prey."

His interest in the flower or the bird lay very deep in his mind, was connected with Nature, — and the meaning of Nature was never attempted to be defined by him. He would not offer a memoir of his observa tions to the Natural History Society. " Why should I ? To detach the description from its connections in my mind would make it no longer true or valuable to me : and they do not wish what belongs to it." His power of observation seemed to indicate additional senses. He saw as with microscope, heard as with ear-trumpet, and his memory was a photographic register of all he saw and heard. And yet none knew better than he that it is not the fact that imports, but the impression or effect of the fact on your mind. Every fact lay in glory in his mind, a type of the order and beauty of the whole.

His determination on Natural History was organic. He confessed that he sometimes felt like a hound or a panther, and, if born among Indians, would have been a fell hunter. But, restrained by his Massachusetts culture, he played out the game in this mild form of botany and ichthyology. His intimacy with animals suggested what Thomas Fuller records of Butler the apiologist, that " either he had told the bees things or the bees had told him." Snakes coiled round his leg; the fishes swam into his hand, and he took them out of the water ; he pulled the woodchuck out of its hole by the tail, and took the foxes under his protection from the hunters. Our naturalist had perfect magnanimity ; he had no secrets: he would carry you to the heron's haunt, or even to his most prized botanical swamp, — possibly knowing that you could never find it again, yet willing to take his risks.

No college ever offered him a diploma, or a profes sor's chair; no academy made him its corresponding secretary, its discoverer, or even its member. Whether these learned bodies feared the satire of his presence. Yet so much knowledge of Nature's secret and genius few others possessed, none in a more large and religious synthesis. For not a particle of respect had he to the opinions of any man or body of men, but homage solely to the truth itself; and as he discovered everywhere among doctors some leaning of courtesy, it discredited them. He grew to be revered and admired by his townsmen, who had at first known him only as an oddity. The farmers who employed him as a surveyor soon discovered his rare accuracy and skill, his knowl-edge of their lands, of trees, of birds, of Indian remains and the like, which enabled him to tell every farmei more than he knew before of his own farm ; so that ho began to feel as if Mr. Thoreau had better rights in his land than he. They felt, too, the superiority of character which addressed all men with a native authority.

Indian relics abound in Concord,— arrow-heads, stone chisels, pestles, and fragments of pottery; and on the river-bank, large heaps of clam-shells and ashes mark spots which the savages frequented. These, and every circumstance touching the Indian, were important in his eyes. His visits to Maine were chiefly for love of the Indian. He had the satisfaction of seeing the manu facture of the bark-canoe, as well as of trying his hand in its management on the rapids. He was inquisitive about the making of the stone arrow-head, and in his last days charged a youth setting out for the Rocky Mountains to find an Indian who could tell him that: " It was well worth a visit to California to learn it." Occasionally, a small party of Penobscot Indians would visit Concord, and pitch their tents for a few weeks in summer on the river-bank. He failed not to make acquaintance with the best of them ; though he well knew that asking questions of Indians is like catechizing beavers and rabbits. In his last visit to Maine he had great satisfaction from Joseph Polis, an intelligent Indian of Oldtown, who was his guide for some weeks.

He was equally interested in every natural fact. The depth of his perception found likeness of law through out Nature, and I know not any genius who so swiftly inferred universal law from the single fact. He was no pedant of a department. His eye was open to beauty, and his ear to music. He found these, not in rare con ditions, but wheresoever he went. He thought the best of music was in single strains; and he found poetic sug gestion in the humming of the telegraph-wire.

His poetry might be bad or good; he no doubt wanted a lyric facility and technical skill; but he had the source of poetry in his spiritual perception. He was a good reader and critic, and his judgment on poetry was to the ground of it. He could not be deceived as to the pres ence or absence of the poetic element in any compo sition, and his thirst for this made him negligent and perhaps scornful of superficial graces. lie would pass by many delicate rhythms, but he would have detected every live stanza or line in a volume, and knew very well where to find an equal poetic charm in prose. lie was so enamored of the spiritual beauty that he held all actual written poems in very light esteem in the com parison. He admired JEschylus and Pindar; but, when some one was commending them, he said that " JEschy-lus and the Greeks, in describing Apollo and Orpheus, had given no song, or no good one. They ought not to have moved trees, but to have chanted to the gods such a hymn as would have sung all their old ideas out of their heads, and new ones in." His own verses are often rude and defective. The gold does not yet run pure, is drossy and crude. The thyme and marjoram are not yet honey. But if he want lyric fineness and technical merits, if he have not the poetic temperament, he never lacks the causal thought, showing that his

genius was better than his talent. He knew the worth of the Imagination for the uplifting and consolation of human life, and liked to throw every thought into a symbol. The fact you tell is of no value, but only the impression. For this reason his presence was poetic, always piqued the curiosity to know more deeply the secrets of his mind. He had many reserves, an umvill-ingness to exhibit to profane eyes what was still sacred in his own, and knew well how to throw a poetic veil over his experience. All readers of "Walden" will remember his mythical record of his disappoint ments : —

" I long ago lost a hound, a bay horse, and a turtle dove, and am still on their trail. Many are the travel lers I have spoken concerning them, describing their tracks, and what calls they answered to. I have met one or two who had heard the hound, and the tramp of the horse, and even seen the dove disappear behind a cloud; and they seemed as anxious to recover them as if they had lost them themselves." *

His riddles were worth the reading, and 1 confide, that, if at any time I do not understand the expression, it is yet just. Such was the wealth of his truth that it ^'^as not worth his while to use words in vain. His <c'"poem entitled " Sympathy" reveals the tenderness un-1 der that triple steel of stoicism, and the intellectual sub-tilty it could animate. His classic poem on " Smoke " suggests Simonides, but is better than any poem of Simonides. His biography is in his verses. His habit ual thought makes all his poetry a hymn to the Cause * " Walden," p. 20.

of causes, the Spirit which vivifies and controls his own.

" I hearing get, who had but ears, And sight, who had but eyes before ; I moments live, who lived but years, And truth discern, who knew but learning's lore."

And still more in these religious lines : —

" Now chiefly is my natal hour, And only now my prime of life; I will not doubt the love untold, Which not my worth or want hath bought, Which wooed me young, and wooes me old, And to this evening hath me brought."

Whilst he used in his writings a certain petulance of remark in reference to churches or churchmen, he was a person of a rare, tender, and absolute religion, a person incapable of any profanation, by act or by thought. Of course, the same isolation which belonged to his original thinking and living detached him from the social relig ious forms. This is neither to be censured nor regretted. Aristotle long ago explained it, when he said, " One\ who surpasses his fellow-citizens in virtue is no longer i a part of the city. Their law is not for him, since he is a law to himself."

Thoreau was sincerity itself, and might fortify the convictions of prophets in the ethical laws by his holy living. It was an affirmative experience which refused to be set aside. A truth-speaker he, capable of the most deep and strict conversation ; a physician to the

wounds of any soul; a friend, knowing not only the secret of friendship, but almost worshipped by those

,'lfew persons who resorted to him as their confessor and prophet, and knew the deep value of his mind and great heart. He thought that without religion or devotion of some kind nothing great was ever accomplished: and he thought that the bigoted sectarian had better bear this in mind.

His virtues, of course, sometimes ran into extremes. It was easy to trace to the inexorable demand on all for exact truth that austerity which made this willing her mit more solitary even than he wished. Himself of a

C^perfect probity, he required not less of others. He had a disgust at crime, and no worldly success could cover it. He detected paltering as readily in dignified and pros perous persons as in beggars, and with equal scorn. Such dangerous frankness was in his dealing that his admirers called him " that terrible Thoreau," as if he spoke when silent, and was still present when he had departed. I think the severity of his ideal interfered to deprive him of a healthy sufficiency of human society. The habit of a realist to find things the reverse of their appeanflice inclined him to put every statement in a paradox. .4 certain habit of antagonism defaced his earlier writings, — a trick of rhetoric not quite out grown in his later, of substituting for the obvious word and thought its diametrical opposite. He praised wild mountains and winter forests for their domestic air, in Bnow and ice he would find sultriness, and commended the wilderness for resembling Rome and Paris. "It was so dry, that ydu might call it wet."

The tendency to magnify the moment, to read all the laws of Nature in the one object or one combination under your eye, is of course comic to those who do not share the philosopher's perception of identity. To him there was no such thing as size. The pond was a small ocean; the Atlantic, a large Walden Pond. He re ferred every minute fact to cosmical laws. Though he meant to be just, he seemed haunted by a certair chronic assumption that the science of the day protend ed completeness, and he had just found out thai the savans had neglected to discriminate a particular tfi/cani-cal variety, had failed to describe the seeds or oi unt the sepals. " That is to say," we replied, " the blockhead? were not born in Concord ; but who said they were <* It was their unspeakable misfortune to be born in Lon don, or Paris, or Rome ; but, poor fellows, they di« what they could, considering that they never saw Bate-man's Pond, or Nine-Acre Corner, or Becky-Stow's Swamp. Besides, what were you sent into the world for, but to add this observation ? "

Had his genius been only contemplative, he had been fitted to his life, but with his energy and practical abil ity he seemed born for great enterprise and for com mand ; and I so much regret the loss of his rare pow ers of action, that I cannot help counting it a fault in him that he had no ambition. Wanting this, instead of engineering for all America, he w r as the captain of a huckleberry party. Pounding beans is good to the end of pounding empires one of these days,; but if, at the end of years, it is still only beans !

But these foibles, real or apparent, were fast vanish-

ing in the incessant growth of a spirit so robust and wise, and which effaced its defeats with new triumphs. His study of Nature was a perpetual ornament to him, and inspired his friends with curiosity to see the world through his eyes, and to hear his adventures. They possessed every kind of interest.

He had many elegances of his own, whilst he scoffed at conventional elegance. Thus, he could not bear to hear the sound of his own steps, the grit of gravel; and therefore never willingly walked in the road, but in the grass, on mountains and in woods. His senses were acute, and he remarked that by night every dwelling-house gives out bad air, like a slaughter-house. He liked the pure fragrance of melilot. He honored cer tain plants with special regard, and, over all, the pond-lily, — then, the gentian, and the Mikania scandens, and " life-everlasting," and a bass-tree which he visited every year when it bloomed, in the middle of July. He thought the scent a more oracular inquisition than the sight, — more oracular and trustworthy. The scent, of course, reveals what is concealed from the other senses. By it he detected earthiness. He delighted in echoes, and said they were almost the only kind of kindred voices that he heard. He loved Nature so well, was so happy in her solitude, that he became very jealous of cities, and the sad work which their refinements and artifices made with man and his dwelling. The axe was always destroying his forest. " Thank God," he said, " they cannot cut down the clouds ! " " All kinds of figures are drawn on the blue ground with this fibrous white paint."

I subjoin a few sentences taken from his unpublished manuscripts, not only as records of his thought and feel ing, but for their power of description and literary excellence.

" Some circumstantial evidence is very strong, as when you find a trout in the milk."

" The chub is a soft fish, and tastes like boiled brown paper salted."

" The youth gets together his materials to build a bridge to the moon, or, perchance, a palace or temple on the earth, and at length the middle-aged man con cludes to built a wood-shed with them."

" The locust z-ing."

" Devil's-needles zigzagging along the Nut-Meadow brook."

" Sugar is not so sweet to the palate as sound to the healthy ear."

" I put on some hemlock-boughs, and the rich salt crackling of their leaves was like mustard to the ear, the crackling of uncountable regiments. Dead trees love the fire."

" The bluebird carries the sky on his back."

" The tanager flies through the green foliage as if it would ignite the leaves."

" If I wish for a horse-hair for my compass-sight, I must go to the stable; but the hair-bird, with her sharp eyes, goes to the road."

" Immortal water, alive even to the superficies."

" Fire is the most tolerable third party."

" Nature made ferns for pure leaves, to show what she could do in that line."

" No tree has so fair a bole and so handsome an in step as the beech."

" How did these beautiful rainbow-tints get into the shell of the fresh-water clam, buried in the mud at the bottom of our dark river ? "

" Hard are the times when the infant's shoes are second-foot."

" We are strictly confined to our men to whom we give liberty."

" Nothing is so much to be feared as fear. Atheism may comparatively be popular with God himself."

" Of what significance the things you can forget ? A little thought is sexton to all the world."

" How can we expect a harvest of thought who have not had a seed-time of character ? "

" Only he can be trusted with gifts who can present a face of bronze to expectations."

" I ask to be melted. You can only ask of the metals that they be tender to the fire that melts them. To nought else can they be tender."

There is a flower known to botanists, one of the same genus with our summer plant called "Life-Everlasting," a Gnaphalium like that, which grows on the most inac cessible cliffs of the Tyrolese mountains, where the chamois dare hardly venture, and which the hunter, tempted by its beauty, and by his love, (for it is im mensely valued by the Swiss maidens,) climbs the cliffs to gather, and is sometimes found dead at the foot, with the flower in his hand. It is called by botanists the Gnaphalium leontopodium, but by the Swiss Edelweisse^

which signifies Noble Purity. Thoreau seemed to me living in the hope to gather this plant, which belonged to him of right. The scale on which his studies pro ceeded was so large as to require longevity, and we were the less prepared for his sudden disappearance. The country knows not yet, or in the least part, how great a son it has lost. It seems an injury that he should leave in the midst his broken task, which none else can finish, — a kind of indignity to so noble a soul, that it should depart out of Nature before yet he has been really shown to his peers for what he is. But he, at least, is content. His soul was made for the noblest society ; he had in a short life exhausted the capabili ties of this world ; wherever there is knowledge, wher ever there is virtue, wherever there is beauty, he will find a home.

EXCURSIONS.

NATURAL HISTORY OF MASSACHUSETTS

[1842.]

BOOKS of natural history make the most cheerful winter reading. I read in Audubon with a thrill of delight, when the snow covers the ground, of the magnolia, and the Florida keys, and their warm sea-breezes ; of the fence-rail, and the cotton-tree, and the migrations of the rice-bird ; of the breaking up of winter in Labrador, and the melting of the snow on the forks of the Missouri; and owe an accession of health to these reminiscences of luxuriant nature.

Within the circuit of this plodding life,
There enter moments of an azure hue,
Untarnished fair as is the violet
Or anemone, when the spring strews them
By some meandering rivulet, which make
The best philosophy untrue that aims
But to console man for his grievances.
I have remembered when the winter came,
High in my chamber in the frosty nights,
When in the still light of the cheerful moon,

* Reports — on the Fishes, Reptiles, and Birds; the Herbaceous Plants and Quadrupeds; the Insects Injurious to Vegetation ; and the Inver tebrate Animals of Massachusetts. Published agreeably to an Order of the Legislature, by tbe Commissioners on thy Zoological and Bo tanical Survev of the Stale.

On every twig and rail and jutting spout,
The icy spears were adding to their length
Against the arrows of the coming sun,
How in the shimmering noon of summer past
Some unrecorded beam slanted across
The upland pastures where the Johnswort grew;

Or heard, amid the verdure of my mind.
The bee's long smothered hum, on the blue flag
Loitering amidst the mead; or busy rill,
Which now through all its course stands still and dumb
Its own memorial, — purling at its play
Along the slopes, and through the meadows next,
Until its youthful sound was hushed at last
In the staid current of the lowland stream;
Or seen the furrows shine but late upturned,
And where the fieldfare followed in the rear,
When all the fields around lay bound and hoar
Beneath a thick integument of snow.
So by God's cheap economy made rich
To go upon my winter's task again.

I am singularly refreshed in winter when I hear of service-berries, poke-weed, juniper. Is not heaven made up of these cheap summer glories ? There is a singular health in those words, Labrador and East Main, which no de sponding creed recognizes. How much more than Federal are these States. If there were no other vicissitudes than the seasons, our interest would never tire. Much more is adoing than Congress wots of. What journal do the per simmon and the buckeye keep, and the sharp-shinned hawk ? What is transpiring from sum-

mer to winter in the Carolinas, and the Great Pine Forest, and the Valley of the Mohawk ? The merely political aspect of the land is never very cheering; men are degraded when consid ered as the members of a political organization. On this side all lands present only the symptoms of decay. I see but Bunker Hill and Sing-Sing, the District of Columbia and Sullivan's Island, with a few avenues connecting them. But pal try are they all beside one blast of the east or the south wind which blows over them.

In society you will not find health, but in nature. Unless our feet at least stood in the midst of nature, all our faces would be pale and livid. Society is always diseased, and the best is the most so. There is no scent in it so whole some as that of the pines, nor any fragrance so penetrating and restorative as the life-everlasting in high pastures. I would keep some book of natural history always by me as a sort of elixir, the reading of which should restore the tone of the system. To the sick, indeed, nature is sick, but to the well, a fountain of health. To him who contemplates a trait of natural beauty no harm nor disappointment can come. The doc trines of despair, of spiritual or political tyranny or servitude, were never taught by such as shared the serenity of nature. Surely good courage will not flag here on the Atlantic border, as

long as we are flanked by the Fur Countries There is enough in that sound to cheer one under any circumstances. The spruce, the hem lock, and the pine will not countenance despair. Methinks some creeds in vestries and churches j do forget the hunter wrapped in furs by the Great Slave Lake, and that the Esquimaux sledges are drawn by dogs, and in the twilight of the northern night, the hunter does not give over to follow the seal and walrus on the ice. They are of sick and diseased imaginations who would toll the world's knell so soon. Cannot these sedentary sects do better than prepare the shrouds and write the epitaphs of those other busy living men ? The practical faith of all men belies the preacher's consolation. What is any man's discourse to me, if I am not sensible of something in it as steady and cheery as the creak of crickets ? In it the woods must be re lieved against the sky. Men tire me when I am not constantly greeted and refreshed as by the flux of sparkling streams. Surely joy is the con dition of life. Think of the young fry that leap^ in ponds, the myriads of insects ushered into being on a summer evening, the incessant note of the hyla with which the woods ring in the spring, the nonchalance of the butterfly carrying accident and change painted in a thousand hues upon its wings, or the brook minnow stoutly

stemming the current, the lustre of whose scales worn bright by the attrition is reflected upon the bank.

We fancy that this din of religion, literature, and philosophy, which is heard in pulpits, lyce-ums, and parlors, vibrates through the universe, and is as catholic a sound as the creaking of the earth's axle; but if a man sleep soundly, he will forget it all between sunset and dawn. It is the three-inch swing of a pendulum in a cup board, which the great pulse of nature vibrates by and through each instant. When we lift our eyelids and open our ears, it disappears with smoke and rattle like the cars on a railroad. When I detect a beauty in any of the recesses of nature, I am reminded, by the serene and retired spirit in which it requires to be contem plated, of the inexpressible privacy of a life,— how silent and unambitious it is. The beauty there is in mosses must be considered from the holiest, quietest nook. What an admirable train ing is science for the more active warfare of life. Indeed, the unchallenged bravery, which these studies imply, is far more impressive than the trumpeted valor of the warrior. I am pleased to learn that Thales was up and stirring by night not unfrequently, as his astronomical dis coveries prove. Linnaeus, setting out for Lap land, surveys his u comb" and "spare shirt,"

" leathern breeches " and " gauze cap to keep off gnats," with as much complacency as Bonaparte a park of artillery for the Russian campaign. The quiet bravery of the man is admirable. His eye is to take in fish, flower, and bird, quadru ped and biped. Science is always brave, for to know, is to know good ; doubt and danger quail before her eye. What the coward overlooks in his hurry, she calmly scrutinizes, breaking ground like a pioneer for the array of arts that follow in her train. But cowardice is unscientific; for there cannot be a science of ignorance. There may be a science of bravery, for that advances; but a retreat is rarely well conducted; if it is, then is it an orderly advance in the face of cir cumstances.

But to draw a little nearer to our promised topics. Entomology extends the limits of being in a new direction, so that I walk in nature with a sense of greater space and freedom. It sug gests besides, that the universe is not rough-hewn, but perfect in its details. Nature will be.ar the closest inspection ; she invites us to lay our eye level with the smallest leaf, and take an insect view of its plain. She has no interstices; every part is full of life. I explore, too, with pleasure, the sources of the myriad sounds which crowd the summer noon, and which seem the very grain and stuff of which eternity is made.

Who does not remember the shrill roll-call of the harvest fly ? There were ears for these sounds in Greece long ago, as Anacreon's ode wilJ show.

" We pronounce thee happy, Cicada, For on the tops of the trees, Drinking a little dew, Like any king thou singest, For thine are they all, Whatever thou seest in the fields, And whatever the woods bear. Thou art the friend of the husbandmen, In no respect injuring any one ; And thou art honored among men, Sweet prophet of summer. The Muses love thee, And Phoebus himself loves thee, And has given thee a shrill song; Age does not wrack thee, Thou skilful, earthborn, song-loving, Unsuirering, bloodless one ; Almost thou art like the gods."

In the autumn days, the creaking of crickets is heard at noon over all the land, and as in summer they are heard chiefly at nightfall, so then by their incessant chirp they usher in the evening of the year. Nor can all the vanities that vex the world alter one whit the measure that night has chosen. Every pulse-beat is in exact time with the cricket's chant and the tick-

ings of the deathwatch in the wall. Alternate with these if you can.

About two hundred and eighty birds either reside permanently in the State, or spend the summer only, or make us a passing visit. Those which spend the winter with us have obtained our warmest sympathy. The nut-hatch and chicadee flitting in company through the dells of the wood, the one harshly scolding at the intruder, the other with a faint lisping note en ticing him on ; the jay screaming in the or chard ; the crow cawing in unison with the storm ; the partridge, like a russet link extended over from autumn to spring, preserving un broken the chain of summers; the hawk with warrior-like firmness abiding the blasts of win ter ; the robin* and lark lurking by warm springs in the woods; the familiar snow-bird culling a few seeds in the garden, or a few crumbs in the yard; and occasionally the shrike, with heed less and unfrozen melody bringing back summer again; —

A white robin and a white quail have occasionally been seen. It is mentioned in Audubon as remarkable that the nest of a robin should be found on the ground; but this bird seems to be less partic ular than most in the choice of a building spot. I have seen its nest placed under the thatched roof of a deserted barn, and in one in stance, where the adjacent country was nearly destitute of trees, together with two of the phoabe, upon the end of a board in the loft of a saw-mill, but a few feet from the saw, which vibrated several inches with the motion of the machinery.

His steady sails he never furls
At any time o' year,
And perching now on Winter's curls,
He whistles in his ear.

As the spring advances, and the ice is melting in the river, our earliest and straggling visitors make their appearance. Again does the old Teiaii poet sing, as well for New England as for Greece, in the

RETURN OF SPRING.

" Behold, how Spring appearing, The Graces send forth roses ; Behold, how the wave of the sea Is made smooth by the calm; Behold, how the duck dives; Behold, how the crane travels ; And Titan shines constantly bright The shadows of the clouds are moving; The works of man shine; The earth puts forth fruits ; The fruit of the olive puts forth. The cup of Bacchus is crowned, Along the leaves, along the branches, The fruit, bending them down, flourishes."

The ducks alight at this season in the still water, in company with the gulls, which do not fail to improve an east wind to visit our meadows, and swim about by twos and threes, pluming themselves, and diving to peck at the root of the lily, and the cranberries which the

frost has not loosened. The first flock of geese is seen beating to north, in long harrows and waving lines; the gingle of the song-sparrow salutes us from the shrubs and fences; the plain tive note of the lark comes clear and sweet from the meadow; and the bluebird, like an azure ray, glances past us in our walk. The fish-hawk, too, is occasionally seen at this season sailing majestically over the water, and he who has once observed it will not soon forget the majesty of its flight. It sails the air like a ship of the line, worthy to struggle with the elements, fall ing back from time to time like a ship on its beam ends, and holding its talons up as if ready for the arrows, in the attitude of the national bird. It is a great presence, as of the master of river and forest. Its eye would not quail before the owner of the soil, but make him feel like an intruder on its domains. And then its retreat, sailing so steadily away, is a kind of advance. I have by me one of a pair of ospreys, which have for some years fished in this vicinity, shot by a neighboring pond, measuring more than two feet in length, and six in the stretch of its wings. Nuttall mentions that " The ancients, particularly Aristotle, pretended that the ospreys taught their young to gaze at the sun, and those who were unable to do so were destroyed. Lin naeus even believed, on ancient authority, that

one of the feet of this bird had all the toes di vided, while the other was partly webbed, so that it could swim with one foot, and grasp a fish with the other." But that educated eye is now dim, and those talons are nerveless. Its shrill scream seems yet to linger in its throat, and the roar of the sea in its wings. There is the tyranny of Jove in its claws, and his wrath in the erectile feathers of the head and neck. It reminds me of the Argonautic expedition, and would inspire the dullest to take flight over Par nassus.

The booming of the bittern, described by Goldsmith and Nuttall, is frequently heard in our fens, in the morning and evening, sounding like a pump, or the chopping of wood in a frosty morning in some distant farm-yard. The man ner in which this sound is produced I have not seen anywhere described. On one occasion, the bird has been seen by one of my neighbors to thrust its bill into the water, and suck up as much as it could hold, then raising its head, it pumped it out again with four or five heaves of the neck, throwing it two or three feet, and making the sound each time.

At length the summer's eternity is ushered in by the cackle of the flicker among the oaks on the hill-side, and a new dynasty begins with calm security.

In May and June the woodland quire is in full tune, and given the immense spaces of hoi-low air, and this curious human ear, one does not see how the void could be better filled.

Each summer sound Is a summer round.

As the season advances, and those birds which make us but a passing visit depart, the woods become silent again, and but few feathers ruffle the drowsy air. But the solitary rambler may still find a response and expression for every mood in the depths of the wood.

Sometimes I hear the veery's* clarion,

Or brazen trump of the impatient jay,

And in secluded woods the chicadee

Doles out her scanty notes, which sing the praise

Of heroes, and set forth the loveliness

Of virtue evermore.

The phoebe still sings in harmony with the sultry weather by the brink of the pond, nor are the desultory hours of noon in the midst of the village without their minstrel.

* This bird, which is so well described by Nuttall, but is appar ently unknown by the author of the Report, is one of the most con-mon in the woods in this vicinity, and in Cambridge I have heard the college yard ring with its trill. The boys call it " yorrick" from the sound of its querulous and chiding note, as it flits near the trav eller through the underwood. The cowbird's egg is occasionally found in its nest", as mentioned by Audubon.

Upon the lofty elm-tree sprays
The vireo rings the changes sweet,
During the trivial summer days,
Striving to lift our thoughts above the street.

With the autumn begins in some measure a new spring. The plover is heard whistling high in the air over the dry pastures, the finches flit from tree to tree, the bobolinks and flickers fly in flocks, and the goldfinch rides on the earliest blast, like a winged hyla peeping amid the rustle of the leaves. The crows, too, begin now to congregate; you may stand and count them as they fly low and straggling over the landscape, singly or by twos and threes, at intervals of half a mile, until a hundred have passed.

I have seen it suggested somewhere that the crow was brought to this country by the white man; but I shall as soon believe that the white man planted these pines and hemlocks. He is no spaniel to follow our steps; but rather flits about the clearings like the dusky spirit of the Indian, reminding me oftener of Philip and Powhatan, than of Winthrop and Smith. He is a relic of the dark ages. By just so slight, by just so lasting a tenure does superstition hold the world ever; there is the rook in England, and the crow in New England.

Thou dusky spirit of the wood, Bird of an ancient brood, 4

Flitting thy lonely way, A meteor in the summer's day, From wood to wood, from hill to hill, Low over forest, field, and rill, What wouldst thou say ? Why shouldst thou haunt the day ? What makes thy melancholy float ? What bravery inspires thy throat, And bears thee up above the clouds, Over desponding human crowds, Which far below Lay thy haunts low ?

The late walker or sailor, in the October eve nings, may hear the murmurings of the snipe, circling over the meadows, the most spirit-like sound in nature; and still later in the autumn, when the frosts have tinged the leaves, a solitary loon pays a visit to our retired ponds, where he may lurk undisturbed till the season of moulting is passed, making the woods ring with his wild laughter. This bird, the Great Northern Diver, well deserves its name; for when pursued with a boat, it will dive, and swim like a fish under water, for sixty rods or more, as fast as a boat can be paddled, and its pursuer, if he would dis cover his game again, must put his ear to the surface to hear where it comes up. When it comes to the surface, it throws the water off with one shake of its wings, and calmly swims about until again disturbed.

These are the sights and sounds which reach our senses oftenest during the year. But some times one hears a quite new note, which has for background other Carolinas and Mexicos than the books describe, and learns that his ornithol ogy has done him no service.

It appears from the Report that there are about forty quadrupeds belonging to the State, and among these one is glad to hear of a few bears, wolves, lynxes, and wildcats.

When our river overflows its banks in the spring, the wind from the meadows is laden with a strong scent of musk, and by its fresh ness advertises me of an unexplored wildness. Those backwoods are not far off then. I am affected by the sight of the cabins of the musk-rat, made of mud and grass, and raised three or four feet along the river, as when I read of the barrows of Asia. The musk-rat is the beaver of the settled States. Their number has even increased within a few years in this vicinity. Among the rivers which empty into the Merri-mack, the Concord is known to the boatmen as a dead stream. The Indians are said to have called it Musketaquid, or Prairie River. Its cur rent being much more sluggish, and its water more muddy than the rest, it abounds more in fish and game of every kind. According to the His tory of the town, " The fur-trade was here once

very important. As early as 1641, a company was formed in the colony, of which Major Wil-lard of Concord was superintendent, and had the exclusive right to trade with the Indians in furs and other articles; and for this right they were obliged to pay into the public treasury one twentieth of all the furs they obtained." There are trappers in our midst still, as well as on the streams of the far West, who night and morning go the round of their traps, without fear of the Indian. One of these takes from one hundred and fifty to two hundred musk-rats in a year, and even thirty-six have been shot by one man in a day. Their fur, which is not nearly as val uable as formerly, is in good condition in the winter and spring only; and upon the breaking up of the ice, when they are driven out of their holes by the water, the greatest number is shot from boats, either swimming or resting on their stools, or slight supports of grass and reeds, by the side of the stream. Though they exhibit considerable cunning at other times, they are easily taken in a trap, which has only to be placed in their holes, or wherever they frequent, without any bait being used, though it is some times rubbed with their musk. In the winter the hunter cuts holes in the ice, and shoots them when they come to the surface. Their burrows are usually in the high banks of the river, with

the entrance under water, and rising within to above the level of high water. Sometimes their nests, composed of dried meadow grass and flags, may be discovered where the bank is low and spongy, by the yielding of the ground under the feet. They have from three to seven or eight young in the spring.

Frequently, in the morning or evening, a long ripple is seen in the still water, where a musk-rat is crossing the stream, with only its nose above the surface, and sometimes a green bough in its mouth to build its house with. When it finds itself observed, it will dive and swim five or six rods under water, and at length conceal itself in its hole, or the weeds. It will remain under water for ten minutes at a time, and on one occasion has been seen, when undisturbed, to form an air-bubble under the ice, which con tracted and expanded as it breathed at leisure. When it suspects danger on shore, it will stand erect like a squirrel, and survey its neighborhood for several minutes, without moving.

In the fall, if a meadow intervene between their burrows and the stream, they erect cabins of mud and grass, three or four feet high, near its edge. These are not their breeding-places, though young are sometimes found in them in late freshets, but rather their hunting-lodges, to which they resort in the winter with their food, and for shelter. Their food consists chiefly of

flags and fresh-water muscles, the shells of the latter being left in large quantities around their lodges in the spring.

The Penobscot Indian wears the entire skin of a musk-rat, with the legs and tail dangling, and the head caught under his girdle, for a pouch, into which he puts his fishing tackle, and essences to scent his traps with.

The bear, wolf, lynx, wildcat, deer, beaver, and marten, have disappeared; the otter is rarely if ever seen here at present; and the mink is less common than formerly.

Perhaps of all our untamed quadrupeds, the fox has obtained the widest and most famil iar reputation, from the time of Pilpay and yEsop to the present day. His recent tracks still give variety to a winter's walk. I tread in the steps of the fox that has gone before me by some hours, or which perhaps I have started, with such a tiptoe of expectation, as if I were on the trail of the Spirit itself which resides in the wood, and expected soon to catch it in its lair. I am curious to know what has deter mined its graceful curvatures, and how surely they were coincident with the fluctuations of some mind. I know which way a mind wended, what horizon it faced, by the setting of these tracks, and whether it moved slowly or rapidly, by their greater or less intervals and distinct ness ; for the swiftest step leaves yet a lasting

trace. Sometimes you will see the trails of many together, and where they have gambolled and gone through a hundred evolution?, which testify to a singular listlessness arid leisure in nature.

When I see a fox run across the pond on the snow, with the carelessness of freedom, or at in tervals trace his course in the sunshine along the ridge of a hill, I give up to him sun and earth as to their true proprietor. He does not go in the sun, but it seems to follow him, and there is a visible sympathy between him and it. Sometimes, when the snow lies light, and but five or six inches deep, you may give chase and come up with one on foot. In such a case he will show a remarkable presence of mind, choos ing only the safest direction, though he may lose ground by it. Notwithstanding his fright, he will take no step which is not beautiful. His pace is a sort of leopard canter, as if he were in nowise impeded by the snow, but were hus banding his strength all the while. When the ground is uneven, the course is a series of grace ful curves, conforming to the shape of the sur face. He runs as though there were not a bone in his back. Occasionally dropping his muzzle io the ground for a rod or two, and then tossing his head aloft, when satisfied of his course When he comes to a declivity, he will put his

forefeet together, and slide swiftly down it, shov ing the snow before him. He treads so softly that you would hardly hear it from any near ness, and yet with such expression that it would not be quite inaudible at any distance.

Of fishes, seventy-five genera and one hun dred and seven species are described in the Re port. The fisherman will be startled to learn that there are but about a dozen kinds in the ponds and streams of any inland town; and almost nothing is known of their habits. Only their names and residence make one love fishes. I would know even the number of their fin-rays, and how many scales compose the lateral line. I am the wiser in respect to all knowledges, and the better qualified for all fortunes, for knowing that there is a minnow in the brook. Methinks I have need even of his sympathy, and to be his fellow in a degree.

I have experienced such simple delight in the trivial matters of fishing and sporting, formerly, as might have inspired the muse of Homer or Shakspeare; and now, when I turn the pages and ponder the plates of the Angler's Souvenir, I am fain to exclaim,—

" Can these things be, And overcome us like a summer's cloud ?"

Next to nature, it seems as if man's actions

were the most natural, they so gently accord with her. The small seines of flax stretched across the shallow and transparent parts of our river, are no more intrusion than the cobweb in the sun. I stay my boat in midcurrent, and look down in the sunny water to see the civil rneshes of his nets, and wonder how the bluster ing people of the town could have done this elvish work. The twine looks like a new river weed, and is to the river as a beautiful me mento of man's presence in nature, discovered as silently and delicately as a footprint in the sand.

When the ice is covered with snow, I do not suspect the wealth under my feet; that there is as good as a mine under me wherever I go. How many pickerel are poised on easy fin fath oms below the loaded wain. The revolution of the seasons must be a curious phenomenon to them. At length the sun and wind brush aside

their curtain, and they see the heavens again.

Early in the spring, after the ice has melted, is the time for spearing fish. Suddenly the wind shifts from northeast and east to west and south, and every icicle, which has tinkled on the meadow grass so long, trickles down its stem, and seeks its level unerringly with a million comrades. The steam curls up from every roof and fence.

I see the civil sun drying earth's tears, Her tears of joy, which only faster flow.

In the brooks is heard the slight grating Bound of small cakes of ice, floating with vari ous speed, full of content and promise, and where the water gurgles under a natural bridge, you may hear these hasty rafts hold conver sation in an undertone. Every rill is a chan nel for the juices of the meadow. In the ponds the ice cracks with a merry and inspirit ing din, and down the larger streams is whirled grating hoarsely, and clashing its way along, which was so lately a highway for the wood man's team and the fox, sometimes with the tracks^ of the skaters still fresh upon it, and the holes cut for pickerel. Town committees anxiously inspect the bridges and causeways, as if by mere eye-force to intercede with the ice, and save the treasury.

The river swelleth more and more, Like some sweet influence stealing o'er The passive town ; and for a while Each tussuck makes a tiny isle, Where, on some friendly Ararat, llesteth the weary water-rat.

No ripple shows Musketaquid,

Her very current e'en is hid,

As deepest souls do calmest rest,

When thoughts are swelling in the breast,

And she that in the summer's drought Doth make a rippling and a rout, Sleeps from Nahshawtuck to the Cliff, Unrufiled by a single skilF. But by a thousand distant hills The louder roar a thousand rills, And ninny a spring which now is dumb, And many a stream with smothered hum,])oth swifter well and faster glide, Though buried deep beneath the tide.

Our village shows a rural Venice, Its broad lagoons where yonder fen is ; As lovely as the Bay of Naples Yon placid cove amid the maples; And in my neighbor's field of corn I recognize the Golden Horn.

Here Nature taught from year to year, When onlv red men came to hear, Methinks 'twas in this school of art Venice and Naples learned their part; But still their mistress, to my mind, Her young disciples leaves behind.

The fisherman now repairs and launches his boat. The best time for spearing is at this sea son, before the weeds have begun to grow, and while the fishes lie in the shallow water, for in summer they prefer the cool depths, and in the autumn they are still more or less concealed by the grass. The first requisite is fuel for you? crate ; and for this purpose the roots of the pitch-pine are commonly used, found under decayed

stumps, where the trees have been felled eight or ten years.

With a crate, or jack, made of iron hoops, to contain your fire, and attached to the bow of i your boat about three feet from the water, a fish-spear with seven tines, and fourteen feet long,, a large basket, or barrow, to carry your fuel and bring back your fish, and a thick outer garment, you are equipped for a cruise. It should be a warm and still evening; and^ then with a fire crackling merrily at the prow, you may launch forth like a cucullo into the night. The dullest soul cannot go upon such an expe dition without some of the spirit of adventure; as if he had stolen the boat of Charon and gone down the Styx on a midnight expedition into the realms of Pluto. And much speculation does this wandering star afford to the musing nightwalker, leading him on and on, jack-o'lan-tern-like, over the meadows ; or, if he is wiser, he amuses himself with imagining what of human life, far in the silent night, is flitting mothlike round its candle. The silent navi gator shoves his craft gently over the water, with a smothered pride and sense of benefaction, as if he were the phosphor, or light-bringer, to these dusky realms, or some sister moon, blessing the spaces with her light. The waters, for a rod or two on either hand and several feet in depth, are

lit up with more than noonday distinctness, and he enjoys the opportunity which so many have desired, for the roofs of a city are indeed raised, and he surveys the midnight economy of the fishes. There they lie in every variety of pos ture ; some on their backs, with their white bel lies uppermost, some suspended in midwater, some sculling gently along with a dreamy mo tion of the fins, and others quite active and wide awake, — a scene not unlike what the human city would present. Occasionally he will en counter a turtle selecting the choicest morsels, or a musk-rat resting on a tussuck. He may exercise his dexterity, if he sees fit, on the more distant and active fish, or fork the nearer into his boat, as potatoes out of a pot, or even take the sound sleepers with his hands. But these last accomplishments he will soon learn to dis pense with, distinguishing the real object of his pursuit, and find compensation in the beauty arid never-ending novelty of his position. The pines growing down to the water's edge will show newly as in the glare of a conflagration ; and as he floats under the willows with his light, the song-sparrow will often wake on her perch, and sing that strain at midnight, which she had meditated for the morning. And when he has done, he may have to steer his way home through the dark by the north star, and he will

feel himself some degrees nearer to it for having lost his way on the earth.

The fishes commonly taken in this way are pickerel, suckers, perch, eels, pouts, breams, and shiners, — from thirty to sixty weight in a night. Some are hard to be recognized in the unnat ural light, especially the perch, which, his dark bands being exaggerated, acquires a ferocious aspect. The number of these transverse bands, which the Report states to be seven, is, however, very variable, for in some of our ponds they have nine and ten even.

It appears that we have eight kinds of tor toises, twelve snakes, — but one of which is venomous, — nine frogs and toads, nine sala manders, and one lizard, for our neighbors.

I am particularly attracted by the motions of the serpent tribe. They make our hands and feet, the wings of the bird, and the fins of the fish seems very superfluous, as if nature had only indulged her fancy in making them. The black snake will dart into a bush when pursued, and circle round and round with an easy and graceful motion, amid the thin and bare twigs, five or six feet from the ground, as a bird flits from bough to bough, or hang in festoons be tween the forks. Elasticity and flexibleness in the simpler forms of animal life are equivalent

to a complex system of limbs in the higher; and we have only to be as wise and wily as the ser pent, to perform as difficult feats without the vulgar assistance of hands and feet.

In May, the snapping turtle, Emysaurus ser-pentina,) is frequently taken on the meadows and in the river. The fisherman, taking sight over Ihe calm surface, discovers its snout projecting above the water, at the distance of many rods, and easily secures his prey through its unwill ingness to disturb the water by swimming has tily away, for, gradually drawing its head under, it remains resting on some limb or clump of grass. Its eggs, which are buried at a distance from the water, in some soft place, as a pigeon-bed, are frequently devoured by the skunk. It will catch fish by daylight, as a toad catches flies, and is said to emit a transparent fluid from its mouth to attract them.

Nature has taken more care than the fondest parent for the education and refinement of her children. Consider the silent influence which flowers exert, no less upon the ditcher in the meadow than the lady in the bower. When I walk in the woods, I am reminded that a wise purveyor has been there before me; my most delicate experience is typified there. I am struck with the pleasing friendships and unanimities of nature, as when the lichen on the trees takes the

form of their leaves. In the most stupendous scenes you will see delicate and fragile features, as slight wreaths of vapor, dewlines, feathery sprays, which suggest a high refinement, a no ble blood and breeding, as it were. It is not hard to account for elves and fairies; they rep resent this light grace, this ethereal gentility. Bring a spray from the wood, or a crystal from the brook, and place it on your mantel, and your household ornaments will seem plebeian beside its nobler fashion and bearing. It will wave superior there, as if used to a more refined and polished circle. It has a salute and a re sponse to all your enthusiasm and heroism.

In the winter, I stop short in the path to ad mire how the trees grow up without forethought, regardless of the time and circumstances. They do not wait as man does, but now is the golden age of the sapling. Earth, air, sun, and rain, are occasion enough; they were no better in primeval centuries. The " winter of their dis content" never comes. Witness the buds of the native poplar standing gayly out to the frost on the sides of its bare switches. They express a naked confidence. With cheerful heart one could be a sojourner in the wilderness, if he were sure to find there the catkins of the willow or the alder. When I read of them in the accounts of northern adventurers, by Baffin's Bay or Mac-

kenzie's river, I see how even there too I could dwell. They are our little vegetable redeemers. Methinks our virtue will hold out till they come again. They are worthy to have had a greater than Minerva or Ceres for their inventor. Who was the benignant goddess that bestowed them on mankind?

Nature is mythical and mystical always, and works with the license and extravagance of genius. She has her luxurious and florid style as well as art. Having a pilgrim's cup to make, she gives to the whole, stem, bowl, handle, and nose, some fantastic shape, as if it were to be the car of some fabulous marine deity, a Ne-reus or Triton.

In the winter, the botanist needs not confine himself to his books and herbarium, and give over his out-door pursuits, but may study a new department of vegetable physiology, what may be called crystalline botany, then. The winter of 1837 was unusually favorable for this. In De cember of that year, the Genius of vegetation seemed to hover by night over its summer haunts with unusual persistency. Such a hoar frost, as is very uncommon here or anywhere, and whose full effects can never be witnessed after sunrise, occurred several times. As I went forth early on a still and frosty morning, the trees looked like airy creatures of darkness caught 5

napping; on this side huddled together with their gray hairs streaming in a secluded valley, which the sun had not penetrated ; on that hur rying off in Indian file along some watercourse, while the shrubs and grasses, like elves and fairies of the night, sought to hide their dimin ished heads in the snow. The river, viewed from the high bank, appeared of a yellowish green color, though all the landscape was white. Every tree, shrub, and spire of grass, that could raise its head above the snow, was covered with a dense ice-foliage, answering, as it were, leaf for leaf to its summer dress. Even the fences had put forth leaves in the night. The centre, diverging, and more minute fibses were per fectly distinct, and the edges regularly indented. These leaves were on the side of the twig or stubble opposite to the sun, meeting it for the most part at right angles, and there were others standing out at all possible angles upon these and upon one another, with no twig or stubble supporting them. When the first rays of the sun slanted over the scene, the grasses seemed hung with innumerable jewels, which jingled merrily as they were brushed by the foot of the traveller, and reflected all the hues of the rain bow as he moved from side to side. It struck me that these ghost leaves, and the green ones whose forms they assume, were the creatures of

but one law; that in obedience to the same law the vegetable juices swell gradually into the per fect leaf, on the one hand, and the crystalline particles troop to their standard in the same order, on the other. As if the material were indifferent, but the law one and invariable, and every plant in the spring but pushed up into and filled a permanent and eternal mould, which, summer and winter forever, is waiting to be filled.

This foliate structure is common to the coral and the plumage of birds, and to how large a part of animate and inanimate nature. The same independence of law on matter is observa ble in many other instances, as in the natural rhymes, when some animal form, color, or odor, has its counterpart in some vegetable. As, in deed, all rhymes imply an eternal melody, inde pendent of any particular sense.

As confirmation of the fact, that vegetation is but a kind of crystallization, every one may observe how, upon the edge of the melting frost on the window, the needle-shaped particles are bundled together so as to resemble fields wav ing with grain, or shocks rising here and there from the stubble; on one side the vegetation of the torrid zone, high-towering palms and wide spread banyans, such as are seen in pictures of oriental scenery; on the other, arctic pines stiff frozen, with downcast branches.

Vegetation has been made the type of all growth; but as in crystals the law is more ob vious, their material being more simple, and for the most part more transient and fleeting, would it not be as philosophical as convenient to con sider all growth, all filling up within the limits of nature, but a crystallization more or less rapid?

On this occasion, in the side of the high bank of the river, wherever the water or other cause had formed a cavity, its throat and outer edge, like the entrance to a citadel, bristled with a glistening ice-armor. In one place you might see minute ostrich-feathers, which seemed the waving plumes of the warriors Sling into the fortress; in another, the glancing, fan-shaped banners of the Lilliputian host; and in another, the needle-shaped particles collected into bun dles, resembling the plumes of the pine, might pass for a phalanx of spears. From the under side of the ice in the brooks, where there was a thicker ice below, depended a mass of crystal lization, four or five inches deep, in the form of prisms, with their lower ends open, which, when the ice was laid on its smooth side, resembled the roofs and steeples of a Gothic city, or the vessels of a crowded haven under a press of canvas. The very mud in the road, where the ice had melted, was crystallized with deep rec tilinear fissures, and the crystalline masses in the sides of the ruts resembled exactly asbestos in the disposition of their needles. Around the roots of the stubble and flower-stalks, the frost was gathered into the form of irregular conical shells, or fairy rings. In some places the ice-crystals were lying upon granite rocks, directly over crystals of quartz, the frost-work of a longer night, crystals of a longer period, but to some eye unprejudiced by the short term of human life, melting as fast as the former.

In the Report on the Invertebrate Animals, this singular fact is recorded, which teaches us to put a new value on time and space. " The distribution of the marine shells is well worthy of notice as a geological fact. Cape Cod, the right arm of the Commonwealth, reaches out into the ocean, some fifty or sixty miles. It is nowhere many miles wide; but this narrow point of land has hitherto proved a barrier to the mi grations of many species of Mollusca. Several genera and numerous species, which are separ ated by the intervention of only a few miles of land, are effectually prevented from mingling by the Cape, and do not pass from one side to the other Of the one hundred and ninety-seven marine species, eighty-three do not pass to the south shore, and fifty are not found on the north shore of the Cape."

That common muscle, the Utiio complanatus.

70 NATURAL HISTORY OF MASSACHUSETTS.

or more properly fluviatilis, left in the spring by the musk-rat upon rocks and stumps, appears to have been an important article of food with the Indians. In one place, where they are said to have feasted, they are found in large quantities, at an elevation of thirty feet above the river, fill ing the soil to the depth of a foot, and mingled with ashes and Indian remains.

The works we have placed at the head of our chapter, with as much license as the preacher selects his text, are such as imply more labor than enthusiasm. The State wanted complete catalogues of its natural riches, with such addi tional facts merely as would be directly useful.

The reports on Fishes, Reptiles, Insects, and Invertebrate Animals, however, indicate labor and research, and have a value independent of the object of the legislature.

Those on Herbaceous Plants and Birds can not be of much value, as long as Bigelow and Nuttall are accessible. They serve but to indi cate, with more or less exactness, what species are found in the State. We detect several errors ourselves, and a more practised eye would no doubt expand the list.

The Quadrupeds deserved a more final and instructive report than they have obtained.

These volumes deal much in measurements and minute descriptions, not interesting to the NATURAL HISTORY OF MASSACHUSETTS. 71

general reader, with only here and there a col ored sentence to allure him, like those plants growing in dark forests, which bear only leaves without blossoms. But the ground was com paratively unbroken, and we will not complain of the pioneer, if he raises no flowers with his first crop. Let us not underrate the value of a fact; it will one day flower in a truth. It is astonishing how few facts of importance are added in a century to the natural history of any animal. The natural history of man himself is still being gradually written. Men are knowing enough after their fashion. Every countryman and dairymaid knows that the coats of the fourth stomach of the calf will curdle milk, and what particular mushroom is a safe and nutritious diet. You cannot go into any field or wood, but it \vill seem as if every stone had been turned, and the bark on every tree ripped up. But, after all, it is much easier to discover than to see when the cover is off. It has been well said that " the attitude of inspection is prone/' Wisdom does not inspect, but behold. We must look a long time before we can see. Slow are the beginnings of philosophy. He has some thing demoniacal in him, who can discern a law or couple two facts.

We can imagine a time when, — "Water runs down hill."—may have been taught in the schools. The tru» man of

science will know nature better by his finer or ganization ; he will smell, taste, see, hear, feel, better than other men. His will be a deeper and finer experience. We do not learn by infer ence and deduction, and the application of math ematics to philosophy, but by direct intercourse and sympathy. It is with science as with eth ics, — we cannot know truth by contrivance and method; the Baconian is as false as any other, and with all the helps of machinery and the arts, the most scientific will still be the healthiest and friendliest man, and possess a more perfect Indian wisdom.

A WALK TO WACHUSETT.

[1843.]

The needles of the pine All to the west incline.

CONCORD, July 19, 1842.

SUMMER and winter our eyes had rested on the dim outline of the mountains in our hori zon, to which distance and indistinctness lent a grandeur not their own, so that they served equally to interpret all the allusions of poets and travellers; whether with Homer, on a spring morning, we sat down on the many-peaked Olympus, or, with Virgil and his compeers, roamed the Etrurian and Thessalian hills, or with Humboldt measured the more modern An des and Teneriffe. Thus we spoke our mind to them, standing on the Concord cliffs.—

With frontier strength ye stand your ground, With grand content ye circle round, Tumultuous silence for all sound, Ye distant nursery of rills, Monadnock, and the Peterboro' hills; Like some vast fleet,

Sailing through rain and sleet,
Through winter's cold and summer's heat;
Still holding on, upon your high emprise,
Until ye find a shore amid the skies ;
Not skulking close to land,
With cargo contraband,
For they who sent a venture out by ye
Have set the sun to see
Their honesty.
Ships of the line, each one,
Ye to the westward run,
Always before the gale,
Under a press of sail,
With weight of metal all untold.
I seem to feel ye, in my firm seat here,
Immeasurable depth of hold,
And breadth of beam, and length of running gear.
Methinks ye take luxurious pleasure
In your novel western leisure;
So cool your brows, and freshly blue,
As Time had nought for ye to do;
For ye lie at your length,
An unappropriated strength,

Unhewn primeval timber,
For knees so stiff, for masts so limber;
The stock of which new earths are made,
One day to be our western trade,
Fit for the stanchions of a world
Which through the seas of space is hurled.
While we enjoy a lingering ray, Ye still o'ertop the western day, Reposing yonder, on God's croft, Like solid stacks of hay.
Edged with silver, and with gold,
The clouds hang o'er in damask fold,
And with such depth of amber light
The west is dight,
Where still a few rays slant,
That even heaven seems extravagant.
On the earth's edge mountains and trees
Stand as they were on air graven,
Or as the vessels in a haven
Await the morning breeze.
I fancy even
Through your defiles windeth the way to heaven ;
And yonder still, in spite of history's page,
Linger the golden and the silver age;
Upon the laboring gale
The news of future centuries is brought,
And of new dynasties of thought,
From your remotest vale.
But special I remember thee,
Wachusett, who like me
Standcst alone without society.
Thy far blue eye,
A remnant of the sky,
Seen through the clearing or the gorge,
Or from the windows on the forge,
Doth leaven all it passes by.
Nothing is true,
But stands 'tween me and you,
Thou western pioneer,
Who know'st not shame nor fear,
By venturous spirit driven,
Under the eaves of heaven,
And can'st expand thee there,
And breathe enough of air ?
Upholding heaven, holding down earth,
Thy pastime from thy birth,
Not steadied by the one, nor leaning on the other;
May I approve myself thy worthy brother!

At length, like Rasselas, and other inhabitants of happy valleys, we resolved to scale the blue wall which bound the western horizon, though not without misgivings, that thereafter no visi ble fairy land would exist for us. But we will not leap at once to our journey's end, though near, but imitate Homer, who conducts his reader over the plain, and along the resound ing sea, though it be but to the tent of Achilles. In the spaces of thought are the reaches of land and water, where men go and come. The land scape lies far and fair within, and the deepest thinker is the farthest travelled.

At a cool and early hour on a pleasant morn ing in July, my companion and I passed rapidly through Acton and Stow, stopping to rest and refresh us on the bank of a small stream, a tribu tary of the Assabet, in the latter tow^n. As we traversed the cool woods of Acton, with stout staves in our hands, we were cheered by the song of the red-eye, the thrushes, the phoebe, and the cuckoo ; and as we passed through the open country, we inhaled the fresh scent of every field, and all nature lay passive, to be viewed and travelled. Every rail, every farm-house,

seen dimly in the twilight, every tinkling sound told of peace and purity, and we moved hap pily along the dank roads, enjoying not such privacy as the day leaves when it withdraws, but such as it has not profaned. It was soli tude with light; which is better than darkness. But anon, the sound of the mower's rifle was heard in the fields, and this, too, mingled with the lowing kine.

This part of our route lay through the coun try of hops, which plant perhaps supplies the want of the vine in American scenery, and may remind the traveller of Italy, and the South of France, whether he traverses the country when the hop-fields, as then, present solid and regular masses of verdure, hanging in graceful festoons from pole to pole; the cool coverts where lurk the gales which refresh the wayfarer; or in Sep tember, when the women and children, and the neighbors from far and near, are gathered to pick the hops into long troughs; or later still, when the poles stand piled in vast pyramids in the yards, or lie in heaps by the roadside.

The culture of the hop, with the processes of picking, drying in the kiln, and packing for the market, as well as the uses to which it is ap plied, so analogous to the culture and uses of the grape, may afford a theme for future poets.

The mower in the adjacent meadow could

not tell us the name of the brook on whose banks we had rested, or whether it had any, but his younger companion, perhaps his brother, knew that it was Great Brook. Though they stood very near together in the field, the things they knew were very far apart; nor did they suspect each other's reserved knowledge, till the stranger came by. In Bolton, while we rested on the rails of a cottage fence, the strains of music which issued from within, probably in compliment to us, sojourners, reminded us that thus far men were fed by the accustomed pleas ures. So soon did we, wayfarers, begin to learn that man's life is rounded with the same few facts, the same simple relations everywhere, and it is vain to travel to find it new. The flowers grow more various ways than he. But coming soon to higher land, which afforded a prospect of the mountains, we thought we had not travelled in vain, if it were only to hear a truer and wilder pronunciation of their names, from the lips of the inhabitants ; not W«2/-tatic, TF«?/-chusett, but TFor-tatic, TFor-chusett. It made us ashamed of our tame and civil pronunciation, and we looked upon them as born and bred farther west than we. Their tongues had a more generous accent than ours, as if breath was cheaper where they wagged. A countryman, who speaks but seldom, talks copiously, as it were, as his wife

sets cream and cheese before you without stint. Before noon we had reached the highlands over looking the valley of Lancaster, (affording the first fair and open prospect into the west,) and there, on the top of a hill, in the shade of some oaks, near to where a spring bubbled out from a leaden pipe, we rested during the heat of the day, reading Virgil, and enjoying the scenery. It was such a place as one feels to be on the outside of the earth, for from it we could, in some measure, see the form and structure of the globe. There lay Wachusett, the object of our journey, lowering upon us with unchanged pro portions, though with a less ethereal aspect than had greeted our morning gaze, while further north, in successive order, slumbered its sister mountains along the horizon.

We could get no further into the .ZEneid than

— atque altas moenia Romce, — and the wall of high Rome,

before we were constrained to reflect by what myriad tests a work of genius has to be tried; that Virgil, away in Rome, two thousand years off, should have to unfold his meaning, the in spiration of Italian vales, to the pilgrim on New England hills. This life so raw and modern, that so civil and ancient; and yet we read Vir gil, mainly to be reminded of the identity of human nature in all ages, and, by the poet's

own account, we are both the children of a late age, and live equally under the reign of Jupiter.

" He shook honey from the leaves, and removed fire, And stayed the wine, everywhere flowing in rivers ; That experience, by meditating, might invent various arts By degrees, and seek the blade of corn in furrows, And strike out hidden fire from the veins of the flint."

The old world stands serenely behind the new, as one mountain yonder towers behind another, more dim and distant. Rome imposes her story still upon this late generation. The very children in the school we had that morn ing passed, had gone through her wars, and recited her alarms, ere they had heard of the wars of neighboring Lancaster. The roving eye still rests inevitably on her hills, and she still holds up the skirts of the sky on that side, and makes the past remote.

The lay of the land hereabouts is well wor thy the attention of the traveller. The hill on which we were resting made part of an exten sive range, running from southwest to north east, across the country, and separating the waters of the Nashua from those of the Con cord, whose banks we had left in the morning . and by bearing in mind this fact, we could ea sily determine whither each brook was bourn? that crossed our path. Parallel to this, and fif

teen miles further west, beyond the deep and broad valley in which lie Groton, Shirley, Lan caster, and Boylston, runs the Wachusett range, in the same general direction. The descent into the valley on the Nashua side, is by far the most sudden ; and a couple of miles brought us to the southern branch of the Nashua, a shal low but rapid stream, flowing between high and gravelly banks. But we soon learned that there were no gclidcs valles into which we had de scended, and missing the coolness of the morn ing air, feared it had become the sun's turn to try his power upon us.

" The sultry sun had gained the middle sky, And not a tree, and not an herb was nigh."

and with melancholy pleasure we echoed the melodious plaint of our fellow-traveller, Hassan, in the desert, —

" Sad was the hour, and luckless was the day, When first from Schiraz' walls I bent my way."

The air lay lifeless between the hills, as in a seething caldron, with no leaf stirring, and in stead of the fresh odor of grass and clover, with which we had before been regaled, the dry scent of every herb seemed merely medicinal. Yield ing, therefore, to the heat, we strolled into the woods, and along the course of a rivulet, on whose banks we loitered, observing at our leisure the products of these new fields. He who traverses the woodland paths, at this season, will have occasion to remember the small droop ing bell-like flowers and slender red stem of the dogs-bane, and the coarser stem and berry of the poke, which are both common in remoter and wilder scenes; and if " the sun casts such a re flecting heat from the sweet fern," as makes him faint, when he is climbing the bare hills, as they complained who first penetrated into these parts, the cool fragrance of the swamp pink restores him again, when traversing the valleys between. As we went on our way late in the afternoon, we refreshed ourselves by bathing our feet in every rill that crossed the road, and anon, as we were able to walk in the shadows of the hills, recovered our morning elasticity. Passing through Sterling, we reached the banks of the Stillwater, in the western part of the town, at evening, where is a small village collected. We fancied that there was already a certain western look about this place, a smell of pines and roar of water, recently confined by dams, belying its name, which were exceedingly grateful. When the first inroad has been made, a few acres lev elled, and a few houses erected, the forest looks wilder than ever. Left to herself, nature is al ways more or less civilized, and delights in a certain refinement; but where the axe has

encroached upon the edge of the forest, the dead and unsightly limbs of the pine, which she had concealed with green banks of verdure, are exposed to sight. This village had, as yet, no post-office, nor any settled name. In the small villages which we entered, the villagers gazed after us, with a complacent, almost compassion ate look, as if we were just making our debut in the world at a late hour. " Nevertheless," did they seem to say, " come and study us, and learn men and manners." So is each one's world but a clearing in the forest, so much open and in closed ground. The landlord had not yet re turned from the field with his men, and the cows had yet to be milked. But we remembered the inscription on the wall of the Swedish inn, " You will find at Trolhate excellent bread, meat, and wine, provided you bring them with you," and were contented. But I must confess it did somewhat disturb our pleasure, in this withdrawn spot, to have our own village news paper handed us by our host, as if the greatest charm the country offered to the traveller was the facility of communication with the town. Let it recline on its own everlasting hills, and not be looking out from their summits for some petty Boston or New York in the horizon.

At intervals we heard the murmuring of wa ter, and the slumberous breathing of crickets throughout the night; and left the inn the next morning in the gray twilight, after it had been hallowed by the night air, and when only the innocent cows were stirring, with a kind of re gret. It was only four miles to the base of the mountain, and the scenery was already more picturesque. Our road lay along the course cf the Stillwater, which was brawling at the bottom of a deep ravine, filled with pines and rocks, tumbling fresh from the mountains, so soon, alas! to commence its career of usefulness. At first, a cloud hung between us and the summit, but it was soon blown away. As we gathered the raspberries, which grew abundantly by the roadside, we fancied that that action was con sistent with a lofty prudence, as if the traveller who ascends into a mountainous region should fortify himself by eating of such light ambrosial fruits as grow there; and, drinking of the springs which gush out from the mountain sides, as he gradually inhales the subtler and purer atmos phere of those elevated places, thus propitiating the mountain gods, by a sacrifice of their own fruits. The gross products of the plains and valleys are for such as dwell therein; but it seemed to us that the juices of this berry had relation to the thin air of the mountain-tops.

In due time we began to ascend the moun tain, passing, first, through a grand sugar maplewood, which bore the marks of the augur, then a denser forest, which gradually became dwarfed, till there were no trees whatever. We at length pitched our tent on the summit. It is but nine teen hundred feet above the village of Princeton, and three thousand above the level of the sea; but by this slight elevation it is infinitely re moved from the plain, and when we reached it, we felt a sense of remoteness, as if we had travelled into distant regions, to Arabia Petrea, or the farthest east. A robin upon a staff, was the highest object in sight. Swallows were flying about us, and the chewink and cuckoo were heard near at hand. The summit consists of a few acres, destitute of trees, covered with bare rocks, interspersed with blueberry bushes, raspberries, gooseberries, strawberries, moss, and a fine wiry grass. The common yellow lily, and dwarf-cornel, grow abundantly in the crevices of the rocks. This clear space, which is gently rounded, is bounded a few feet lower by a thick shrubbery of oaks, with maples, aspens, beeches, cherries, and occasionally a mountain-ash inter mingled, among which we found the bright blue berries of the Solomon's Seal, and the fruit of the pyrola. From the foundation of a wooden observatory, which was formerly erected on the highest point, forming a rude, hollow structure of stone, a dozen feet in diameter, and five or

six in height, we could see Monadnock, in simple grandeur, in the northwest, rising nearly a thousand feet higher, still the " far blue moun tain," though with an altered profile. The first day the weather was so hazy that it was in vain we endeavored to unravel the ob scurity. It was like looking into the sky again, and the patches of forest here and there seemed to flit like clouds over a lower heaven. As to voyagers of an aerial Polynesia, the earth seemed like a larger island in the ether; on every side, even as low as we. the sky shutting down, like an unfathomable deep, around it, a blue Pacific island, where who knows what islanders in habit ? and as we sail near its shores we see the waving of trees, and hear the lowing of kine.

We read Virgil and Wordsworth in our tent, with new pleasure there, while waiting for a clearer atmosphere, nor did the weather prevent our appreciating the simple truth and beauty of Peter Bell:

. " And he had lain beside his asses, On lofty Cheviot hills."

" And he had trudged through Yorkshire dales, Among the rocks and winding scars, Where deep and low the hamlets lie Beneath their little patch of sky, And little lot of stars."

Who knows but this hill may one day be a

Helvellyn, or even a Parnassus, and the Muses haunt here, and other Homers frequent the neighboring plains,

Not unconcerned Wachusett rears his head Above the field, so late from nature won,

With patient brow reserved, as one who read New annals in the history of man.

The blue-berries which the mountain afforded, added to the milk we had brought, made our frugal supper, while for entertainment the even song of the wood-thrush rung along the ridge. Our eyes rested on no painted ceiling nor car peted hall, but on skies of nature's painting, and hills and forests of her embroidery. Be fore sunset, we rambled along the ridge to the north, while a hawk soared still above us. It was a place where gods might wander, so sol emn and solitary, and removed from all conta gion with the plain. As the evening came on, the haze was condensed in vapor, and the land scape became more distinctly visible, and nu merous sheets of water were brought to light.

Et jam summa procul villarum culmina fumant, Majoresque cadunt altis de montibus umbra?.

And now the tops of the villas smoke afar off,

And the shadows fall longer from the high mountains.

As we stood on the stone tower while the sun was setting, we saw the shades of night creep

gradually over the valleys of the east, and the inhabitants went into their houses, and shut their doors, while the moon silently rose up, and took possession of that part. And then the same scene was repeated on the west side, as far as the Connecticut and the Green Moun tains, and the sun's rays fell on us two alone, of all New England men.

It was the night but one before the full of the moon, so bright that we could see to read dis tinctly by moonlight, and in the evening strolled over the summit without danger. There was, by chance, a fire blazing on Monadnock that night, which lighted up the whole western hori zon, and by making us aware of a community of mountains, made our position seem less soli tary. But at length the wind drove us to the shelter of our tent, and we closed its door for the night, and fell asleep.

It was thrilling to hear the wind roar over the rocks, at intervals when we waked, for it had grown quite cold and windy. The night was in its elements, simple even to majesty in that bleak place,— a bright moonlight and a piercing wind. It was at no time darker than twilight within the tent, and we could easily see the moon through its transparent roof as we lay ; for there was the moon still above us, with Jupiter and Saturn on either hand, looking down on Wachu-

sett, and it was a satisfaction to know that they were our fellow-travellers still, as high and out of our reach as our own destiny. Truly the stars were given for a consolation to man. We should not know but our life were fated to be always grovelling, but it is permitted to behold them, and surely they are deserving of a fair destiny. We see laws which never fail, of whose failure we never conceived ; and their lamps burn all the night, too, as well as all day,— so rich and lavish is that nature which can afford this superfluity of light.

The morning twilight began as soon as the moon had set, and we arose and kindled our fire, whose blaze might have been seen for thirty miles around. As the daylight increased, it was remarkable how rapidly the wind went down. There was no dew on the summit, but coldness supplied its place. When the dawn had reached its prime, we enjoyed the view of a distinct hori zon line, and could fancy ourselves at sea, and the distant hills the waves in the horizon, as seen from the deck of a vessel. The cherry-birds flit ted around us, the nuthatch and flicker were heard among the bushes, the titmouse perched within a few feet, and the song of the wood-thrush again rung along the ridge. At length we saw the sun rise up out of the sea, and shine on Massachusetts; and from this moment the at-

mosphere grew more and more transparent till the time of our departure, and we began to real ize the extent of the view, and how the earth, in some degree, answered to the heavens in breadth, the white villages to the constellations in the sky. There was little of the sublimity and grandeur which belong to mountain scenery, but an immense landscape to ponder on a sum mer's day. We could see how ample and roomy is nature. As far as the eye could reach, there was little life in the landscape; the few birds that flitted past did not crowd. The travellers on the remote highways, which intersect the country on every side, had no fellow-travellers for miles, before or behind. On every side, the eye ranged over successive circles of towns, ris ing one above another, like the terraces of a vineyard, till they were lost in the horizon. Wachusett is, in fact, the observatory of the State. There lay Massachusetts, spread out be fore us in its length and breadth, like a map. There was the level horizon, which told of the sea on the east and south, the well-known hills of New Hampshire on the north, and the misty summits of the Hoosac and Green Mountains, first made visible to us the evening before, blue and unsubstantial, like some bank of clouds which the morning wind would dissipate, on the northwest and west. These last distant ranges,

on which the eye rests unwearied, commence with an abrupt boulder in the north, beyond the Connecticut, and travel southward, with three or four peaks dimly seen. But Monadnock, rear ing its masculine front in the northwest, is the grandest feature. As we beheld it, w r e knew that it was the height of land between the two rivers, on this side the valley of the Merrimack, or that of the Connecticut, fluctuating with their blue seas of air, — these rival vales, al ready teeming with Yankee men along their respective streams, born to what destiny who shall tell ? Watatic, and the neighboring hills in this State and in New Hampshire, are a continuation of the same elevated range on which we were standing. But that New Hamp shire bluff,— that promontory of a State,—low ering day and night on this our State of Massa chusetts, will longest haunt our dreams.

We could, at length, realize the place moun tains occupy on the land, and how they come into the general scheme of the universe. When firs" we climb their summits and observe their lesser irregularities, we do not give credit to the comprehensive intelligence which shaped them ; but when afterward we behold their outlines in the - horizon, we confess that the hand which moulded their opposite slopes, making one to "balance the other, worked round a deep centre,

and was privy to the plan of the universe. So is the least part of nature in its bearings refer red to all space. These lesser mountain ranges, as well as the Alleghanies, run from northeast to southwest, and parallel with these mountain streams are the more fluent rivers, answering to the general direction of the coast, the bank of the great ocean stream itself. Even the clouds, with their thin bars, fall into the same direction by preference, and such even is the course of the prevailing winds, and the migration of men and birds. A mountain-chain determines many things for the statesman and philosopher. The improvements of civilization rather creep along its sides than cross its summit. How often is it a barrier to prejudice and fanaticism ? In pass ing over these heights of land, through their thin atmosphere, the follies of the plain are refined and purified; and as many species of plants do not scale their summits, so many species of folly no doubt do not cross the Alleghanies; it is only the hardy mountain plant that creeps quite over the ridge, and descends into the valley beyond.

We get a dim notion of the flight of birds, especially of such as fly high in the air, by having ascended a mountain. We can now see what landmarks mountains are to their migra tions ; how the Catskills and Highlands have hardly sunk to them, when Wachusett and

Monadnock open a passage to the northeast; how they are guided, too, in their course by the rivers and valleys; and who knows but by the stars, as well as the mountain ranges, and not by the petty landmarks which we use. The bird whose eye takes in the Green Mountains on the one side, and the ocean on the other, need not be at a loss to find its way.

At noon we descended the mountain, and having returned to the abodes of men, turned our faces to the east again; measuring our prog ress, from time to time, by the more ethereal hues which the mountain assumed. Passing swiftly through Stillwater and Sterling, as with a downward impetus, we found ourselves almost at home again in the green meadows of Lancas ter, so like our own Concord, for both are wa tered by two streams which unite near their centres, and have many other features in com mon. There is an unexpected refinement about this scenery; level prairies of great extent, inter spersed with elms and hop-fields and groves of trees, give it almost a classic appearance. This, it will be remembered, was the scene of Mrs. Rowlandson's capture, and of other events in the Indian wars, but from this July afternoon, and under that mild exterior, those times seemed as remote as the irruption of the Goths. They were the dark age of

New England. On be-

holding a picture of a New England village as it then appeared, with a fair open prospect, and a light on trees and river, as if it were broad noon, we find we had not thought the sun shone in those days, or that men lived in broad day light then. We do not imagine the sun shining on hill and valley during Philip's war, nor on the war-path of Paugus, or Standish, or Church, or Lovell, with serene summer weather, but a dim twilight or night did those events transpire in. They must have fought in the shade of their own dusky deeds.

At length, as we plodded along the dusty roads, our thoughts became as dusty as they; all thought indeed stopped, thinking broke down, or proceeded only passively in a sort of rhythmi cal cadence of the confused material of thought, and we found ourselves mechanically repeating some familiar measure which timed with our tread; some verse of the Robin Hood ballads, for instance, which one can recommend to travel

by-
" Swearers are swift, sayd lyttle John,
As the wind blows over the hill; For if it be never so loud this night,
To-morrow it may be still."

And so it went up hill and down till a stone interrupted the line, when a new verse was chosen.

" His shoote it was but loosely shot, Yet flewe not the arrowe in vaine,
For it met one of the sheriffe's men, And Williani-a-Trent was slaine."

There is, however, this consolation to the most way-worn traveller, upon the dustiest road, that the path his feet describe is so perfectly symbolical of human life, — now climbing the hills, now descending into the vales. From the summits he beholds the heavens and the horizon, from the vales he looks up to the heights again. He is treading his old lessons still, and though he may be very weary and travel-worn, it is yet sincere experience.

Leaving the Nashua, we changed our route a little, and arrived at Stillriver Village, in the western part of Harvard, just as the sun was set ting. From this place, which lies to the north ward, upon the western slope of the same range of hills on which we had spent the noon before, in the adjacent town, the prospect is beautiful, and the grandeur of the mountain outlines un surpassed. There was such a repose and quiet here at this hour, as if the very hill-sides were enjoying the scene, and we passed slowly along, looking back over the country we had traversed, and listening to the evening song of the robin, we could not help contrasting the equanimity of nature with the bustle and impatience of man.

His words and actions presume always a crisis near at hand, but she is forever silent and unpre tending.

And now that we have returned to the desul tory life of the plain, let us endeavor to import a little of that mountain grandeur into it. We will remember within what walls we lie, and understand that this level life too has its summit, and why from the mountain-top the deepest val leys have a tinge of blue; that there is elevation in every hour, as no part of the earth is so low that the heavens may not be seen from, and we have only to stand on the summit of our hour to command an uninterrupted horizon.

We rested that night at Harvard, and the next morning, while one bent his steps to the nearer village of Groton, the other took his separate and solitary way to the peaceful meadows of Con cord ; but let him not forget to record the brave hospitality of a farmer and his wife, who gener ously entertained him at their board, though the poor wayfarer could only congratulate the one on the continuance of hayweather, and silently accept the kindness of the other. Refreshed by this instance of generosity, no less than by the substantial viands set before him, he pushed for ward with new vigor, and reached the banks of the Concord before the sun had climbed many degrees into the heavens.

THE LANDLORD.

[1843.]

UNDER the one word, house, are included the school-house, the alms-house, the jail, the tavern, the dwelling-house ; and the meanest shed or cave in which men live contains the elements of all these. But nowhere on the earth stands the entire and perfect house. The Parthenon, St. Peter's, the Gothic minster, the palace, the hovel, are but imperfect executions of an imperfect idea. Who would dwell in them ? Perhaps to the eye of the gods, the cottage is more holy than the Parthenon, for they look down with no especial favor upon the shrines formally ded icated to them, and that should be the most sacred roof which shelters most of humanity. Surely, then, the gods who are most interested in the human race preside over the Tavern, where especially men congregate. Methinks I see the thousand shrines erected to Hospitality shining afar in all countries, as well Mahometan and Jewish, as Christian, khans, and caravansa ries, and inns, whither all pilgrims without dis tinction resort.

Likewise we look in vain, east or west over the earth, to find the perfect man; bat each rep resents only some particular excellence. The Landlord is a man of more open and general sympathies, who possesses a spirit of hospitality which is its own reward, and feeds and shelters men from pure love of the creatures. To be sure, this profession is as often filled by imper fect characters, and such as have sought it from unworthy motives, as any other, but so much the more should we prize the true and honest Landlord when we meet with him.

Who has not imagined to himself a country inn, where the traveller shall really feel in, and at home, and at his public-house, who was before at his private house; whose host is indeed a host, and a lord of the land, a self-appointed brother of his race; called to his place, beside, by all the winds of heaven and his good genius, as truly as the preacher is called to preach; a man of such uni versal sympathies, and so broad and genial a human nature, that he would fain sacrifice the tender but narrow ties of private friendship, to a broad, sunshiny, fair-weather-and-foul friendship for his race; who loves men, not as a philoso pher, with philanthropy, nor as an overseer of the poor, with charity, but by a necessity of his nature, as he loves dogs and horses ; and stand ing at his open door from morning till night,

would fain see more and more of them come along the highway, and is never satiated. To him the sun and moon are but travellers, the one by day and the other by night; and they too patronize his house. To his imagination all things travel save his sign-post and himself; and though you may be his neighbor for years, he will show you only the civilities of the road. But on the other hand, while nations and indi viduals are alike selfish and exclusive, he loves all men equally ; and if he treats his nearest neighbor as a stranger, since he has invited all nations to share his hospitality, the farthest trav elled is in some measure kindred to him who takes him into the bosom of his family.

He keeps a house of entertainment at the sign of the Black Horse or the Spread Eagle, and is known far and wide, and his fame travels with increasing radius every year. All the neigh borhood is in his interest, and if the traveller ask how far to a tavern, he receives some such an swer as this : " Well, sir, there's a house about three miles from here, where they haven't taken down their sign yet; but it's only ten miles to Slocum's, and that's a capital house, both for man and beast." At three miles he passes a cheerless barrack, standing desolate behind its sign-post, neither public nor private, and has glimpses of a discontented couple who have mistaken their calling. At ten miles see where the Tavern stands, — really an entertaining pros pect,— so public and inviting that only the rain and snow do not enter. It is no gay pavilion, made of bright stuffs, and furnished with nuts and gingerbread, but as plain and sincere as a caravansary; located in no Tarry town, where you receive only the civilities of commerce, but far in the fields it exercises a primitive hospital ity, amid the fresh scent of new hay and rasp berries, if it be summer time, and the tinkling of cow-bells from invisible pastures; for it is a land flowing with milk and honey, and the newest milk courses in a broad, deep stream across the premises.

In these retired places the tavern is first of all a house — elsewhere, last of all, or never, — and warms and shelters its inhabitants. It is as sim ple and sincere in its essentials as the caves in which the first men dwelt, but it is also as open and public. The traveller steps across the thresh old, and lo! he too is master, for he only can be called proprietor of the house here who behaves with most propriety in it. The Landlord stands clear back in nature, to my imagination, with his axe and spade felling trees and raising pota toes with the vigor of a pioneer; with Prome thean energy making nature yield her increase to supply the wants of so many; and he is not so

exhausted, nor of so short a stride, but that he comes forward even to the highway to this wide hospitality and publicity. Surely, he has solved some of the problems of life. He comes in at his backdoor, holding a log fresh cut for the hearth upon his shoulder with one hand, while he greets the newly arrived traveller with the other.

Here at length we have free range, as not in palaces, nor cottages, nor temples, and intrude nowhere. All the secrets of housekeeping are exhibited to the eyes of men, above and below, before and behind. This is the necessary way to live, men have confessed, in these days, and shall he skulk and hide ? And why should we have any serious disgust at kitchens ? Perhaps they are the holiest recess of the house. There is the hearth, after all, — and the settle, and the fagots, and the kettle, and the crickets. We have pleasant reminiscences of these. They are the heart, the left ventricle, the very vital part of the house. Here the real and sincere life which we meet in the streets was actually fed and sheltered. Here burns the taper that cheers the lonely traveller by night, and from this hearth ascend the smokes that populate the valley to his eyes by day. On the whole, a man may not be so little ashamed of any other part of his house, for here is his sincerity and earnest, at

least. It may not be here that the besoms are plied most, — it is not here that they need to be, for dust will not settle on the kitchen floor more than in nature.

Hence it will not do for the Landlord to pos sess too fine a nature. He must have health above the common accidents of life, subject to no modern fashionable diseases ; but no taste, rather a vast relish or appetite. His sentiments on all subjects will be delivered as freely as the wind blows ; there is nothing private or individ ual in them, though still original, but they are public, and of the hue of the heavens over his house, — a certain out-of-door obviousness and transparency not to be disputed. What he does, his manners are not to be complained of, though abstractly offensive, for it is what man does, and in him the race is exhibited. When he eats, he is liver and bowels, and the whole digestive apparatus to the company, and so all admit the thing is done. He must have no idiosyncrasies, no particular bents or tendencies to this or that, but a general, uniform, and healthy development, such as his portly person indicates, offering him self equally on all sides to men. He is not one of your peaked and inhospitable men of genius, with particular tastes, but, as we said before, has one uniform relish, and taste which never aspires higher than a tavern-sign, or the cut of

a weather-cock. The man of genius, like a dog with a bone, or the slave who has swallowed a diamond, or a patient with the gravel, sits afar and retired, off the road, hangs out no sign of refreshment for man and beast, but says, by all possible hints and signs, I wish to be alone — good-by — farewell. But the landlord can af ford to live without privacy. He entertains no private thought, he cherishes no solitary hour, no Sabbath day, but thinks, — enough to assert the dignity of reason, — and talks, and reads the newspaper. What he does not tell to one trav eller, he tells to another. He never wants to be alone, but sleeps, wakes, eats, drinks, sociably, still remembering his race. He walks abroad through the thoughts of men, and the Iliad and Shakspeare are tame to him, who hears the rude but homely incidents of the road from every traveller. The mail might drive through his brain in the midst of his most lonely soliloquy, without disturbing his equanimity, provided it brought plenty of news and passengers. There can be no j5ro-fanity where there is no fane be hind, and the whole world may see quite round him. Perchance his lines have fallen to him in dustier places, and he has heroically sat down where two roads meet, or at the Four Corners, or the Five Points, and his life is sublimely triv ial for the good of men. The dust of travel

blows ever in his eyes, and they preserve their clear, complacent look. The hourlies and half-hourlies, the dailies and weeklies, whirl on well-worn tracks, round and round his house, as if it were the goal in the stadium, and still he sits within in unruffled serenity, with no show of retreat. His neighbor dwells timidly behind a screen of poplars and willows, and a fence with sheaves of spears at regular intervals, or defended against the tender palms of visitors by sharp spikes, — but the traveller's wheels rattle over the door-step of the tavern, and he cracks his whip in the entry. He is truly glad to see you, and sincere as the bull's-eye over his door. The traveller seeks to find, wherever he goes, some one who will stand in this broad and catholic re lation to him, who will be an inhabitant of the land to him a stranger, and represent its human nature, as the rock stands for its inanimate na ture ; and this is he. As his crib furnishes prov ender for the traveller's horse, and his larder provisions for his appetite, so his conversation furnishes the necessary aliment to his spirits. He knows very well what a man wants, for he is a man himself, and as it were the farthest travelled, though he has never stirred from his door. He understands his needs and destiny, He would be well fed and lodged, there can be no doubt, and have the transient sympathy of a

cheerful companion, and of a heart which always prophesies fair weather. And after all the great est men, even, want much more the sympathy which every honest fellow can give, than that which the great only can impart. If he is not the most upright, let us allow him this praise, that he is the most downright of men. He has a hand to shake and to be shaken, and takes a sturdy and unquestionable interest in you, as if he had assumed the care of you, but if you will break your neck, he will even give you the best advice as to the method.

The great poets have not been ungrateful to their landlords. Mine host of the Tabard Inn, in the Prologue to the Canterbury Tales, was an honor to his profession : -

" A semely man our Hoste was, with alle,
For to ban been an marshal in an halle.
A large man he was, with eyen stepe ;
A fairer burgeis is ther non in Chepe :
Bold of his speche, and wise, and well ytaught,
And of manhood him lacked righte naught.
Eke thereto, was he right a mery man,
And after souper plaien he began,
And spake of mirthe amonges other thinges,
Whan that we hadden made our reckoninges."

He is the true house-band, and centre of the company — of greater fellowship and practical social talent than any. He it is that proposes

that each shall tell a tale to while away the time to Canterbury, and leads them himself, and concludes with his own tale: —

" Now, by my fader's soule that is ded,

But ye be mery, smiteth of my bed :

Hold up your hondes withouten more speche."

If we do not look up to the Landlord, we look round for him on all emergencies, for he is a man of infinite experience, who unites hands with wit. He is a more public character than a statesman, — a publican, and not conse quently a sinner; and surely, he, if any, should be exempted from taxation and military duty.

Talking with our host is next best and in structive to talking with one's self. It is a more conscious soliloquy; as it were, to speak generally, and try what we would say provided we had an audience. He has indulgent and open ears, and does not require petty and par ticular statements. " Heigho ! " exclaims the traveller. Them's my sentiments, thinks mine host, and stands ready for what may come next, expressing the purest sympathy by his demeanor. " Hot as blazes ! " says the other,

" Hard weather, sir, — not much stirring

nowadays," says he. He is wiser than to con tradict his guest in any case; he lets him go on, he lets him travel.

The latest sitter leaves him standing far in the night, prepared to live right on, while suns rise and set, and his " good night " has as brisk a sound as his " good morning;" and the earliest riser finds him tasting his liquors in the bar ere flies begin to buzz, with a countenance fresh as the morning star over the sanded floor, — and not as one who had watched all night for trav ellers. And yet, if beds be the subject of con versation, it will appear that no man has been a sounder sleeper in his time.

Finally, as for his moral character, we do not hesitate to say, that he has no grain of vice or meanness in him, but represents just that de gree of virtue which all men relish without be ing obliged to respect. He is a good man, as his bitters are good, — an unquestionable good ness. Not what is called a good man, — good to be considered, as a work of art in galleries and museums, — but a good fellow, that is, good^o be associated with. Who ever thought of the religion of an innkeeper — whether he was joined to the Church, partook of the sacrament, said his prayers, feared God, or the like ? No doubt he has had his experiences, has felt a change, and is a firm believer in the persever ance of the saints. In this last, we suspect, does the peculiarity of his religion consist. But he keeps an inn, and not a conscience. How

many fragrant charities and sincere social vir tues are implied in this daily offering of him self to the public. He cherishes good will to all, and gives the wayfarer as good and honest advice to direct him on his road as the priest.

To conclude, the tavern will compare favor ably with the church. The church is the place where prayers and sermons are delivered, but the tavern is where they are to take effect, and if the former are good, the latter cannot be bad.

A WINTER WALK.

[1843.]

THE wind has gently murmured through the blinds, or puffed with feathery softness against the windows, and occasionally sighed like a summer zephyr lifting the leaves along, the live long night. The meadow-mouse has slept in his snug gallery in the sod, the owl has sat in a hollow tree in the depth of the swamp, the rab bit, the squirrel, and the fox have all been housed. The watch-dog has lain quiet on the hearth, and the cattle have stood silent in their stalls. The earth itself has slept, as it were its first, not its last sleep, save when some street-sign or wood-house door has faintly creaked upon its hinge, cheering forlorn nature at her midnight work, — the only sound awake twixt Venus and Mars, — advertising us of a remote inward warmth, a divine cheer and fellowship, where gods are met together, but where it is very bleak for men to stand. But while the earth has slumbered, all the air has been alive with feathery flakes descending, as if some northern

Ceres reigned, showering her silvery grain over all the fields.

We sleep, and at length awake to the still reality of a winter morning. The snow lies warm as cotton or down upon the window-sill; the broadened sash and frosted panes admit a dim and private light, which enhances the snug cheer within. The stillness of the morning is impressive. The floor creaks under our feet as we move toward the window to look abroad through some clear space over the fields. We see the roofs stand under their snow burden. From the eaves and fences hang stalactites of snow, and in the yard stand stalagmites cover ing some concealed core. The trees and shrubs rear white arms to the sky on every side; and where were walls and fences, we see fantastic forms stretching in frolic gambols across the dusky landscape, as if nature had strewn her fresh designs over the fields by night as models for man's art.

Silently we unlatch the door, letting the drift fall in, and step abroad to face the cutting air. Already the stars have lost some of their sparkle, and a dull, leaden mist skirts the horizon. A lurid brazen light in the east proclaims the ap proach of day, while the western landscape is dim and spectral still, and clothed in a sombre Tartarian light, like the shadowy realms. They

are Infernal sounds only that you hear, — the crowing of cocks, the barking of dogs, the chop ping of wood, the lowing of kine, all seem to come from Pluto's barn-yard and beyond the Styx; — not for any melancholy they suggest, but their twilight bustle is too solemn and mys terious for earth. The recent tracks of the fox or otter, in the yard, remind us that each hour of the night is crowded with events, and the primeval nature is still working and making tracks in the snow. Opening the gate, we tread briskly along the lone country road, crunching the dry and crisped snow under our feet, or aroused by the sharp clear creak of the wood-sled, just starting for the distant market, from the early farmer's door, where it has lain the summer long, dreaming amid the chips and stubble; while far through the drifts and pow dered windows we see the farmer's early candle, like a paled star, emitting a lonely beam, as if some severe virtue were at its matins there. And one by one the smokes begin to ascend from the chimneys amidst the trees and snows.

The sluggish smoke curls up from some deep dell, The stiffened air exploring in the dawn, And making slow acquaintance with the day Delaying now upon its heavenward course, In wreathed letterings dallying with itself, With as uncertain purpose and slow deed,

A WINTER WALK.

As its half-wakened master by the hearth, Whose mind still slumbering and sluggish thoughts Have not yet swept into the onward current Of the new day ; — and now it streams afar, The while the chopper goes with step direct, And mind intent to swing the early axe.

First in the dusky dawn he sends abroad His early scout, his emissary, smoke, The earliest, latest pilgrim from the roof, To feel the frosty air, inform the day ; And while he crouches still beside the hearth, Nor musters courage to unbar the door, It has gone down the glen with the light wind, And o'er the plain unfurled its venturous wreath, Draped the tree-tops, loitered upon the hill, And warmed the pinions of the early bird ; And now, perchance, high in the crispy air, Has caught sight of the day o'er the earth's edge, And greets its master's eye at his low door, As some refulgent cloud in the upper sky.

We hear the sound of wood-chopping at the farmers' doors, far over the frozen earth, the bay ing of the house-dog, and the distant clarion of the cock. Though the thin and frosty air con veys only the finer particles of sound to our ears, with short and sweet vibrations, as the waves subside soonest on the purest and lightest liquids, in which gross substances sink to the bottom. They come clear and bell-like, and from a greater distance in the horizon, as if there were fewer impediments than in summer to make them faint and ragged. The ground is sonorous, like seasoned wood, and even the or dinary rural sounds are melodious, and the jing ling of the ice on the trees is sweet and liquid. There is the least possible moisture in the at mosphere, all being dried up, or congealed, and it is of such extreme tenuity and elasticity, that it becomes a source of delight. The withdrawn and tense sky seems groined like the aisles of a cathedral, and the polished air sparkles as if there were crystals of ice floating in it. As they who have resided in Greenland tell us, that, when it freezes, " the sea smokes like burning turf-land, and a fog or mist arises, called frost-smoke," which " cutting smoke frequently raises blisters on the face and hands, and is very per nicious to the health." But this pure stinging cold is an elixir to the lungs, and not so much a frozen mist, as a crystallized midsummer haze, refined and purified by cold.

The sun at length rises through the distant woods, as if with the faint clashing swinging sound of cymbals, melting the air with his beams, and with such rapid steps the morning travels, that already his rays are gilding the distant western mountains. Meanwhile we step hastily along through the powdery snow, warmed by an inward heat, enjoying an Indian summer still, in the increased glow of thought and feel-8

ing. Probably if our lives were more conformed to nature, we should not need to defend our selves against her heats and colds, but find her our constant nurse and friend, as do plants and quadrupeds. If our bodies were fed with pure and simple elements, and not with a stimulating and heating diet, they would afford no more pasture for cold than a leafless twig, but thrive like the trees, which find even winter genial to their expansion.

The wonderful purity of nature at this season is a most pleasing fact. Every decayed stump and moss-grown stone and rail, and the dead leaves of autumn, are concealed by a clean nap kin of snow. In the bare fields and tinkling woods, see what virtue survives. In the coldest and bleakest places, the warmest charities still maintain a foothold. A cold and searching wind drives away all contagion, and nothing can withstand it but what has a virtue in it; and accordingly, whatever we meet with in cold and bleak places, as the tops of mountains, we respect for a sort of sturdy innocence, a Puritan toughness. All things beside seem to be called in for shelter, and what stays out must be part of the original frame of the universe, and of such valor as God himself. It is invigorating to breathe the cleansed air. Its greater fineness and purity are visible to the eye, and we would

fain stay out long and late, that the 1 gales may sigh through us, too, as through the leafless trees, and fit us for the winter: — as if we hoped so to borrow some pure and steadfast virtue, which will stead us in all seasons.

There is a slumbering subterranean fire in nature which never goes out, and which no cold can chill. It finally melts the great snow, and in January or July is only buried under a thicker or thinner covering. In the coldest day it flows somewhere, and the snow melts around every tree. This field of winter rye, which sprouted late in the fall, and now speedily dissolves the snow, is where the fire is very thinly covered. We feel warmed by it. In the winter, warmth stands for all virtue, and we resort in thought to a trickling rill, with its bare stones shining in the sun, and to warm springs in the woods, with as much eagerness as rabbits and robins. The steam which rises from swamps and pools, is as dear and domestic as that of our own kettle. What fire could ever equal the sunshine of a winter's day, when the meadow mice come out by the wallsides, and the chicadee lisps in the defiles of the wood ? The warmth comes di rectly from the sun, and is not radiated from the earth, as in summer; and when we feel his beams on our backs as we are treading some snowy dell, we are grateful as for a special kind-ness, and bless the sun which has followed us into that by-place.

This subterranean fire has its altar in each man's breast, for in the coldest day, and on the bleakest hill, the traveller cherishes a warmer fire within the folds of his cloak than is kindled on any hearth. A healthy man, indeed, is the com plement of the seasons, and in winter, summer is in his heart. There is the south. Thither have all birds and insects migrated, and around the warm springs in his breast are gathered the robin and the lark.

At length, having reached the edge of the woods, and shut out the gadding town, we enter within their covert as we go under the roof of a cottage, and cross its threshold, all ceiled and banked up with snow. They are glad and warm still, and as genial and cheery in winter as in summer. As we stand in the midst of the pines, in the flickering and checkered light which strag gles but little way into their maze, we wonder if the towns have ever heard their simple story. It seems to us that no traveller has ever explored them, and notwithstanding the wonders which science is elsewhere revealing every day, who would not like to hear their annals? Our hum ble villages in the plain are their contribution. We borrow from the forest the boards which shelter, and the sticks which warm us. How

important is their evergreen to the winter, that portion of the summer which does not fade, the permanent year, the unwithered grass. Thus simply, and with little expense of altitude, is the surface of the earth diversified. What would human life be without forests, those natural cities? From the tops of mountains they ap pear like smooth shaven lawns, yet whither shall we walk but in this taller grass ?

In this glade covered with bushes of a year's growth, see how the silvery dust lies on every seared leaf and twig, deposited in such infinite and luxurious forms as by their very variety atone for the absence of color. Observe the tiny tracks of mice around every stem, and the tri angular tracks of the nib bit. A pure elastic heaven hangs over all, as if the impurities of the summer sky, refined and shrunk by the chaste winter's cold, had been winnowed from the heavens upon the earth.

Nature confounds her summer distinctions at this season. The heavens seem to be nearer the earth. The elements are less reserved and dis tinct. Water turns to ice, rain to snow. The day is but a Scandinavian night. The winter is an arctic summer.

How much more living is the life that is in nature, the furred life which still survives the stinging nights, and, from amidst fields and

woods covered with frost and snow, sees the sun rise.

" The foodless wilds Pour forth their brown inhabitants."

The gray squirrel and rabbit are brisk and play-ftL in the remote glens, even on the morning of the cold Friday. Here is our Lapland and Lab rador, and for our Esquimaux and Knistenaux, Dog-ribbed Indians, Novazemblaites, and Spitz-bergeners, are there not the ice-cutter and wood-chopper, the fox, musk-rat, and mink ?

Still, in the midst of the arctic day, we may trace the summer to its retreats, and sympathize with some contemporary life. Stretched over the brooks, in the midst of the frost-bound meadows, we may observe the submarine cottages of the caddice-worms, the larvae of the Plicipennes. Their small cylindrical cases built around them selves, composed of flags, sticks, grass, and with ered leaves, shells, and pebbles, in form and color like the wrecks which strew the bottom, — now drifting along over the pebbly bottom, now whirling in tiny eddies and dashing down steep falls, or sweeping rapidly along with the current, or else swaying to and fro at the end of some grass-blade or root. Anon they will leave their sunken habitations, and, crawling up the stems of plants, or to the surface, like gnats, as perfect

insects henceforth, flutter over the surface of the water, or sacrifice their short lives in the flame of our candles at evening. Down yonder little glen the shrubs are drooping under their burden, and the red alder-berries contrast with the white ground. Here are the marks of a myriad feet which have already been abroad. The sun rises as proudly over such a glen, as over the valley of the Seine or the Tiber, and it seems the residence of a pure and self-subsistent valor, such as they never witnessed ; which never knew defeat nor fear. Here reign the simplicity and purity of a primitive age, and a health and hope far remote from towns and cities. Stand ing quite alone, far in the forest, while the wind is shaking down snow from the trees, and leaving the only human tracks behind us, we find our reflections of a richer variety than the life of cities. The chicadee and nut hatch are more inspiring society than statesmen and philosophers, and we shall return to these last, as to more vulgar companions. In this lonely glen, with its brook draining the slopes, its creased ice and crystals of all hues, where the spruces and hemlocks stand up on either side, and the rush and sere wild oats in the rivulet itself, our lives are more serene and worthy to contemplate.

As the day advances, the heat of the sun is

reflected by the hill-sides, and we hear a faint but sweet music, where flows the rill released from its fetters, and the icicles are melting on the trees; and the nuthatch and partridge are heard and seen. The south wind melts the snow at noon, and the bare ground appears with its withered grass and leaves, and we are invigorated by the perfume which exhales from it, as by the scent of strong meats.

Let us go into this deserted woodman's hut, and see how he has passed the long winter nights and the short and stormy days. For here man has lived under this south hill-side, and it seems a civilized and public spot. We have such associations as when the traveller stands by the ruins of Palmyra or Hecatornpolis. Singing birds and flowers perchance have begun to appear here, for flowers as well as weeds fol low in the footsteps of man. These hemlocks whispered over his head, these hickory logs were his fuel, and these pitch-pine roots kindled his fire; yonder fuming rill in the hollow, whose thin and airy vapor still ascends as busily as ever, though he is far off now, was his well. These hemlock boughs, and the straw upon this raised platform, were his bed, and this broken dish held his drink. But he has not been here this season, for the phaebes built their nest upon this shelf last summer. I find some embers left,

as if he had but just gone out, where he baked his pot of beans; and while at evening he smoked his pipe, whose stemless bowl lies in the ashes, chatted with his only companion, if perchance he had any, about the depth of the snow on the morrow, already falling fast and thick without, or disputed whether the last sound was the screech of an owl, or the creak of a bough, or imagination only; and through this broad chim ney throat, in the late winter evening, ere he stretched himself upon the straw, he looked up to learn the progress of the storm, and, seeing the bright stars of Cassiopeia's chair shining brightly down upon him, fell contentedly asleep. See how many traces from which we may learn the chopper's history. From this stump we may guess the sharpness of his axe, and, from the slope of the stroke, on which side he stood, and whether he cut down the tree with out going round it or changing hands; and, from the flexure of the splinters, we may know which way it fell. This one chip contains in scribed on it the whole history of the wood-chopper and of the world. On this scrap of paper, which held his sugar or salt, perchance, or was the wadding of his gun, sitting on a log in the forest, with what interest we read the tat tle of cities, of those larger huts, empty and to let, like this, in High Streets and Broadways.

The eaves are dripping on the south side of this simple roof, while the titmouse lisps in the pine, and the genial warmth of the sun around the door is somewhat kind and human.

After two seasons, this rude dwelling does not deform the scene. Already the birds resort to it, to build their nests, and you may track to its door the feet of many quadrupeds. Thus, for a long time, nature overlooks the encroachment and profanity of man. The wood still cheer fully and unsuspiciously echoes the strokes of the axe that fells it, and while they are few and seldom, they enhance its wildness, and all the elements strive to naturalize the sound.

Now our path begins to ascend gradually to the top of this high hill, from whose precipitous south side we can look over the broad country, of forest and field and river, to the distant snowy mountains. See yonder thin column of smoke curling up through the woods from some invisible farm-house; the standard raised over some rural homestead. There must be a warmer and more genial spot there below, as where we detect the vapor from a spring forming a cloud above the trees. What fine relations are estab lished between the traveller who discovers this airy column from some eminence in the forest, and him who sits below. Up goes the smoke as silently and naturally as the vapor exhales

from the leaves, and as busy disposing itself in wreathes as the housewife on the hearth below. It is a hieroglyphic of man's life, and suggests more intimate and important things than the boiling of a pot. Where its fine column rises above the forest, like an ensign, some human life has planted itself, — and such is the begin ning of Rome, the establishment of the arts, and the foundation of empires, whether on the prai ries of America, or the steppes of Asia.

And now we descend again to the brink of this woodland lake, which lies in a hollow of the hills, as if it were their expressed juice, and that of the leaves, which are annually steeped in it. Without outlet or inlet to the eye, it has still its history, in the lapse of its waves, in the rounded pebbles on its shore, and in the pines which grow down to its brink. It has not been idle, though sedentary, but, like Abu Musa, teaches that " sitting still at home is the heavenly way; the going out is the way of the world." Yet in its evaporation it travels as far as any. In sum mer it is the earth's liquid eye; a mirror in the breast of nature. The sins of the wood are washed out in it. See how the woods form an amphitheatre about it, and it is an arena for all the genialness of nature. All trees direct the traveller to its brink, all paths seek it out, birds fly to it, quadrupeds flee to it, and the very

ground inclines toward it, It is nature's saloon, where she has sat down to her toilet. Consider her silent economy and tidiness ; how the sun comes with his evaporation to sweep the dust from its surface each morning, and a fresh sur face is constantly welling up; and annually, after whatever impurities have accumulated herein, its liquid transparency appears again in the spring. In summer a hushed music seems to sweep across its surface. But now a plain sheet of snow conceals it from our eyes, except where the wind has swept the ice bare, and the sere leaves are gliding from side to side, tacking and veering on their tiny voyages. Here is one just keeled up against a pebble on shore, a dry beech-leaf, rocking still, as if it would start again. A skilful engineer, methinks, might pro ject its course since it fell from the parent stem. Here are all the elements for such a calculation. Its present position, the direction of the wind, the level of the pond, and how much more is given. In its scarred edges and veins is its log rolled up.

We fancy ourselves in the interior of a larger house. The surface of the pond is our deal table or sanded floor, and the woods rise abruptly from its edge, like the walls of a cottage. The lines set to catch pickerel through the ice look like a larger culinary preparation, and the men

stand about on the white ground like pieces of forest furniture. The actions of these men, at the distance of half a mile over the ice and snow, impress us as w r hen we read the exploits of Alexander in history. They seem not un worthy of the scenery, and as momentous as the conquest of kingdoms.

Again we have wandered through the arches of the wood, until from its skirts we hear the distant booming of ice from yonder bay of the river, as if it were moved by some other and subtler tide than oceans know. To me it has a strange sound of home, thrilling as the voice of one's distant and noble kindred. A mild sum mer sun shines over forest and lake, and though there is but one green leaf for many rods, yet nature enjoys a serene health. Every sound is fraught with the same mysterious assurance of health, as well now the creaking of the boughs in January, as the soft sough of the wind in July.

When Winter fringes every bougb
With his fantastic wreath, And puts the seal of silence now
Upon the leaves beneath;
When every stream in its pent-house
Goes gurgling on its way, And in his gallery the mouse
Nibbleth the meadow hay;
Methinks the summer still is nigh, And lurketh underneath,
As that same meadow-mouse doth lie Snug in that last year's heath.
And if perchance the chicadee
Lisp a faint note anon, The snow is summer's canopy,
Which she herself put on.
Fair blossoms deck the cheerful trees, And dazzling fruits depend,
The north wind sighs a summer breeze, The nipping frosts to fend,
Bringing glad tidings unto me, The while I stand all ear,
Of a serene eternity, Which need not winter fear.
Out on the silent pond straightway The restless ice doth crack,
And pond sprites merry gambols play Amid the deafening rack.
Eager I hasten to the vale, As if I heard brave news,
How nature held high festival, Which it were hard to lose.
I gambol with my neighbor ice, And sympathizing quake,
As each new crack darts in a trice Across the gladsome lake.
One with the cricket in the ground, And fagot on the hearth,
Resounds the rare domestic sound Along the forest path.

Before night we will take a journey on skates along the course of this meandering river, as full of novelty to one who sits by the cottage fire all the winter's day, as if it were over the polar ice, with Captain Parry or Franklin; following the winding of the stream, now flowing amid hills, now spreading out into fair meadows, and form ing a myriad coves and bays where the pine and hemlock overarch. The river flows in the rear of the towns, and we see all things from a new and wilder side. The fields and gardens come down to it with a frankness, and freedom from pretension, which they do not wear on the high way. It is the outside and edge of the earth. Our eyes are not offended by violent contrasts. The last rail of the farmer's fence is some sway ing willow bough, which still preserves its fresh ness, and here at length all fences stop, and we no longer cross any road. We may go far up within the country now by the most retired and level road, never climbing a hill, but by broad levels ascending to the upland meadows. It is a beautiful illustration of the law of obedience, the flow of a river; the path for a sick man, a highway down which an acorn cup may float secure with its freight. Its slight occasional falls, whose precipices would not diversify the landscape, are celebrated by mist and spray, and attract the traveller from far and near. From

the remote interior, its current conducts him by broad and easy steps, or by one gentle inclined plane, to the sea. Thus by an early and con stant yielding to the inequalities of the ground, it secures itself the easiest passage.

No domain of nature is quite closed to man at all times, and now we draw near to the em pire of the fishes. Our feet glide swiftly over unfathomed depths, where in summer our line tempted the pout and perch, and where the stately pickerel lurked in the long corridors formed by the bulrushes. The deep, impenetra ble marsh, where the heron waded, and bittern squatted, is made pervious to our swift shoes, as if a thousand railroads had been made into it. With one impulse we are carried to the cabin of the musk-rat, that earliest settler, and see him dart away under the transparent ice, like a furred fish, to his hole in the bank ; and we glide rapidly over meadows where lately " the mower whet his scythe," through beds of frozen cran berries mixed with meadow grass. We skate near to where the blackbird, the pewee, and the kingbird hung their nests over the water, and the hornets builded from the maple in the swamp. How many gay warblers following the sun, have radiated from this nest of silver-birch and thistle down. On the swamp's outer edge was hung the supermarine village, where no foot pene-

trated. In this hollow tree the wood-duck reared her brood, and slid away each day to forage in yonder fen.

In winter, nature is a cabinet of curiosities, full of dried specimens, in their natural order and position. The meadows and forests are a hortus siccus. The leaves and grasses stand perfectly pressed by the air without screw or gum, and the birds' nests are not hung on an artificial twig, but where they builded them. We go about dryshod to inspect the summer's work in the rank swamp, and see what a growth have got the alders, the willows, and the rnaples; testifying to how many warm suns, and fertiliz ing clews and showers. See what strides their boughs took in the luxuriant summer, — and anon these dormant buds will carry them on ward and upward another span into the heavens.

Occasionally we wade through fields of snow, under whose depths the river is lost for many rods, to appear again to the right or left, where we least expected; still holding on its way underneath, with a faint, stertorous, rumbling sound, as if, like the bear and marmot, it too had hibernated, and we had followed its faint summer-trail to where it earthed itself in snow and ice. At first we should have thought thatrivers would be empty and dry in midwinter, or else frozen solid till the spring thawed them ;

but their volume is not diminished even, for only a superficial cold bridges their surface. The thousand springs which feed the lakes and streams are flowing still. The issues of a few surface springs only are closed, and they go to swell the deep reservoirs. Nature's wells are below the frost. The summer brooks are not filled with snow-water, nor does the mower quench his thirst with that alone, The streams are swollen when the snow melts in the spring, because nature's work has been delayed, the water being turned into ice and snow, whose particles are less smooth and round, and do not find their level so soon.

Far over the ice, between the hemlock woods and snow-clad hills, stands the pickerel fisher, his lines set in some retired cove, like a Fin-lander, with his arms thrust into the pouches of his dreadnought; with dull, snowy, fishy thoughts, himself a finless fish, separated a few inches from his race; dumb, erect, and made to be enveloped in clouds and snows, like the pines on shore. In these wild scenes, men stand about in the scenery, or move deliberately and heavily, having sacrificed the sprightliness and vivacity of towns to the dumb sobriety of nature. He does not make the scenery less wild, more than the jays and musk-rats, but stands there as a part of it, as the natives are represented in the

voyages of early navigators, at Nootka Sound, and on the Northwest coast, with their furs about them, before they were tempted to loquac ity by a scrap of iron. He belongs to the nat ural family of man, and is planted deeper in nature and has more root than the inhabitants of towns. Go to him, ask what luck, and you will learn that he too is a worshipper of the un seen. Hear with what sincere deference and waving gesture in his tone, he speaks of the lake pickerel, which he has never seen, his prim itive and ideal race of pickerel. He is connected with the shore still, as by a fish-line, and yet re members the season when he took fish through the ice on the pond, while the peas were up in his garden at home.

O

But now, while we have loitered, the clouds have gathered again, and a few straggling snow-flakes are beginning to descend. Faster and faster they fall, shutting out the distant objects from sight. The snow falls on every wood and field, and no crevice is forgotten ; by the river and the pond, on the hill and in the valley. Quadrupeds are confined to their coverts, and the birds sit upon their perches this peaceful hour. There is not so much sound as in fair weather, but silently and gradually every slope, and the gray walls and fences, and the polished ice, and the sere leaves, which were not buried

before, are concealed, and the tracks of men and beasts are lost. With so little effort does nature reassert her rule and blot out the traces of men. Hear how Homer has described the same. " The snow-flakes fall thick and fast on a winter's day. The winds are lulled, and the snow falls inces sant, covering the tops of the mountains, and the hills, and the plains where the lotus-tree grows, and the cultivated fields, and they are falling by the inlets and shores of the foaming sea, but are silently dissolved by the waves." The snow levels all things, and infolds them deeper in the bosom of nature, as, in the slow summer, vegetation creeps up to the entablature of the temple, and the turrets of the castle, and helps her to prevail over art.

The surly night-wind rustles through the wood, and warns us to retrace our steps, while the sun goes down behind the thickening storm, and birds seek their roosts, and cattle their stalls.

" Drooping the lab'rer ox

Stands covered o'er with snow, and now demands The fruit of all his toil."

Though winter is represented in the almanac as an old man, facing the wind and sleet, and drawing his cloak about him, we rather think of him as a merry wood-chopper, and warm-blooded youth, as blithe as summer. The unexplored

grandeur of the storm keeps up the spirits of the traveller. It does not trifle with us, but has a sweet earnestness. In winter we lead a more inward life. Our hearts are warm and cheery, like cottages under drifts, whose windows and doors are half concealed, but from whose chim neys the smoke cheerfully ascends. The im prisoning drifts increase the sense of comfort which the house affords, and in the coldest days we are content to sit over the hearth and see the sky through the chimney top, enjoying the quiet and serene life that may be had in a warm corner by the chimney side, or feeling our pulse by listening to the low of cattle in the street, or the sound of the flail in distant barns all the long afternoon. No doubt a skilful physician could determine our health by observing how these simple and natural sounds affected us. We enjoy now, not an oriental, but a boreal leisure, around warm stoves and fireplaces, and watch the shadow of motes in the sunbeams.

Sometimes our fate grows too homely and familiarly serious ever to be cruel. Consider how for three months the human destiny is wrapped in furs. The good Hebrew Revelation takes no cognizance of all this cheerful snow. Is there no religion for the temperate and frigid zones ? We know of no scripture which records the pure benignity of the gods on a New Eng-

land winter night. Their praises have never been sung, only their wrath deprecated. The best scripture, after all, records but a meagre faith. Its saints live reserved and austere. Let a brave devout man spend the year in the woods of Maine or Labrador, and see if the Hebrew Scriptures speak adequately to his condition and experience, from the setting in of winter to the breaking up oi the ice,

Now commences the long winter evening around the farmer's hearth, when the thoughts of the indwellers travel far abroad, and men are by nature and necessity charitable and liberal to all creatures. Now is the happy resistance to cold, when the farmer reaps his reward, and thinks of his preparedness for winter, and, through the glittering panes, sees with equanimity " the mansion of the northern bear," for now the storm is over,

" The full ethereal round, Infinite worlds disclosing to the view, Shines out intensely keen ; and all one cope Of starry glitter glows from pole to pole."

THE SUCCESSION OF FOREST TREES.*

[I860.]

EVERY man is entitled to come to Cattle-show, even a transcendentalist; and for my part I am more interested in the men than in the cattle. I wish to see once more those old famil iar faces, whose names I do not know, which for me represent the Middlesex country, and come as near being indigenous to the soil as a white man can ; the men who are not above their busi ness, whose coats are not too black, whose shoes do not shine very much, who never wear gloves to conceal their hands. It is true, there are some queer specimens of humanity attracted to our festival, but all are welcome. I am pretty sure to meet once more that weak-minded and whimsical fellow, generally weak-bodied too, who prefers a crooked stick for a cane; per fectly useless, you would say, only bizarre, fit for a cabinet, like a petrified snake. A ram's horn would be as convenient, and is yet more curiously twisted. He brings that much in dulged bit of the country with him, from some town's end or other, and introduces it to Con*

* An Address read to the Middlesex Agricultural Society, in Con cord, September, I860.

cord groves, as if he had promised it so much sometime. So some, it seems to me, elect their rulers for their crookedness. But I think that a straight stick makes the best cane, and an up right man the best ruler. Or why choose a man to do plain work who is distinguished for his oddity ? However, I do not know but you will think that they have committed this mistake who invited me to speak to you to-day.

In my capacity of surveyor, I have often talked with some of you, my employers, at your dinner-tables, after having gone round and round and behind your farming, and ascertained exactly what its limits were. Moreover, taking a sur veyor's and a naturalist's liberty, I have been in the habit of going across your lots much oftener than is usual, as many of you, perhaps to your sorrow, are aware. Yet many of you, to my relief, have seemed not to be aware of it; and when I came across you in some out-of-the-way nook of your farms, have inquired, with an air of surprise, if I were not lost, since you had never seen me in that part of the town or county before; when, if the truth were known, and it had not been for betraying my secret, I might with more propriety have inquired if you were not lost, since I had never seen you there before I have several times shown the proprietor th shortest way out of his wood-lot.

Therefore, it would seem that I have some title to speak to you to-day; and considering what that title is, and the occasion that has called us together, I need offer no apology if I invite your attention, for the few moments that are allotted me, to a purely scientific subject.

At those dinner-tables referred to, I have often been asked, as many of you have been, if I could tell how it happened, that when a pine wood was cut down an oak one commonly sprang up, and vice versa. To which I have answered, and now answer, that I can tell,— that it is no mystery to me. As I am not aware that this has been clearly shown by any one, I shall lay the more stress on this point. Let me lead you back into your wood-lots again.

When, hereabouts, a single forest tree or a forest springs up naturally where none of its kind grew before, I do not hesitate to say, though in some quarters still it may sound par adoxical, that it came from a seed. Of the va rious ways by which trees are known to be prop agated, — by transplanting, cuttings, and the like, — this is the only supposable one under these circumstances. No such tree has ever been known to spring from anything else. If any one asserts that it sprang from something else, or from nothing, the burden of proof lies with him.

It remains, then, only to show how the seed is transported from where it grows, to where it is planted. This is done chiefly by the agency of the wind, water, and animals. The lighter seeds, as those of pines and maples, are transported chiefly by wind and water; the heavier, as acorns and nuts, by animals.

In all the pines, a very thin membrane, in ap pearance much like an insect's wing, grows over and around the seed, and independent of it, while the latter is being developed within its base. Indeed this is often perfectly developed, though the seed is abortive; nature being, you would say, more sure to provide the means of transporting the seed, than to provide the seed to be transported. In other words, a beautiful thin sack is woven around the seed, with a han dle to it such as the wind can take hold of, and it is then committed to the wind, expressly that it may transport the seed and extend the range of the species ; and this it does, as effectually, as when seeds are sent by mail in a different kind of sack from the patent-office. There is a pat ent-office at the seat of government of the uni verse, whose managers are as much interested in the dispersion of seeds as anybody at Wash ington can be, and their operations are infinitely more extensive and regular.

There is then no necessity for supposing that

the pines have sprung up from nothing, and I am aware that I am not at all peculiar in assert ing that they come from seeds, though the mode of their propagation by nature has been but little attended to. They are very extensively raised from the seed in Europe, and are beginning to be here.

When you cut down an oak wood, a pine wood will not at once spring up there unless there are, or have been, quite recently, seed-bear ing pines near enough for the seeds to be blown from them. But, adjacent to a forest of pines, if you prevent other crops from growing there, you will surely have an extension of your pine forest, provided the soil is suitable.

As for the heavy seeds and nuts which are not furnished with wings, the notion is still a very common one that, when the trees which bear these spring up where none of their kind were noticed before, they have come from seeds or other principles spontaneously generated there in an unusual manner, or which have lain dor mant in the soil for centuries, or perhaps been called into activity by the heat of a burning. I do not believe these assertions, and I will state some of the ways in which, according to my observation, such forests are planted and raised.

Every one of these seeds, too, will be found to be winged or legged in another fashion.

Surely it is not wonderful that cherry-trees of all kinds are widely dispersed, since their fruit is well known to be the favorite food of various birds. Many kinds are called bird-cherries, and they appropriate many more kinds, which are not so called. Eating cherries is a bird-like employment, and unless we disperse the seeds occasionally, as they do, I shall think that the birds have the best right to them. See how art fully the seed of a cherry is placed in order that a bird may be compelled to transport it — in the very midst of a tempting pericarp, so that the creature that would devour this must commonly take the stone also into its mouth or bill. If you ever ate a cherry, and did not make two bites of it, you must have perceived it — right in the centre of the luscious morsel, a large earthy residuum left on the tongue. We thus take into our mouths cherry stones as big as peas, a dozen at once, for Nature can persuade us to do almost anything when she would com pass her ends. Some wild men and children instinctively swallow these, as the birds do when in a hurry, it being the shortest way to get rid of them. Thus, though these seeds are not pro vided with vegetable wings, Nature has impelled the thrush tribe to take them into their bills and fly away with them; and they are winged in another sense, and more effectually than the

seeds of pines, for these are carried even against the wind. The consequence is, that cherry-trees grow not only here but there. The same is true of a great many other seeds.

But to come to the observation which sug gested these remarks. As I have said, I sus pect that I can throw some light on the fact, that when hereabouts a dense pine wood is cut down, oaks and other hard woods may at once take its place. I have got only to show that the acorns and nuts, provided they are grown in the neighborhood, are regularly planted in such woods; for I assert that if an oak-tree has not grown within ten miles, and man has not car ried acorns thither, then an oak wood will not spring up at once, when a pine wood is cut down.

Apparently, there were only pines there be fore. They are cut off, and after a year or two you see oaks and other hard woods springing up there, with scarcely a pine amid them, and the wonder commonly is, how the seed could have lain in the ground so long without decay ing. Bat the truth is, that it has not lain in the ground so long, but is regularly planted each year by various quadrupeds and birds.

In this neighborhood, where oaks and pines are about equally dispersed, if you look through the thickest pine wood, even the seemingly

unmixed pitch-pine ones, you will commonly detect many little oaks, birches, and other hard woods, sprung from seeds carried into the thicket by squirrels and other animals, and also blown thither, but which are over shadowed and choked by the pines. The denser the evergreen wood, the more likely it is to be well planted with these seeds, because the planters incline to resort with their forage to the closest covert. They also carry it into birch and other woods. This planting is carried on an nually, and the oldest seedlings annually die ; but when the pines are cleared off, the oaks, having got just the start they want, and now secured favorable conditions, immediately spring up to trees.

The shade of a dense pine wood, is more unfavorable to the springing up of pines of the same species than of oaks within it, though the former may come up abundantly when the pines are cut, if there chance to be sound seed in the ground.

But when you cut off a lot of hard wood, very often the little pines mixed with it have a similar start, for the squirrels have carried off the nuts to the pines, and not to the more open wood, and they commonly make pretty clean work of it; and moreover, if the wood was old, the sprouts will be feeble or entirely fail; to say nothing about the soil being, in a measure, ex hausted for this kind of crop.

If a pine wood is surrounded by a white oak one chiefly, white oaks may be expected to suc ceed when the pines are cut. If it is surrounded instead by an edging of shrub-oaks, then you will probably have a dense shrub-oak thicket.

I have no time to go into details, but will say, in a word, that while the wind is conveying the seeds of pines into hard woods and open lands, the squirrels and other animals are conveying the seeds of oaks and walnuts into the pine woods, and thus a rotation of crops is kept up.

I affirmed this confidently many years ago, and an occasional examination of dense pine woods confirmed me in my opinion. It has long been known to observers that squirrels bury nuts in the ground, but I am not aware that any one has thus accounted for the regular succession of forests.

On the 24th of September, in 1857, as I was paddling down the Assabet, in this town, I saw a red squirrel run along the bank under some herbage, with something large in its mouth. It stopped near the foot of a hemlock, within a couple of rods of me, and, hastily pawing a hole with its forefeet, dropped its booty into it, covered it up, and retreated part way up the trunk of the tree. As I approached the shore

to examine the deposit, the squirrel, descending part way, betrayed no little anxiety about its treasure, and made two or three motions to recover it before it finally retreated. Digging there, I found two green pig-nuts joined to gether, with the thick husks on, buried about an inch and a half under the reddish soil of decayed hemlock leaves, — just the right depth to plant it. In short, this squirrel was then engaged in accomplishing two objects, to wit, laying up a store of winter food for itself, and planting a hickory wood for all creation. If the squirrel was killed, or neglected its de posit, a hickory would spring up. The nearest hickory tree was twenty rods distant. These nuts were there still just fourteen days later, but were gone when I looked again, November 21, or six weeks later still.

I have since examined more carefully several dense woods, which are said to be, and are ap parently exclusively pine, and always with the same result. For instance, I walked the same day to a small, but very dense and handsome white-pine grove, about fifteen rods square, in the east part of this town. The trees are large for Concord, being from ten to twenty inches in diameter, and as exclusively pine as any wood that I know. Indeed, I selected this wood be cause I thought it the least likely to contain

anything else. It stands on an open plain or pasture, except that it adjoins another small pine wood, which has a few little oaks in it, on the southeast side. On every other side, it was at least thirty rods from the nearest woods. Standing on the edge of this grove and looking through it, for it is quite level and free from underwood, for the most part bare, red-carpeted ground, you would have said that there was not a hard wood tree in it, young or old. But on looking carefully along over its floor I discov ered, though it was not till my eye had got used to the search, that, alternating with thin ferns, and small blueberry bushes, there was, not mere ly here and there, but as often as every five feet and with a degree of regularity, a little oak, from three to twelve inches high, and in one place I found a green acorn dropped by the base of a pine.

I confess, I \vas surprised to find my theory so perfectly proved in this case. One of the prin cipal agents in this planting, the red squirrels, were all the while curiously inspecting me, while I was inspecting their plantation. Some of the little oaks had been browsed by cows, which re sorted to this wood for shade.

After seven or eight years, the hard woods evidently find such a locality unfavorable tc their growth, the pines being allowed to stand. 10

As an evidence of this, I observed a diseased red-maple twenty-five feet long, which had been recently prostrated, though it was still covered with green leaves, the only maple in any posi tion in the wood.

But although these oaks almost invariably die if the pines are not cut down, it is probable that they do better for a few years under their shelter than they would anywhere else.

The very extensive and thorough experiments of the English, have at length led them to adopt a method of raising oaks almost precisely like this, which somewhat earlier had been adopted by nature and her squirrels here; they have simply rediscovered the value of pines as nurses for oaks. The English experimenters seem early and generally, to have found out the importance of using trees of some kind, as nurse-plants for the young oaks. I quote from Loudon what he describes as " the ultimatum on the subject of planting and sheltering oaks," —" an abstract of the practice adopted by the government officers in the national forests " of England, prepared by Alexander Milne.

At first some oaks had been planted by them selves, and others mixed with Scotch pines; " but in all cases," says Mr. Milne, " where oaks were planted actually among the pines, and surrounded by them, [though the soil might

be inferior,] the oaks were found to be much the best." " For several years past, the plan pursued has been to plant the inclosures with Scotch pines only, [a tree very similar to our pitch-pine,] and when the pines have got to the height of five or six feet, then to put in good strong oak plants of about four or five years' growth among the pines, — not cutting away any pines at first, unless they happen to be so strong and thick as to overshadow the oaks. In about two years, it becomes necessary to shred the branches of the pines, to give light and air to the oaks, and in about t\vo or three more years to begin gradually to remove the pines altogether, taking out a certain number each year, so that, at the end of twenty or twen ty-five years, not a single Scotch pine shall be left; although, for the first ten or twelve years, the plantation may have appeared to contain noth ing else but pine. The advantage of this mode of planting has been found to be that the pines dry and ameliorate the soil, destroying the coarse grass and brambles which frequently choke and injure oaks ; and that no mending over is neces sary, as scarcely an oak so planted is found to fail."

Thus much the English planters have discov ered by patient experiment, and, for aught I know, they have taken out a patent for it; but

they appear not to have discovered that it Was discovered before, and that they are merely adopting the method of Nature, which she long ago made patent to all. She is all the while planting the oaks amid the pines without our knowledge, and at last, instead of government officers, we send a party of wood-choppers to cut down the pines, and so rescue an oak forest, at which we wonder as if it had dropped from the skies.

As I walk amid hickories, even in August, I hear the sound of green pig-nuts falling from time to time, cut off by the chickaree over my head. In the fall, I notice on the ground, either within or in the neighborhood of oak woods, on all sides of the town, stout oak twigs three or four inches long, bearing half-a-dozen empty acorn-cups, which twigs have been gnawed off by squirrels, on both sides of the nuts, in order to make them more portable. The jays scream and the red squirrels scold while you are clubbing and shaking the chestnut trees, for they are there on the same errand, and two of a trade never agree. I frequently see a red or gray squirrel cast down a green chestnut bur, as I am going through the woods, and I used to think, some times, that they were cast at me. In fact, they are so busy about it, in the midst of the chest nut season, that you cannot stand long in the

woods without hearing one fall. A sportsman told me that he had, the day before, — that was in the middle of October, — seen a green chest nut bur dropt on our great river meadow, fifty rods from the nearest wood, and much further from the nearest chestnut-tree, and he could not tell how it came there. Occasionally, when chestnutting in midwinter, I find thirty or forty nuts in a pile, left in its gallery, just under the leaves, by the common wood-mouse (mus Icucopus).

But especially, in the winter, the extent to which this transportation and planting of nuts is carried on is made apparent by the snow. In almost every wood, you will see where the red or gray squirrels have pawed down through the snow in a hundred places, sometimes two feet deep, and almost always directly to a nut or a pine-cone, as directly as if they had started from it and bored upward, — which you and I could not have done. It would be difficult for us to find one before the snow falls. Commonly, no doubt, they had deposited them there in the fall. You wonder if they remember the localities, or discover them by the scent. The red squirrel commonly has its winter abode in the earth under a thicket of evergreens, frequently under a small clump of evergreens in the midst of a deciduous wood. If there are any nut-trees,

which still retain their nuts, standing at a dis tance without the wood, their paths often lead directly to and from them. We, therefore, need not suppose an oak standing here and there in the wood in order to seed it, but if a few stand within twenty or thirty rods of it, it is sufficient.

I think that I may venture to say that every white-pine cone that falls to the earth naturally in this town, before opening and losing its seeds, and almost every pitch-pine one that falls at all, is cut off by a squirrel, and they begin to pluck them long before they are ripe, so that when the crop of white-pine cones is a small one, as it commonly is, they cut off thus almost every one of these before it fairly ripens. I think, more over, that their design, if I may so speak, in cut ting them off green, is, partly, to prevent their opening and losing their seeds, for these are the ones for which they dig through the snow, and the only white-pine cones which contain any thing then. I have counted in one heap, within a diameter of four feet, the cores of 239 pitch-pine cones which had been cut off and stripped by the red squirrel the previous winter.

The nuts thus left on the surface, or buried just beneath it, are placed in the most favorable circumstances for germinating. I have some times wondered how those which merely fell on the surface of the earth got planted ; but, by the

end of December, I find the chestnut of the same year partially mixed with the mould, as it were, under the decaying and mouldy leave?, where there is all the moisture and manure they want, for the nuts fall first. In a plentiful year, a large proportion of the nuts are thus covered loosely an inch deep, and are, of course, somewhat con cealed from squirrels. One winter, when the crop had been abundant, I got, with the aid of a rake, many quarts of these nuts as late as the tenth of January, and though some bought at the store the same day were more than half of them mouldy, I did not find a single mouldy one among these which I picked from under the wet and mouldy leaves, where they had been snowed on once or twice. Nature knows how to pack them best. They were still plump and tender. Ap parently, they do not heat there, though wet. In the spring they were all sprouting.

Loudon says that " when the nut [of the com mon walnut of Europe] is to be preserved through the winter for the purpose of planting in the following spring, it should be laid in a rot-heap, as soon as gathered, with the husk on ; and the heap should be turned over frequently in the course of the winter."

Here, again, he is stealing Nature's "thunder." How can a poor mortal do otherwise ? for it is she that finds fingers to steal with, and the treas-

ure to be stolen. In the planting of the seeds of most trees, the best gardeners do no more than follow Nature, though they may not know it. Generally, both large and small ones are most sure to germinate, and succeed best, when only beaten into the earth with the back of a spade, and then covered with leaves or straw. These results to which planters have arrived, remind us of the experience of Kane and his companions at the North, who, when learning to live in that climate, were surprised to find themselves stead ily adopting the customs of the natives, simply becoming Esquimaux. So, when we experiment in planting forests, we find ourselves at last do ing as Nature does. Would it not be well to consult with Nature in the outset ? for she is the most extensive and experienced planter of us all, not excepting the Dukes of Athol.

In short, they who have not attended particu larly to this subject are but little aware to what an extent quadrupeds and birds are employed, especially in the fall, in collecting, and so dissem inating and planting the seeds of trees. It is the almost constant employment of the squirrels at that season and you rarely meet with one that has not a nut in its mouth, or is not just going to get one. One squirrel-hunter of this town told me that he knew of a walnut-tree which bore particularly good nuts, but that on

going to gather them one fall, he found that he had been anticipated by a family of a dozen red squirrels. He took out of the tree, which was hollow, one bushel and three pecks by measure ment, without the husks, and they supplied him and his family for the winter. It would be easy to multiply instances of this kind. How com monly in the fall you see the cheek-pouches of the striped squirrel distended by a quantity of nuts! This species gets its scientific name Ta-mias, or the steward, from its habit of storing up nuts and other seeds. Look under a nut-tree a month after the nuts have fallen, and see what proportion of sound nuts to the abortive ones and shells you will find ordinarily. They have been already eaten, or dispersed far and wide. The ground looks like a platform before a gro cery, where the gossips of the village sit to crack nuts and less savory jokes. You have come, you would say, after the feast was over, and are presented with the shells only.

Occasionally, when threading the woods in the fall, you will hear a sound as if some one had broken a twig, and, looking up, see a jay pecking at an acorn, or you will see a flock of them at once about it, in the top of an oak, and hear them break them off. They then fly to a suitable limb, and placing the acorn under one foot, hammer away at it busily, making a sound

like a woodpecker's tapping, looking round from time to time to see if any foe is approaching, and soon reach the meat, and nibble at it, hold ing up their heads to swallow, while they hold the remainder very firmly with their claws. Nev ertheless, it often drops to the ground before the bird has done with it. I can confirm what Wm. Bartram wrote to Wilson, the Ornithologist, that " The jay is one of the most useful agents in the economy of nature, for disseminating forest trees and other nuciferous and hard-seeded vegetables on which they feed. Their chief employment during the autumnal season is foraging to sup ply their winter stores. In performing this ne cessary duty they drop abundance of seed in their flight over fields, hedges, and by fences, where they alight to deposit them in the post-holes, &c. It is remarkable what numbers of young trees rise up in fields and pastures after a wet winter and spring. These birds alone are capable, in a few years' time, to replant all the cleared lands."

I have noticed that squirrels also frequently drop their nuts in open land, which will still further account for the oaks and walnuts which spring up in pastures, for, depend on it, every new tree comes from a seed. When I examine the little oaks, one or two years old, in such places, I invariably find the empty acorn from which they sprung.

THE SUCCESSION OF FOREST TREES. 155

So far from the seed having lain dormant in the soil since oaks grew there before, as many believe, it is well known that it is difficult to preserve the vitality of acorns long enough to transport them to Europe; and it is recom mended in London's Arboretum, as the safest course, to sprout them in pots on the voyage. The same authority states that " very few acorns of any species will germinate after having been kept a year," that beechmast, " only retains its vital properties one year," and the black-walnut, " seldom more than six months after it has ri pened." I have frequently found that in Novem ber, almost every acorn left on the ground had sprouted or decayed. What with frost, drouth, moisture, and worms, the greater part are soon destroyed. Yet it is staled by one botanical writer that " acorns that have lain for centuries, on being ploughed up, have soon vegetated."

Mr. George B. Emerson, in his valuable Report on the Trees and Shrubs of this State, says of the pines : " The tenacity of life of the seeds is re markable. They will remain for many years un changed in the ground, protected by the coolness and deep shade of the forest above them. But when the forest is removed, and the warmth of the sun admitted, they immediately vegetate." Since he does not tell us on what observation his remark is founded, I must doubt its truth.

156 THE SUCCESSION OF FOREST TREES.

Besides, the experience of nurserymen makes it the more questionable.

The stories of wheat raised from seed buried with an ancient Egyptian, and of raspberries raised from seed found in the stomach of a man in England, who is supposed to have died six teen or seventeen hundred years ago, are gen erally discredited, simply because the evidence is not conclusive.

Several men of science, Dr. Carpenter among them, have used the statement that beach-plums sprang up in sand which was dug up forty miles inland in Maine, to prove that the seed had lain there a very long time, and some have inferred that the coast has receded so far. But it seems to me necessary to their argument to show, first, that beach-plums grow only on a beach. They are not uncommon here, which is about half that distance from the shore; and I remember a dense patch a few miles north of us, twenty-five miles inland, from which the fruit was annually car ried to market. How much further inland they grow, I know not. Dr. Chas. T. Jackson speaks of finding " beach-plums " (perhaps they were this kind) more than one hundred miles inland in Maine.

It chances that similar objections lie against all the more notorious instances of the kind on record.

THE SUCCESSION OF FOREST TREES. 157

Yet I am prepared to believe that some seeds, especially small ones, may retain their vitality for centuries under favorable circumstances. In the spring of 1859, the old Hunt House, so called, in this town, whose chimney bore the date 1703, was taken down. This stood on land which belonged to John Winthrop, the first Governor of Massachusetts, and a part of the house was evidently much older than the above date, and belonged to the Winthrop family. For many years, I have ransacked this neigh borhood for plants, and I consider myself famil iar with its productions. Thinking of the seeds which are said to be sometimes dug up at an unusual depth in the earth, and thus to repro duce long extinct plants, it occurred to me last fall that some new or rare plants might have sprung up in the cellar of this house, which had been covered from the light so long. Searching there on the 22d of September, I found, among other rank weeds, a species of nettle (Urtica urens), which I had not found before ; dill, which I had not seen growing spontaneously ; the Je rusalem oak (Chenopodium botrys), which I had seen wild in but one place ; black nightshade (Solatium nigrum), which is quite rare here abouts, and common tobacco, which, though it was often cultivated here in the last century, has for fifty years been an unknown plant in

this town, and a few months before this not even I had heard that one man in the north part of the town, was cultivating a few plants for his own use. I have no doubt that some or all of these plants sprang from seeds which had long been buried under or about that house, and that that tobacco is an additional evidence that the plant was formerly cultivated here. The cellar has been filled up this year, and four of those plants, including the tobacco, are now again extinct in that locality.

It is true, I have shown that the animals con sume a great part of the seeds of trees, and so> at least, effectually prevent their becoming trees ; but in all these cases, as I have said, the con sumer is compelled to be at the same time the disperser and planter, and this is the tax which he pays to nature. I think it is Linnaeus, who says, that while the swine is rooting for acorns,, he is planting acorns.

Though I do not believe that a plant will spring up where no seed has been, I have great faith in a seed — a, to me, equally mysterious ori gin for it. Convince me that you have a seed there, and I am prepared to expect wonders. I shall even believe that the millennium is at hand, and that the reign of justice is about to commence, when the Patent Office, or Govern ment, begins to distribute, and the people to plant the seeds of these things.

In the spring of 1857, I planted six seeds sent to rne from the Patent Office, and labelled, I think, " Poitritie jautie grosse" large yellow squash. Two came up, and one bore a squash which weighed 123| pounds, the other bore four, weighing together 186* pounds. Who would have believed that there was 310 pounds of poitrine jaunc grosse in that corner of my gar den ? These seeds were the bait I used to catch it, my ferrets which I sent into its burrow, my brace of terriers which unearthed it. A little mysterious hoeing and manuring was all the abra cadabra presto-change, that I used, and lo! true to the label, they found for me 310 pounds of poitrine jaune grosse there, where it never was known to be, nor was before. These talismen had perchance sprung from America at first, and returned to it with unabated force. The big squash took a premium at your fair that fall, and I understood that the man who bought it, intended to sell the seeds for ten cents a piece. (Were they not cheap at that?) But I have more hounds of the same breed. I learn that one which I despatched to a distant town, true to its instinct, points to the large yellow squash there, too, where no hound ever found it before, as its ancestors did here and in France.

Other seeds I have which will find other things in that corner of my garden, in like fashion, almost any fruit you wish, every yeat for ages, until the crop more than fills the whole garden. You have but little more to do, than throw up your cap for entertainment these American days. Perfect alchemists I keep, who can transmute substances without end; and thus the corner of my garden is an inex haustible treasure-chest. Here you can dig, not gold, but the value which gold merely repre sents ; and there is no Signer Blitz about it. Yet farmers' sons will stare by the hour to see a juggler draw ribbons from his throat, though he tells them it is all deception. Surely, men love darkness rather than light.

WALKING.

[1862.]

I WISH to speak a word for Nature, for abso lute freedom and wildness, as contrasted with a freedom and culture merely civil, — to regard man as an inhabitant, or a part and parcel of Nature, rather than a member of society. I wish to make an extreme statement, if so I may make an emphatic one, for there are enough champions of civilization : the minister and the school-committee, and every one of you will take care of that.

I have met with but one or two persons in the course of my life who understood the art of Walking, that is, of taking walks, — who had a genius, so to speak, for sauntering: which word is beautifully derived " from idle people who roved about the country, in the Middle Ages, and asked charity, under pretence of going a la Sainte Terre" to the Holy Land, till the chil dren exclaimed, " There goes a Sainte- Terrer" a Saunterer, — a Holy-Lander. They who never go to the Holy Land in their walks, as they pretend, are indeed mere idlers and vaga bonds ; but they who do go there are saunterers in the good sense, such as I mean. Some, however, would derive the word from sans terre, without land or a home, which, therefore, in the good sense, will mean, having no particular home, but equally at home everywhere. For this is the secret of successful sauntering. He who sits still in a house all the time may be the greatest vagrant of all; but the saunterer, in the good sense, is no more vagrant than the mean dering river, which is all the while sedulously seeking the shortest course to the sea. But I prefer the first, which, indeed, is the most prob able derivation. For every walk is a sort of crusade, preached by some Peter the Hermit in us, to go forth and reconquer this Holy Land from the hands of the Infidels.

It is true, we are but faint-hearted crusaders, even the walkers, nowadays, who undertake no persevering, never-ending enterprises. Our ex peditions are but tours, and come round again at evening to the old hearth-side from which we set out. Half the walk is but retracing our steps. We should go forth on the shortest walk, perchance, in the spirit of undying adven ture, never to return, — prepared to send back our embalmed hearts only as relics to our deso late kingdoms. If you are ready to leave father and mother, and brother and sister, and wife and child and friends, and never see them again, — if you have paid your debts, and made your will, and settled all your affairs,'and are a free man, then you are ready for a walk.

To come down to my own experience, my companion and I, for I sometimes have a com panion, take pleasure in fancying ourselves knights of a new, or rather an old, order, — not Equestrians or Chevaliers, not Ritters or riders, but Walkers, a still more ancient and honorable class, I trust. The chivalric and heroic spirit which once belonged to the Rider seems now to reside in, or perchance to have subsided into, the Walker, — not the Knight, but Walker Er rant. He is a sort of fourth estate, outside of Church and State and People.

We have felt that we almost alone hereabouts practised this noble art; though, to tell the truth, at least, if their own assertions are to be received, most of my townsmen would fain walk some times, as I do, but they cannot. No wealth can buy the requisite leisure, freedom, and indepen dence, which are the capital in this profession. It comes only by the grace of God. It requires a direct dispensation from Heaven to become a walker. You must be born into the family of the Walkers. Ambulator nasciiur^non fit. Some of my townsmen, it is true, can remember and

have described to me some walks which they took ten years ago, in which they were so blessed as to lose themselves for half an hour in the woods; but I know very well that they have confined themselves to the highway ever since, whatever pretensions they may make to belong to this select class. No doubt they were ele vated for a moment as by the reminiscence of a previous state of existence, when even they were foresters and outlaws.

" When he came to grene wode,
In a mery mornynge, There he herde the notes small Of byrdes mery syngynge.
" It is ferre gone, sayd Robyn,
That I was last here ; Me lyste a lytell for to shote At the donne dere."

I think that I cannot preserve my health and spirits, unless I spend four hours a day at least,— and it is commonly more than that, — sauntering through the woods and over the hills and fields, absolutely free from all worldly engagements. You may safely say, A penny for your thoughts, or a thousand pounds. When sometimes I am reminded that the mechanics and shopkeepers stay in their shops not only all the forenoon, but all the afternoon too, sitting with crossed legs, so many of them, — as if the legs were made to

sit upon, and not to stand or walk upon, — I think that they deserve some credit for not hav ing all committed suicide long ago.

I, who cannot stay in my chamber for a single day without acquiring some rust, and when sometimes I have stolen forth for a walk at the eleventh hour of four o'clock in the afternoon, too late to redeem the day, when the shades of night were already beginning to be mingled with the daylight, have felt as if I had committed some sin to be atoned for, — T confess that I am astonished at the power of endurance, to say nothing of the moral insensibility, of my neigh bors who confine themselves to shops and offices the whole day for weeks and months, ay, and years almost together. I know not what man ner of stuff they are of, — sitting there now at three o'clock in the afternoon, as if it were three o'clock in the morning. Bonaparte may talk of the three-o'clock-in-the-morning courage, but it is nothing to the courage which can sit down cheerfully at this hour in the afternoon over against one's self whom you have known all the morning, to starve out a garrison to whom you are bound by such strong ties of sympathy. I wonder that about this time, or say between four and five o'clock in the afternoon, too late for the morning papers and too early for the evening ones, there is not a general explosion

heard up and down the street, scattering a legion of antiquated and house-bred notions and whims to the four winds for an airing, — and so the evil cure itself.

How womankind, who are confined to the house still more than men, stand it I do not know; but I have ground to suspect that most of them do not stand it at all. When, early in a summer afternoon, we have been shaking the dust of the village from the skirts of our gar ments, making haste past those houses with purely Doric or Gothic fronts, which have such an air of repose about them, my companion whispers that probably about these times their occupants are all gone to bed. Then it is that I appreciate the beauty and the glory of architec ture, which itself never turns in, but forever stands out and erect, keeping watch over the slumberers.

No doubt temperament, and, above all, age, have a good deal to do with it. As a man grows older, his ability to sit still and follow in door occupations increases. He grows vesper-tinal in his habits as the evening of life ap proaches, till at last he comes forth only just before sundown, and gets all the walk that he requires in half an hour.

But the walking of which I speak has nothing in it akin to taking exercise, as it is called, as

the sick take medicine at stated hours, — as the swinging of dumb-bells or chairs ; but is itself the enterprise and adventure of the day. If you would get exercise, go in search of the springs of life. Think of a man's swinging dumb-bells for his health, when those springs are bubbling up in far-off pastures unsought by him !

Moreover, you must walk like a camel, which is said to be the only beast which ruminates when walking. When a traveller asked Words worth's servant to show him her master's study, she answered, " Here is his library, but his study is out of doors."

Living much out of doors, in the sun and wind, will no doubt produce a certain roughness of character, — will cause a thicker cuticle to grow over some of the finer qualities of our na ture, as on the face and hands, or as severe man ual labor robs the hands of some of their deli cacy of touch. So staying in the house, on the other hand, may produce a softness and smooth ness, not to say thinness of skin, accompanied by an increased sensibility to certain impressions. Perhaps we should be more susceptible to some influences important to our intellectual and moral growth, if the sun had shone and the wind blown on us a little less ; and no doubt it is a nice matter to proportion rightly the thick and thin skin. But methinks that is a scurf that

will fall off fast enough, — that the natural rem edy is to be found in the proportion which the night bears to the day, the winter to the sum mer, thought to experience. There will be so much the more air and sunshine in our thoughts. The callous palms of the laborer are conversant with finer tissues of self-respect and heroism, whose touch thrills the heart, than the languid fingers of idleness. That is mere sentimentality that lies abed by day and thinks itself white, far from the tan and callus of experience.

When we walk, we naturally go to the fields and woods : what would become of us, if we walked only in a garden or a mall ? Even some sects of philosophers have felt the necessity of importing the woods to themselves, since they did not go to the woods. " They planted groves and walks of Platanes," where they took subdi-ales ambulationes in porticos open to the air. Of course it is of no use to direct our steps to the woods, if they do not carry us thither. I am alarmed when it happens that I have walked a mile into the woods bodily, without getting there in spirit. In my afternoon walk I would fain forget all my morning occupations and my obligations to society. But it sometimes hap pens that I cannot easily shake off the village. The thought of some work will run in my head, and I am not where my body is, — I am out of

my senses. In my walks I would fain return to my senses. What business have I in the woods, if I am thinking of something out of the woods ? I suspect myself, and cannot help a shudder, when I find myself so implicated even in what are called good works, — for this may sometimes happen.

My vicinity affords many good walks ; and though for so many years I have walked almost every day, and sometimes for several days to gether, I have not yet exhausted them. An ab solutely new prospect is a great happiness, and I can still get this any afternoon. Two or three hours' walking will carry me to as strange a country as I expect ever to see. A single farm house which I had not seen before is sometimes as good as the dominions of the King of Daho mey. There is in fact a sort of harmony dis coverable between the capabilities of the land scape within a circle of ten miles' radius, or the limits of an afternoon walk, and the threescore years and ten of human life. It will never be come quite familiar to you.

Nowadays almost all man's improvements, so called, as the building of houses, and the cut ting down of the forest and of all large trees, simply deform the landscape, and make it more and more tame and cheap. A people who would begin by burning the fences and let the

forest stand ! I saw the fences half consumed, their ends lost in the middle of the prairie, ana some worldly miser with a surveyor looking after his bounds, while heaven had taken place around him, and he did not see the angels going to and fro, but was looking for an old post-hole in the midst of paradise. I looked again, and saw him standing in the middle of a boggy, stygian fen, surrounded by devils, and he had found his bounds without a doubt, three little stones, where a stake had been driven, and look ing nearer, I saw that the Prince of Darkness was his surveyor.

I can easily walk ten, fifteen, twenty, any number of miles, commencing at my own door, without going by any house, without crossing a road except where the fox and the mink do: first along by the river, and then the brook, and then the meadow and the wood-side. There are square miles in my vicinity which have no in habitant. From many a hill I can see civili zation and the abodes of man afar. The farm ers and their works are scarcely more obvious than woodchucks and their burrows. Man and his affairs, church and state and school, trade and commerce, and manufactures and agricul ture, even politics, the most alarming of them all, — I am pleased to see how little space they occupy in the landscape. Politics is but a nar-

row field, and that still narrower highway yon der leads to it. I sometimes direct the traveller thither. If you would go to the political world, follow the great road, — follow that market-man, keep his dust in your eyes, and it will lead you straight to it; for it, too, has its place merely, and does not occupy all space. I pass from it as from a bean-field into the forest, and it is for gotten. In one half-hour I can walk off to some portion of the earth's surface where a man does not stand from one year's end to another, and there, consequently, politics are not, for they are but as the cigar-smoke of a man.

The village is the place to which the roads tend, a sort of expansion of the highway, as a lake of a river. It is the body of which roads are the arms and legs, — a trivial or quadrivial place, the thoroughfare and ordinary of travel lers. The word is from the Latin villa, which, together with via, a way, or more anciently ved and vella, Varro derives from veho, to carry, be cause the villa is the place to and from which things are carried. They who got their living by teaming were said vellaturam facere. Hence, too, apparently, the Latin word vilis and our vile ; also villain. This suggests what kind of degeneracy villagers are liable to. They are wayworn by the travel that goes by and over them, without travelling themselves.

Some do not walk at all; others walk in the highways; a few walk across lots. Roads are made for horses and men of business. I do not travel in them much, comparatively, because I am not in a hurry to get to any tavern or grocery or livery-stable or depot to which they lead. I am a good horse to travel, but not from choice a roadster. The landscape-painter uses the fig ures of men to mark a road. He would not make that use of my figure. I walk out into a Nature such as the old prophets and poets, Menu, Moses, Homer, Chaucer, walked in. You may name it America, but it is not America : neither Americus Vespucius, nor Columbus, nor the rest were the discoverers of it. There is a truer ac count of it in mythology than in any history of America, so called, that I have seen.

However, there are a few old roads that may be trodden with profit, as if they led somewhere now that they are nearly discontinued. There is the Old Marlborough Road, which does not go to Marlborough now, methinks, unless that is Marlborough where it carries me. I am the bolder to speak of it here, because I presume that there are one or two such roads in every town

THE OLD MARLBOROUGH ROAD.

Where they once dug for money,
But never found any;
Where sometimes Martial Miles
Singly files,
And Elijah Wood,
I fear for no good :
No other man,
Save Elisha Dugan, —
O man of wild habits,
Partridges and rabbits,
Who hast no cares
Only to set snares,
W T ho liv'st all alone,
Close to the bone,
And where life is sweetest
Constantly eatest.
When the spring stirs my blood With the instinct to travel, I can get enough gravel
On the Old Marlborough Road. Nobody repairs it, For nobody wears it; It is a living way,
As the Christians say.

Not many there be Who enter therein,
Only the guests of the Irishman Quin.
What is it, what is it,
But a direction out there,
And the bare possibility Of going somewhere ?
Great guide-boards of stone, But travellers none ; Cenotaphs of the towns Named on their
crowns. It is worth going to see Where you might be.

What king
Did the thing,
I am still wondering;
Set up how or when,
By what selectmen,
Gourgas or Lee,
Clark or Darby ?
They 're a great endeavor
To be something forever;
Blank tablets of stone,
Where a traveller might groan,
And in one sentence
Grave all that is known ;
Which another might read,
In his extreme need.
I know one or two
Lines that would do,
Literature that might stand

All over the land,
Which a man could remember
Till next December,
And read again in the spring,
After the thawing. If with fancy unfurled
You leave your abode, You may go round the world By the Old Marlborough Road.

At present, in this vicinity, the best part of the land is not private property; the landscape is not owned, and the walker enjoys compara tive freedom. But possibly the day will come when it will be partitioned off into so-called pleasure-grounds, in which a few will take a

narrow and exclusive pleasure only, — when fen ces shall be multiplied, and man-traps and other engines invented to confine men to the public road, and walking over the surface of God's earth shall be construed to mean trespassing on some gentleman's grounds. To enjoy a thing ex clusively is commonly to exclude yourself from the true enjoyment of it. Let us improve our opportunities, then, before the evil days come.

What is it that makes it so hard sometimes to determine whither we will walk ? I believe that there is a subtile magnetism in Nature, which, if we unconsciously yield to it, will direct us aright. It is not indifferent to us which way we walk. There is a right way ; but we are very liable from heedlessness and stupidity to take the wrong one. We would fain take that walk, never yet taken by us through this actual world, V which is perfectly symbolical of the path which we love to travel in the interior and ideal world; and sometimes, no doubt, we find it difficult to choose our direction, because it does not yet exist distinctly in our idea.

When I go out of the house for a walk, un certain as yet whither I will bend my steps, and submit myself to my instinct to decide for me, I find, strange and whimsical as it may seem, that I finally and inevitably settle southwest,

toward some particular wood or meadow or d& serted pasture or hill in that direction. My nee die is slow to settle, — varies a few degrees, ancr does not always point due southwest, it is true, and it has good authority for this variation, but it always settles between west and south-south west. The future lies that way to me, and the earth seems more unexhausted and richer on that side. The outline which would bound my walks would be, not a circle, but a parabola, or rather like one of those cometary orbits which have been thought to be non-returning curves, in this case opening westward, in which my house oc cupies the place of the sun. I turn round and round irresolute sometimes for a quarter of an hour, until I decide, for a thousandth time, that I will walk into the southwest or west. East ward I go only by force; but westward I go free. Thither no business leads me. It is hard for me to believe that I shall find fair landscapes or sufficient wildness and freedom behind the eastern horizon. I am not excited by the pros pect of a walk thither; but I believe that the forest which I see in the western horizon stretch es uninterruptedly toward the setting sun, and there are no towns nor cities in it of enough consequence to disturb me. Let me live where I will, on this side is the city, on that the wilder ness, and ever I am leaving the city more and

more, and withdrawing into the wilderness. I should not lay so much stress on this fact, if I did not believe that something like this is the prevailing tendency of my countrymen. I must walk toward Oregon, and not toward Eu rope. And that way the nation is moving, and I may say that mankind progress from east to west. Within a few years we have witnessed the phe nomenon of a southeastward migration, in the settlement of Australia; but this affects us as a retrograde movement, and, judging from the moral and physical character of the first genera tion of Australians, has not yet proved a success ful experiment. The eastern Tartars think that there is nothing west beyond Thibet. " The world ends there," say they, " beyond there is nothing but a shoreless sea." It is unmitigated East where they live.

We go eastward to realize history and study the works of art and literature, retracing _the steps of the race; we go westward as into the future, with a spirit of enterprise and adventure. The Atlantic is a Lethean stream, in our pas sage over which we have had an opportunity to forget the Old World and its institutions. If we do not succeed this time, there is perhaps one more chance for the race left before it arrives on the banks of the Styx; and that is in the Lethe of the Pacific, which is three times as wide.

12

I know not how significant it is, or how far it is an evidence of singularity, that an individual should thus consent in his pettiest walk with the general movement of the race; but I know that something akin to the migratory instinct in birds and quadrupeds, — which, in some instances, is known to have affected the squirrel tribe, impel ling them to a general and mysterious movement, in which they were seen, say some, crossing the broadest rivers, each on its particular chip, with its tail raised for a sail, and bridging narrower streams with their dead, — that something like the furor which affects the domestic cattle in the spring, and which is referred to a worm in their tails, — affects both nations and individuals, either perennially or from time to time. Not a flock of wild geese cackles over our town, but it to some extent unsettles the value of real estate here, and, if I were a broker, I should probably take that disturbance into account.

" Than longen folk to gon on pilgrimages, And palmeres for to seken strange strondes."

Every sunset which I witness inspires me with the desire to go to a West as distant and as fair as that into which the sun goes down. He appears to migrate westward daily, and tempt us to follow him. He is the Great Western Pioneer whom the nations follow.

We dream all night of those mountain-ridges in the horizon, though they may be of vapor only, which were last gilded by his rays. The island of Atlantis, and the islands and gardens of the Hesperides, a sort of terrestrial par adise, appear to have been the Great West of the ancients, enveloped in mystery and poetry. Who has not seen in imagination, when look ing into the sunset sky, the gardens of the Hes perides, and the foundation of all those fables ? Columbus felt the westward tendency more strongly than any before. He obeyed it, and found a New World for Castile and Leon. The herd of men in those days scented fresh pastures from afar.

" And now the sun had stretched out all the hills, And now was dropped into the western bay; At last lie rose, and twitched his mantle blue ; To-morrow to fresh woods and pastures new."

Where on the globe can there be found an area of equal extent with that occupied by the bulk of our States, so fertile and so rich and varied in its productions, and at the same time so habitable by the European, as this is ? Michaux, who knew but part of them, says that " the species of large trees are much more numerous in North America than in Eu rope ; in the United States there are more than

one hundred and forty species that exceed thirty feet in height; in France there are but thirty that attain this size." Later botanists more than confirm his observations. Humboldt came to America to realize his youthful dreams of a tropical vegetation, and he beheld it in its greatest perfection in the primitive forests of the Amazon, the most gigantic wilderness on the earth, which he has so eloquently described The geographer Guyot, himself a European, goes farther, — farther than I am ready to fol low him; yet not when he says, —" As the plant is made for the animal, as the vegetable world is made for the animal world, America

is made for the man of the Old World

The man of the Old World sets out upon his way. Leaving the highlands of Asia, he de scends from station to station towards Europe. Each of his steps is marked by a new civili zation superior to the preceding, by a greater power of development. Arrived at the Atlantic, he pauses on the shore of this unknown ocean, the bounds of which he knows not, and turns upon his footprints for an instant." When he has exhausted the rich soil of Europe, and rein-vigorated himself, " then recommences his ad venturous career westward as in the earliest ages." So far Guyot.

From this western impulse coming in contact

with the barrier of the Atlantic sprang the com merce and enterprise of modern times. The younger Michaux, in his " Travels West of the Alleghanies in 1802," says that the common inquiry in the newly settled West was, "' From what part of the world have you come ?' As if these vast and fertile regions would naturally be the place of meeting and common country of all the inhabitants of the globe."

To use an obsolete Latin word, I might say, Ex Oriente lux ; ex Occidente FRUX. From the East light; from the West fruit.

Sir Francis Head, an English traveller and a Governor-General of Canada, tells us that " in both the northern and southern hemi spheres of the New World, Nature has not only outlined her works on a larger scale, but has painted the whole picture with brighter and more costly colors than she used in delineating

and in beautifying the Old World The

heavens of America appear infinitely higher, the sky is bluer, the air is fresher, the cold is intenser, the moon looks larger, the stars are brighter, the thunder is louder, the lightning is vivider, the wind is stronger, the rain is heavier, the mountains are higher, the rivers longer, the for ests bigger, the plains broader." This statement will do at least to set against BufFon's account of this part of the world and its productions.

Linnaeus said long ago, " Nescio quae facies Iceta, glabra plantis Americanis : I know not what there is of joyous and smooth in the aspect of American plants ;" and I think that in this country there are no, or at most very few, Africance bestice, African beasts, as the Romans called them, and that in this respect also it is peculiarly fitted for the habitation of man. We are told that within three miles of the centre of the East-Indian city of Singa pore, some of the inhabitants are annually car ried off by tigers; but the traveller can lie down in the woods at night almost anywhere in North America without fear of wild beasts.

These are encouraging testimonies. If the moon looks larger here than in Europe, prob ably the sun looks larger also. If the heavens of America appear infinitely higher, and the stars brighter, I trust that these facts are sym bolical of the height to which the philosophy and poetry and religion of her inhabitants may one day soar. At length, perchance, the imma terial heaven will appear as much higher to the American mind, and the intimations that star it as much brighter. For I believe that climate « / does thus react on man,— as there is something in the mountain-air that feeds the spirit ana inspires. Will not man grow to greater perfec tion intellectually as well as physically under

these influences? Or is it unimportant how many foggy days there are in his life ? I trust that we shall be more imaginative, that our thoughts will be clearer, fresher, and more ethereal, as our sky, — our understanding more comprehensive and broader, like our plains, — our intellect generally on a grander scale, like our thunder and lightning, our rivers and moun tains and forests,— and our hearts shall even correspond in breadth and depth and grandeur to our inland seas. Perchance there will ap pear to the traveller something, he knows not what, of Iccta and glabra, of joyous and se rene, in our very faces. Else to what end does the world go on, and why was America dis covered ?

To Americans I hardly need to say, —

" Westward the star of empire takes its way."

As a true patriot, I should be ashamed to think that Adam in paradise was more favorably sit uated on the whole than the backwoodsman in this country.

Our sympathies in Massachusetts are not confined to New England; though we may be estranged from the South, we sympathize with the West. There is the home of the younger sons, as among the Scandinavians they took to the sea for their inheritance. It is too late to

be studying Hebrew; it is more important to understand even the slang of to-day.

Some months ago I went to see a pano rama of the Rhine. It was like a dream of the Middle Ages. I floated down its historic stream in something more than imagination, under bridges built by the Romans, and re* paired by later heroes, past cities and castles whose very names were music to my ears, and each of which was the subject of a legend. There were Ehrenbreitstein and Rolandseck and Coblentz, which I knew only in history. They were ruins that interested me chiefly. There seemed to come up from its waters and its vine-clad hills and valleys a hushed music as of Crusaders departing for the Holy Land. I floated along under the spell of en chantment, as if I had been transported to an heroic age, and breathed an atmosphere of chivalry.

Soon after, I went to see a panorama of the Mississippi, and as I worked my way up the river in the light of to-day, and saw the steam boats wooding up, counted the rising cities, gazed on the fresh ruins of Nauvoo, beheld the Indians moving west across the stream, and, as before I had looked up the Moselle now looked up the Ohio and the Missouri and heard the legends of Dubuau«5 and ot

Wenona's Cliff, — still thinking more of the future than of the past or present,— I saw that this was a Rhine stream of a different kind ; that the foundations of castles were yet to be laid, and the famous bridges were yet to be thrown over the river; and I felt that this was the heroic age itself, though we know it not, for the hero is commonly the simplest and obscurest * of men.

The West of which I speak is but another name for the Wild; and what I have been pre paring to say is, that in Wildness is the preser vation of the World. Every tree sends its fibres forth in search of the Wild. The cities import it at any price. Men plough and sail for it. From the forest and wilderness come the tonics and barks which brace mankind. Our ancestors were savages. The story of Romulus and Re mus being suckled by a wolf is not a meaning less fable. The founders of every State which has risen to eminence have drawn their nourish ment and vigor from a similar wild source. It was because the children of the Empire were not suckled by the wolf that they were con quered and displaced by the children of the Northern forests who were.

I believe in the forest, and in the meadow, and in the night in which the corn grows. We require an infusion of hemlock-spruce or arbor vitse in our tea. There is a difference between eating and drinking for strength and from mere gluttony. The Hottentots eagerly devour the marrow of the koodoo and other antelopes raw, as a matter of course. Some of our Northern Indians eat raw the marrow of the Arctic rein deer, as well as various other parts, including the summits of the antlers, as long as they are soft. And herein, perchance, they have stolen a march on the cooks of Paris. They get what usually goes to feed the fire. This is probably better than stall-fed beef and slaughter-house pork to make a man of. Give me a wildness whose glance no civilization can endure, — as if we lived on the marrow of koodoos devoured raw.

There are some intervals which border the strain of the wood-thrush, to which I would migrate, — wild lands where no settler has squat ted ; to which, methinks, I am already accli mated.

The African hunter Cummings tells us that the skin of the eland, as well as that of most other antelopes just killed, emits the most de licious perfume of trees and grass. I would have every man so much like a wild antelope, so much a part and parcel of Nature, that his very person should thus sweetly advertise our

senses of his presence, and remind us of those parts of Nature which he most haunts. I feel no disposition to be satirical, when the trapper's coat emits the odor of musquash even ; it is a sweeter scent to me than that which commonly exhales from the merchant's or the scholar's gar ments. When I go into their wardrobes and handle their vestments, I am reminded of no grassy plains and flowery meads which they have frequented, but of dusty merchants' ex changes and libraries rather.

A tanned skin is something more than re spectable, and perhaps olive is a fitter color than white for a man, — a denizen of the woods. " The pale white man! " I do not wonder that the African pitied him. Darwin the naturalist says, " A white man bathing by the side of a Tahitian was like a plant bleached by the gardener's art, compared with a fine, dark green one, growing vigorously in the open fields."

Ben Jonson exclaims, —

" How near to good is what is fair ! " So I would say, —

How near to good is what is wild !

Life consists with wildness. The most alive is the wildest. Not yet subdued to man, its pres ence refreshes him. One who pressed forward incessantly and never rested from his labors,

who grew fast and made infinite demands on life, would always find himself in a new country or wilderness, and surrounded by the raw mate rial of life. He would be climbing over the prostrate stems of primitive forest-trees.

Hope and the future for me are not in lawns and cultivated fields, not in towns and cities, but in the impervious and quaking swamps. When, formerly, I have analyzed my partiality for some farm which I had contemplated pur chasing, I have frequently found that I was attracted solely by a few square rods of imper meable and unfathomable bog, — a natural sink in one corner of it. That was the jewel which dazzled me. I derive more of my subsistence from the swamps which surround my native town than from the cultivated gardens in the village. There are no richer parterres to my eyes than the dense beds of dwarf andromeda (Cassandra calyculata) which cover these ten der places on the earth's surface. Botany can not go farther than tell me the names of the shrubs which grow there, — the high-blueberry, panicled andromeda, lamb-kill, azalea, and rho-dora, — all standing in the quaking sphagnum. I often think that I should like to have my house front on this mass of dull red bushes, omitting other flower plots and borders, trans planted spruce and trim box, even gravelled

walks, — to have this fertile spot under my windows, not a few imported barrow-fulls of soil only to cover the sand which was thrown out in digging the cellar. Why not put my house, my parlor, behind this plot, instead of behind that meagre assemblage of curiosities, that poor apology for a Nature and Art, which I call my front-yard ? It is an effort to clear up and make a decent appearance when the car penter and mason have departed, though done as much for the passer-by as the dweller within. The most tasteful front-yard fence was never an agreeable object of study to me; the most elab orate ornaments, acorn-tops, or what not, soon wearied and disgusted me. Bring your sills up to the very edge of the swamp, then, (though it may not be the best place for a dry cellar,) so that there be no access on that side to citizens. Front-yards are not made to walk in, but, at most, through, and you could go in the back way.

Yes, though you may think me perverse, if it were proposed to me to dwell in the neighbor hood of the most beautiful garden that ever hu man art contrived, or else of a Dismal swamp, I should certainly decide for the swamp. How vain, then, have been all your labors, citizens, for me!

My spirits infallibly rise in proportion to the \j outward dreariness. Give me the ocean, the

desert or the wilderness! In the desert, pure air and solitude compensate for want of moist ure and fertility. The traveller Burton says of it,—" Your morale improves ; you become frank and cordial, hospitable and single-minded. . . . In the desert, spirituous liquors excite only dis gust. There is a keen enjoyment in a mere animal existence." They who have been trav elling long on the steppes of Tartary say,— " On reentering cultivated lands, the agitation, perplexity, and turmoil of civilization oppressed and suffocated us; the air seemed to fail us, and we felt every moment as if about to die of asphyxia." When I would recreate myself, I seek the darkest wood, the thickest and most interminable, and, to the citizen, most dismal swamp. I enter a swamp as a sacred place, — a sanctum sanctorum. There is the strength, the marrow of Nature. The wild-wood covers the* virgin mould, — and the same soil is good foi men and for trees. A man's health requires as many acres of meadow to his prospect as his farm does loads of muck. There are the strong meats on which he feeds. A town is saved, not more by the righteous men in it than by the woods and swamps that surround it. A town ship where one primitive forest waves abovt,, while another primitive forest rots below, — such a town is fitted to raise not only coin

and potatoes, but poets and philosophers for the coming ages. In such a soil grew Homer and Confucius and the rest, and out of such a wilderness comes the Reformer eating locusts and wild honey.

To preserve wild animals implies generally the creation of a forest for them to dwell in or resort to. So it is with man. A hundred years ago they sold bark in our streets peeled from our own woods. In the very aspect of those primitive and rugged trees, there was, methinks, a tanning principle which hardened and consol idated the fibres of men's thoughts. Ah! already I shudder for these comparatively degenerate days of my native village, when you cannot col lect a load of bark of good thickness, — and we no longer produce tar and turpentine.

The civilized nations — Greece, Rome, Eng land— have been sustained by the primitive for ests which anciently rotted where they stand. They survive as long as the soil is not exhausted. Alas for human culture! little is to be expected . of a nation, when the vegetable mould is exhaust ed, and it is compelled to make manure of the k bones of its fathers. There the poet sustains himself merely by his own superfluous fat, and the philosopher comes down on his marrow-bones.

It is said to be the task of the American " to work the virgin soil," and that " agriculture here

already assumes proportions unknown every where else." I think that the farmer displaces the Indian even because he redeems the meadowjr and so makes himself stronger and in some re spects more natural. I was surveying for a man the other day a single straight line one hundred and thirty-two rods long, through a swamp, at whose entrance might have been written the words which Dante read over the entrance to the infernal regions, — " Leave all hope, ye that enter,"— that is, of ever getting out again; where at one time I saw my employer actually up to his neck and swimming for his life in his prop erty, though it was still winter. He had an other similar swamp which I could not survey at all, because it was completely under water, and nevertheless, with regard to a third swamp, which I did survey from a distance, he remarked to me, true to his instincts, that he would not part with it for any consideration, on account of the mud which it contained. And that man intends to put a girdling ditch round the whole in the course of forty months, and so redeem it by the magic of his spade. I refer to him only as the type of a class.

The weapons with which we have gained our most important victories, which should be handed down as heirlooms from father to son, are not the sword and the lance, but the bush-

whack, the turf-cutter, the spade, and the bog-hoe, rusted with the blood of many a meadow, and begrimed with the dust of many a hard-fought field. The very winds blew the Indian's corn field into the meadow, and pointed out the way which he had not the skill to follow. He had no better implement with which to intrench himself in the land than a clam-shell. But the farmer is armed with plough and spade.

In Literature it is only the wild that attracts us. Dulness is but another name for tameness. It is the uncivilized free and wild thinking in " Hamlet" and the " Iliad," in all the Scriptures and Mythologies, not learned in the schools, that delights us. As the wild duck is more swift and beautiful than the tame, so is the wild — the mallard — thought, which 'mid falling dews wings its way above the fens. A truly good book is something as natural, and as unexpect edly and unaccountably fair and perfect, as a wild flower discovered on the prairies of the West or in the jungles of the East. Genius is a light which makes the darkness visible, like the lightning's flash, which perchance shatters the temple of knowledge itself, — and not a taper lighted at the hearth-stone of the race, which pales before the light of common day.

English literatuie, from the days of the min strels to the Lake Poets, — Chaucer and Spen-13

ser and Milton, and even Shakspeare, included,

— breathes no quite fresh and in this sense wild strain. It is an essentially tame and civilized literature, reflecting Greece and Rome. Her wilderness is a green wood, — her wild man a Robin Hood. There is plenty of genial love of Nature, but not so much of Nature herself. Her chronicles inform us when her wild animals, but not when the wild man in her, became extinct.

The science of Humboldt is one thing, poetry is another thing. The poet to-day, notwith standing all the discoveries of science, and the accumulated learning of mankind, enjoys no advantage over Homer.

Where is the literature which gives expres sion to Nature ? He would be a poet who could impress the winds and streams into his service, to speak for him; who nailed words to their primitive senses, as farmers drive down stakes in the spring, which the frost has heaved; who derived his words as often as he used them,

— transplanted them to his page with earth ad hering to their roots; whose words were so true and fresh and natural that they would appear to expand like the buds at the approach of spring, though they lay half-smothered between two musty leaves in a library, — ay, to bloom and bear fruit there, after their kind, annually, for the faithful reader, in sympathy with surround ing Nature.

I do not know of any poetry to quote which adequately expresses this yearning for the Wild. Approached from this side, the best poetry is tarne. I do not know where to find in any lit erature, ancient or modern, any account which contents me of that Nature with which even I am acquainted. You will perceive that I de mand something which no Augustan nor Eliza bethan age, which no culture, in short, can give. Mythology comes nearer to it than anything. How much more fertile a Nature, at least, has Grecian mythology its root in than English lit erature ! Mythology is the crop which the Old World bore before its soil was exhausted, before the fancy and imagination were affected with blight; and which it still bears, wherever its pristine vigor is unabated. All other literatures endure only as the elms which overshadow our houses; but this is like the great dragon-tree of the Western Isles, as old as mankind, and, whether that does or not, will endure as long; for the decay of other literatures makes the soil in which it thrives.

The West is preparing to add its fables to those of the East. The valleys of the Ganges, the Nile, and the Rhine, having yielded their crop, it remains to be seen what the valleys of the Amazon, the Plate, the Orinoco, the St. Law rence, and the Mississippi will produce. Per-

chance, when, in the course of ages, American liberty has become a fiction of the past, — as it is to some extent a fiction of the present, — the poets of the world will be inspired by American mythology.

The wildest dreams of wild men, even, are not the less true, though they may not recom mend themselves to the sense which is most common among Englishmen and Americans to day. It is not every truth that recommends itself to the common sense. Nature has a place for the wild clematis as well as for the cabbage. Some expressions of truth are reminiscent,— others merely sensible^ as the phrase is, — others prophetic. Some forms of disease, even, may prophesy forms of health. The geologist has discovered that the figures of serpents, griffins, flying dragons, and other fanciful embellish ments of heraldry, have their prototypes in the forms of fossil species which were extinct be fore man was created, and hence " indicate a faint and shadowy knowledge of a previous state of organic existence." The Hindoos dreamed that the earth rested on an elephant, and the elephant on a tortoise, and the tortoise on a ser pent; and though it may be an unimportant coincidence, it will not be out of place here to state, that a fossil tortoise has lately been dis covered in Asia large enough to support an ele-

phant. I confess that I am partial to these wild fancies, which transcend the order of time and •. development. They are the sublimest recrea tion of the intellect. The partridge loves peas, but not those that go with her into the pot.

In short, all good things are wild and free. There is something in a strain of music, whether produced by an instrument or by the human voice, — take the sound of a bugle in a summer night, for instance,—which by its wildness, to speak without satire, reminds me of the cries emitted by wild beasts in their native forests. It is so much of their wildness as I can under stand. Give me for my friends and neighbors wild men, not tame ones. The wildness of the savage is but a faint symbol of the awful ferity with which good men and lovers meet.

I love even to see the domestic animals re assert their native rights, — any evidence that they have not wholly lost their original wild habits and vigor; as when my neighbor's cow breaks out of her pasture early in the spring and boldly swims the river, a cold, gray tide, twenty-five or thirty rods wide, swollen by the melted snow. It is the buffalo crossing the Mis-

O

sissippi. This exploit confers some dignity on the herd in my eyes, — already dignified. The seeds of instinct are preserved under the thick hides of cattle and horses, like seeds in the bow els of the earth, an indefinite period.

Any sportiveness in cattle is unexpected. I saw one day a herd of a dozen bullocks and cows running about and frisking in unwieldly sport, like huge rats, even like kittens. They shook their heads, raised their tails, and rushed up and down a hill, and I perceived by their horns, as well as by their activity, their relation to the deer tribe. But, alas! a sudden loud Whoa ! would have damped their ardor at once, reduced them from venison to beef, and stiffened their sides and sinews like the locomotive. Who but the Evil One has cried, " Whoa! " to man kind? Indeed, the life of cattle, like that of many men, is but a sort of locomotiveness ; they move a side at a time, and man, by his machin ery, is meeting the horse and the ox half-way. Whatever part the whip has touched is thence forth palsied. Who would ever think of a side of any of the supple cat tribe, as we speak of a side of beef?

I rejoice that horses and steers have to be broken before they can be made the slaves of men, and that men themselves have some wild oats still left to sow before they become submis sive members of society. Undoubtedly, all men are not equally fit subjects for civilization; and because the majority, like dogs and sheep, are tame by inherited disposition, this is no reason V why the others should have their natures broken

that they may be reduced to the same level. Men are in the main alike, but they were made several in order that they might be various. If a low use is to be served, one man will do nearly or quite as well as another ; if a high one, indi vidual excellence is to be regarded. Any man can stop a hole to keep the wind away, but no other man could serve so rare a use as the au thor of this illustration did. Confucius says, — " The skins of the tiger and the leopard, when they are tanned, are as the skins of the dog and the sheep tanned." But it is not the part of a true culture to tame tigers, any more than it is to make sheep ferocious; and tanning their skins for shoes is not the best use to which they can be put

When looking over a list of men's names in a foreign language, as of military officers, or of authors who have written on a particular subject, I am reminded once more that there is nothing in a name. The name Menschikoff, for instance, has nothing in it to my ears more human than a whisker, and it may belong to a rat. As the names of the Poles and Russians are to us, so are ours to them. It is as if they had been named by the child's rigmarole, — lery wiery ichery van, tittie-lol-tan. I see in my mind a herd of wild Creatures swarming over the earth, and to each

the herdsman has affixed some barbarous sound in his own dialect. The names of men are of course as cheap and meaningless as Bose and Tray, the names of dogs.

Methinks it would be some advantage to phi losophy, if men were named merely in the gross, as they are known. It would be necessary only to know the genus and perhaps the race or va riety, to know the individual. We are not pre pared to believe that every private soldier in a Roman army had a name of his own, — because we have not supposed that he had a character of his own. At present our only true names are nicknames. I knew a boy who, from his pecu liar energy, was called " Buster" by his play mates, and this rightly supplanted his Christian name. Some travellers tell us that an Indian had no name given him at first, but earned it, and his name was his fame; and among some tribes he acquired a new name with every new exploit. It is pitiful when a man bears a name for convenience merely, who has earned neither name nor fame.

I will not allow mere names to make distinc tions for me, but still see men in herds for all them. A familiar name cannot make a man less strange to me. It may be given to a savage who retains in secret his own wild title earned in the woods. We have a wild savage in us,

and a savage name is perchance somewhere re corded as ours. I see that my neighbor, who bears the familiar epithet William, or Edwin, takes it off with his jacket. It does not adhere to him when asleep or in anger, or aroused by any passion or inspiration. I seem to hear pro nounced by some of his kin at such a time his original wild name in some jaw-breaking or else melodious tongue.

Here is this vast, savage, howling mother of ours, Nature, lying all around, with such beauty, and such affection for her children, as the leop ard ; and yet we are so early weaned from her breast to society, to that culture which is exclu sively an interaction of man on man, — a sort of breeding in and in, which produces at most a merely English nobility, a civilization destined to have a speedy limit.

In society, in the best institutions of men, it is easy to detect a certain precocity. When we should still be growing children, we are already little men. Give me a culture which imports much muck from the meadows, and deepens the soil, — not that which trusts to heating manures, and improved implements and modes of culture only!

Many a poor sore-eyed student that I have heard of would grow faster, both intellectually and physically, if, instead of sitting up so very late, he honestly slumbered a fool's allowance.

There may be an excess even of informing light. Niepce, a Frenchman, discovered " actin ism," that power in the sun's rays which pro duces a chemical effect, — that granite rocks, and stone structures, and statues of metal, " are all alike destructively acted upon during the hours of sunshine, and, but for provisions of Nature no less wonderful, would soon perish under the deli cate touch of the most subtile of the agencies of the universe." But he observed that " those bodies which underwent this change during the daylight possessed the power of restoring them selves to their original conditions during the hours of night, when this excitement was no longer influencing them." Hence it has been in ferred that " the hours of darkness are as neces sary to the inorganic creation as we know night and sleep are to the organic kingdom." Not even does the moon shine every night, but gives place to darkness.

I would not have every man nor every part of a man cultivated, any more than I would have every acre of earth cultivated: part will be till age, but the greater part will be meadow and forest, not only serving an immediate use, but preparing a mould against a distant future, by the annual decay of the vegetation which it supports.

There are other letters for the child to learn than those which Cadmus invented. The Span iards have a good term to express this wild and dusky knowledge, — Gramatica parda, tawny grammar,— a kind of mother-wit derived from that same leopard to which I have referred.

We have heard of a Society for the Diffusion of Useful Knowledge. It is said that knowledge is power; and the like. Methinks there is equal need of a Society for the Diffusion of Useful Ig norance, what we will call Beautiful Knowledge^ a knowledge useful in a higher sense: for what is most of our boasted so-called knowledge but a conceit that we know something, which robs us of the advantage of our actual ignorance ? What we call knowledge is often our positive ignorance; ignorance our negative knowledge. By long years of patient industry and reading of the newspapers, — for what are the libraries of science but files of newspapers ? — a man accu mulates a myriad facts, lays them up in his memory, and then when in some spring of his life hd saunters abroad into the Great Fields of thought, he, as it were, goes to grass like a horse, and leaves all his harness behind in the stable. I would say to the Society for the Diffusion of Useful Knowledge, sometimes, — Go to grass. You have eaten hay long enough. The spring has come with its green crop. The very cows

are driven to their country pastures before the end of May ; though I have heard of one un natural farmer who kept his cow in the barn and fed her on hay all the year round. So, fre quently, the Society for the Diffusion of Useful Knowledge treats its cattle.

A man's ignorance sometimes is not only useful, but beautiful, — while his knowledge, so called, is oftentimes worse than useless, besides being ugly. Which is the best man to deal with, — he who knows nothing about a subject, and, what is extremely rare, knows that he knows nothing, or he who really knows some thing about it, but thinks that he knows all ?

My desire for knowledge is intermittent; but my desire to bathe my head in atmospheres un known to my feet is perennial and constant. The highest that we can attain to is not Knowl edge, but Sympathy with Intelligence. I do not know that this higher knowledge amounts to anything more definite than a novel and grand surprise on a sudden revelation of the in sufficiency of all that we called Knowledge be fore, — a discovery that there are more things in heaven and earth than are dreamed of in our philosophy. It is the lighting up of the mist by the sun. Man cannot know in any higher sense than this, any more than he can look serenely and with impunity in the face of sun : 'Os r\

ov KCLVOV voyo-eis, — " You will not perceive that, as perceiving a particular thing," say the Chal dean Oracles.

There is something servile in the habit of seeking after a law which we may obey. We may study the laws of matter at and for our convenience, but a successful life knows no law. It is an unfortunate discovery certainly, that of a law which binds us where we did not know before that we were bound. Live free, child of the mist, — and with respect to knowledge we are all children of the mist. The man who takes the liberty to live is superior to all the laws, by virtue of his relation to the law-maker. " That is active duty," says the Vishnu Purana, "which is not for our bondage ; that is knowledge which is for our liberation : all other duty is good only unto weariness ; all other knowledge is only the cleverness of an artist."

It is remarkable how few events or crises there are in our histories ; how little exercised we have been in our minds ; how few experi ences we have had. I would fain be assured that I am growing apace and rankly, though my very growth disturb this dull equanimity,— though it be with struggle through long, dark, muggy nights or seasons of gloom. It would be well, if all our lives were a divine tragedy

even, instead of this trivial comedy or farce. Dante, Bunyan, and others, appear to have been exercised in their minds more than we : they were subjected to a kind of culture such as our district schools and colleges do not contemplate. Even Mahomet, though many may scream at his name, had a good deal more to live for, ay, and to die for, than they have commonly.

When, at rare intervals, some thought visits one, as perchance he is walking on a railroad, then indeed the cars go by without his hearing them. But soon, by some inexorable law, our life goes by and the cars return.

" Gentle breeze, that wanderest unseen, And bendest the thistles round Loira of storms, Traveller of the windy glens, Why hast thou left my ear so soon ? "

While almost all men feel an attraction draw ing them to society, few are attracted strongly to Nature. In their relation to Nature men ap pear to me for the most part, notwithstanding their arts, lower than the animals. It is not often a beautiful relation, as in the case of the animals. How little appreciation of the beauty of the landscape there is among us! We have to be told that the Greeks called the world KoV/xos, Beauty, or Order, but we do not see clearly why they did so, and we esteem it at best only a curious philological fact.

For my part, I feel that with regard to Nature I live a sort of border life, on the confines of a world into which I make occasional and tran-sional and transient forays only, and my patriot ism and allegiance to the State into whose ter ritories I seern to retreat are those of a moss trooper. Unto a life which I call natural I would gladly follow even a will-o'-the-wisp through bogs and sloughs unimaginable, but no moon nor fire-fly has shown me the causeway to it. Nature is a personality so vast and univer sal that we have never seen one of her features. The walker in the familiar fields which stretch around my native town sometimes finds him self in another land than is described in their owners' deeds, as it were in some far-away field on the confines of the actual Concord, where her jurisdiction ceases, and the idea which the word Concord suggests ceases to be suggested. These farms which I have myself surveyed, these bounds which I have set up, appear dimly still as through a mist; but they have no chemistry to fix them; they fade from the surface of the glass ; and the picture which the painter painted stands out dimly from beneath. The world with which we are commonly acquainted leaves no trace, and it will have no anniversary.

I took a walk on Spaulding's Farm the other afternoon. I saw the setting sun lighting up the opposite side of a stately pine wood. It3 golden rays straggled into the aisles of the wood as into some noble hall. I was impressed as if some ancient and altogether admirable and shin ing family had settled there in that part of the land called Concord, unknown to ine, — to whom the sun was servant, — who had not gone into society in the village, — who had not been called on. I saw their park, their pleasure-ground, beyond through the wood, in Spauld-ing's cranberry-meadow. The pines furnished them with gables as they grew. Their house was not obvious to vision ; the trees grew through it. I do not know whether I heard the sounds of a suppressed hilarity or not. They seemed to recline on the sunbeams. They have sons and daughters. They are quite well. The farmer's cart-path, which leads directly through their hall, does not in the least put them out, — as the muddy bottom of a pool is sometimes seen through the reflected skies. They never heard of Spaulding, and do not know that he is their neighbor, — notwithstanding I heard him whistle as he drove his team through the house. Nothing can equal the serenity of their lives. Their coat of arms is simply a lichen. I saw it painted on the pines and oaks. Their attics were in the tops of the trees. They are of no politics. There was no noise of labor. I did

not perceive that they were weaving or spin ning. Yet I did detect, when the wind lulled and hearing was done away, the finest imagin able sweet musical hum, — as of a distant hive in May, which perchance was the sound of then thinking. They had no idle thoughts, and no one without could see their work, for their in dustry was not as in knots and excrescences embayed.

But I find it difficult to remember them. They fade irrevocably out of my mind even now while I speak and endeavor to recall them, and recol lect myself. It is only after a long and serious effort to recollect my best thoughts that I be come again aware of their cohabitancy. If it were not for such families as this, I think I should move out of Concord.

We are accustomed to say in New England that few and fewer pigeons visit us every year. Our forests furnish no mast for them. So, it would seem, few and fewer thoughts visit each growing man from year to year, for the grove in our minds is laid waste, — sold to feed unneces sary fires of ambition, or sent to mill, and there is scarcely a twig left for them to perch on. They no longer build nor breed with us. In some more genial season, perchance, a faint shadow flits across the landscape of the mind,

14

J

cast by the wing's of some thought in its vernal or autumnal migration, but, looking up, we are unable to detect the substance of the thought itself. Our winged thoughts are turned to poul try. They no longer soar, and they attain only to a Shanghai and Cochin-China grandeur. Those gra-a-ate thoughts, those gra-a-ate men you hear of!

We hug the earth, — how rarely we mount! Methinks we might elevate ourselves a little more. We might climb a tree, at least. I found my account in climbing a tree once. It was a tall white pine, on the top of a hill; and though I got well pitched, I was well paid for it, for I discovered new mountains in the hori zon which I had never seen before, — so much more of the earth and the heavens. I might have walked about the foot of the tree for three score years and ten, and yet I certainly should never have seen them. But, above all, I dis covered around me, — it was near the end of June, — on the ends of the topmost branches only, a few minute and delicate red cone-like blossoms, the fertile flower of the white pine looking heavenward. I carried straightway to the village the topmost spire, and showed it to stranger jurymen who walked the streets, — for it was court-week, — and to farmers and mm-

ber-dealers and wood-choppers and hunters, and not one had ever seen the like before, but they wondered as at a star dropped down. Tell of ancient architects finishing their works on the tops of columns as perfectly as on the lower and more visible parts! Nature has from the first expanded the minute blossoms of the forest only toward the heavens, above men's heads and unobserved by them. We see only the flowers that are under our feet in the meadows. The pines have developed their delicate blossoms on the highest twigs of the wood every summer for ages, as well over the heads of Nature's red children as of her white ones; yet scarcely a farmer or hunter in the land has ever seen them.

Above all, we cannot afford not to live in the present. He is blessed over all mortals who loses no moment of the passing life in remem bering the past. Unless our philosophy hears the cock crow in every barn-yard within our horizon, it is belated. That sound commonly reminds us that we are growing rusty and an tique in our employments and habits of thought. His philosophy comes down to a more recent time than ours. There is something suggested by it that is a newer testament, — the gospel according to this moment. He has not fallen astern; he has got up early, and kept up early,

and to be where he is to be in season, in the foremost rank of time. It is an expression of the health and soundness of Nature, a brag for all the world, — healthiness as of a spring burst forth, a new fountain of the Muses, to celebrate this last instant of time. Where he lives no fugitive slave laws are passed. Who has not betrayed his master many times since last he heard that note?

The merit of this bird's strain is in its free dom from all plaintiveness. The singer can easily move us to tears or to laughter, but where is he who can excite in us a pure morn ing joy? When, in doleful dumps, breaking the awful stillness of our wooden sidewalk on a Sunday, or, perchance, a watcher in the house of mourning, I hear a cockerel crow far or near, I think to myself, " There is one of us well, at any rate," — and with a sudden gush return to my senses.

We had a remarkable sunset one day last November. I was walking in a meadow, the source of a small brook, when the sun at last, just before setting, after a cold gray day, reached a clear stratum in the horizon, and the softest brightest morning sunlight fell on the dry grass and on the stems of the trees in the opposite horizon, and on the leaves of the shrub-oaks on

the hill-side, while our shadows stretched long over the meadow eastward, as if we were the only motes in its beams. It was such a light as we could not have imagined a moment be fore, and the air also was so warm and serene that nothing was wanting to make a paradise of that meadow. When we reflected that this was not a solitary phenomenon, never to hap pen again, but that it would happen forever and ever an infinite number of evenings, and cheer and reassure the latest child that walked there, it was more glorious still.

O

The sun sets on some retired meadow, where no house is visible, with all the glory and splen dor that it lavishes on cities, and perchance, as it has never set before, — where there is but a solitary marsh-hawk to have his wings gilded by it, or only a musquash looks out from his cabin, and there is some little black-veined brook in the midst of the marsh, just begin ning to meander, winding slowly round a de caying stump. We walked in so pure and bright a light, gilding the withered grass and leaves, so softly and serenely bright, I thought I had never bathed in such a golden flood, with out a ripple or a murmur to it. The west side of every wood and rising ground gleamed like the boundary of Elysium, and the sun on our backs seemed like a gentle herdsman driving us home at evening.

So we saunter toward the Holy Land, till one day the sun shall shine more brightly than ever he has done, shall perchance shine into our minds and hearts, and light up our whole lives with a great awakening light, as warm and se rene and golden as on a bank-side in autumn.

AUTUMNAL TINTS.

[1862.]

EUROPEANS coming to America are surprised by the brilliancy of our autumnal foliage. There is no account of such a phenomenon in English poetry, because the trees acquire but few bright colors there. The most that Thomson says on this subject in his " Au tumn" is contained in the lines,—

" But see the fading many-colored woods, Shade deepening over shade, the country round Imbrown ; a crowded umbrage, dusk and dun, Of every hue, from wan declining green to sooty dark": —

and in the line in which he speaks of

" Autumn beaming o'er the yellow woods."

The autumnal change of our woods has not made a deep impression on our own literature yet. October has hardly tinged our poetry.

A great many, who have spent their lives in cities, and have never chanced to come into the country at this season, have never seen this, the flower, or rather the ripe fruit, of the year. I remember riding with one such citizen, who, though a fortnight too late for the most bril liant tints, was taken by surprise, and would not believe that there had been any brighter. He had never heard of this phenomenon before. Not only many in our towns have never wit nessed it, but it is scarcely remembered by the majority from year to year.

Most appear to confound changed leaves with withered ones, as if they were to confound ripe apples with rotten ones. I think that the change to some higher color in a leaf is an evidence that it has arrived at a late and perfect maturity, an swering to the maturity of fruits. It is generally the lowest and oldest leaves which change first. But as the perfect winged and usually bright* col ored insect is short-lived, so the leaves ripen but to faU.

Generally, every fruit, on ripening, and just before it falls, when it commences a more inde pendent and individual existence, requiring less nourishment from any source, and that not so much from the earth through its stem as from the sun and air, acquires a bright tint. So do leaves. The physiologist says it is " due to an increased absorption of oxygen." That is the scientific account of the matter, — only a reas-sertion of the fact. But I am more interested in the rosy cheek than I am to know what par-

ticular diet the maiden fed on. The very forest and herbage, the pellicle of the earth, must ac quire a bright color, an evidence of its ripeness, — as if the globe itself were a fruit on its stem, with ever a cheek toward the sun.

Flowers are but colored leaves, fruits but ripe ones. The edible part of most fruits is, as the physiologist says, "the parenchyma or fleshy tissue of the leaf," of which they are formed.

Our appetites have commonly confined our views of ripeness and its phenomena, color, mellowness, and perfectness, to the fruits which we eat, and we are wont to forget that an im mense harvest which we do not eat, hardly use at all, is annually ripened by Nature. At our annual Cattle Shows and Horticultural Exhibi tions, we make, as we think, a great show of fair fruits, destined, however, to a rather ignoble end, fruits not valued for their beauty chiefly. But round about and within our towns there is annually another show of fruits, on an in finitely grander scale, fruits which address our taste for oeauty alone.

October is the month for painted leaves. Their rich glow now flashes round the world. ^s fruits and leaves and the day itself acquire a. bright tint just before they fall, so the year near its setting. October is its sunset sky; No vember the later twilight.

I formerly thought that it would be worth the while to get a specimen leaf from each chang ing tree, shrub, and herbaceous plant, when it had acquired its brightest characteristic color, in its transition from the green to the brown state, outline it, and copy its color exactly, with paint in a book, which should be entitled, " October, or Autumnal Tints " ; — beginning with the ear liest reddening, — Woodbine and the lake of radical leaves, and coming down through the Maples, Hickories, and Sumachs, and many beautifully freckled leaves less generally known, to the latest Oaks and Aspens. What a me mento such a book would be ! You would need only to turn over its leaves to take a ramble through the autumn woods whenever you pleased. Or if I could preserve the leaves themselves, unfaded, it would be better still. I have made but little progress toward such a book, but I have endeavored, instead, to describe all these bright tints in the order in which they present themselves. The following are some extracts from my notes.

THE PURPLE GRASSES.

BY the twentieth of August, everywhere in woods and swamps, we are reminded of the fall, both by the richly spotted Sarsapaiilla

leaves and Brakes, and the withering and black ened Skunk-Cabbage and Hellebore, and, by the river-side, the already blackening Pontedc-ria.

The Purple Grass (Eragrostis pectindcea) is now in the height of its beauty. I remember still when I first noticed this grass particularly. Standing on a hillside near our river, I saw, thirty or forty rods off, a stripe of purple half a dozen rods long, under the edge of a wood, where the ground sloped toward a meadow. It was as high-colored and interesting, though not quite so bright, as the patches of Rhexia, being a darker purple, like a berry's stain laid on close and thick. On going to and examining it, I found it to be a kind of grass in bloom, hardly a foot high, with but few green bkides, and a fine spreading panicle of purple flowers, a shal low, purplish mist trembling around me. Close at hand it appeared but a dull purple, and made little impression on the eye ; it was even diffi cult to detect; and if you plucked a single plant, you were surprised to find how thin it was, and how little color it had. But viewed at a dis tance in a favorable light, it was of a fine lively purple, flower-like, enriching the earth. Such puny causes combine to produce these decided effects. I was the more surprised and charmed because grass is commonly of a sober and hum ble color.

With its beautiful purple blush it reminds me, and supplies the place, of the Rhexia, which is now leaving off, and it is one of the most in teresting phenomena of August. The finest patches of it grow on waste strips or selvages of land at the base of dry hills, just above the edge of the meadows, where the greedy mower does not deign to swing his scythe; for this is a thin and poor grass, beneath his notice. Or, it may be, because it is so beautiful he does not know that it exists; for the same eye does not see this and Timothy. He carefully gets the meadow hay and the more nutritious grasses which "grow next to that, but he leaves this fine purple mist for the walker's harvest, — fodder for his fancy stock. Higher up the hill, per chance, grow also Blackberries, John's-Wort, and neglected, withered, and wiry June-Grass. How fortunate that it grows in such places, and not in the midst of the rank grasses which are annually cut! Nature thus keeps use and beauty distinct. I know many such localities, where it does not fail to present itself annually, and paint the earth with its blush. It grows on the gentle slopes, either in a continuous patch or in scattered and rounded tufts a foot in diameter, and it lasts till it is killed by the first smart frosts.

In most plants the corolla or calyx is the part which attains the highest color, and is the most attractive; in many it is the seed-vessel or fruit; in others, as the Red Maple, the leaves; and in others still it is the very culm itself which is the principal flower or blooming part.

The last is especially the case with the Poke or Garget (Phytolacca decdndra). Some which stand under our cliffs quite dazzle rne with their purple stems now and early in September. They are as interesting to me as most flowers, and one of the most important fruits of our autumn. Every part is flower, (or fruit,) such is its superfluity of color, — stem, branch, peduncle, pedicel, petiole, and even the ut length yellowish purple-veined leaves. Its cylindrical racemes of berries of various hues, from green to dark purple, six or seven inches long, are gracefully drooping on all sides, offer ing repasts to the birds ; and even the sepals from which the birds have picked the berries are a brilliant lake-red, with crimson flame-like re flections, equal to anything of the kind, — all on fire with ripeness. Hence the lacca, from lac, lake. There are at the same time flower-buds, flowers, green berries, dark purple or ripe ones, and these flower-like sepals, all on the same plant.

We love to see any redness in the vegetation of the temperate zone. It is the color of colors.

This plant speaks to our blood. It asks a bright sun on it to make it show to best advantage and it must be seen at this season of the year. On warm hillsides its stems are ripe by the twenty-third of August. At that date I walked through a beautiful grove of them, six or seven feet high, on the side of one of our cliffs, where they ripen early. Quite to the ground they were a deep brilliant purple with a bloom, con trasting with the still clear green leaves. It ap pears a rare triumph of Nature to have pro duced and perfected such a plant, as if this were enough for a summer. What a perfect maturity it arrives at! It is the emblem of a successful life concluded by a death not prema ture, which is an ornament to Nature. What if we were to mature as perfectly, root and branch, glowing in the midst of our decay, like the Poke! I confess that it excites me to be hold them. I cut one for a cane, for I would fain handle and lean on it. I love to press the berries between my fingers, and see their juice staining my hand. To walk amid these up right, branching casks of purple wine, which retain and diffuse a sunset glow, tasting each one with your eye, instead of counting the pipes on a London dock, what a privilege! For Nature's vintage is not confined to the vine. Our poets have sung of wine, the pro-

duct of a foreign plant which commonly they never saw, as if our own plants had no juice in them more than the singers. Indeed, this has been called by some the American Grape, and, though a native of America, its juices are used in some foreign countries to improve the color of the wine ; so that the poetaster may be celebrating the virtues of the Poke without knowing it. Here are berries enough to paint afresh the western sky, and play the bacchanal with, if you will. And what flutes its ensan guined stems would make, to be used in such a dance! It is truly a royal plant. I could spend the evening of the year musing amid the Poke-stems. And perchance amid these groves might arise at last a new school of philosophy or poetry. It lasts all through September.

At the same time with this, or near the end of August, a to me very interesting genus of grasses, Andropogons, or Beard-Grasses, is in its prime. Andropogon furcatus, Forked Beard-Grass, or call it Purple-Fingered Grass; Andro pogon scopariuSj Purple Wood-Grass; and An dropogon (now called Sorghum) nutans, Indian-Grass. The first is a very tall and slender-culmed grass, three to seven feet high, with four or five purple finger-like spikes raying up ward from the top. The second is also quite vender, growing in tufts two feet high by

one wide, with culms often somewhat curving, which, as the spikes go out of bloom, have a whitish fuzzy look. These two are prevail ing grasses at this season on dry and sandy fields and hillsides. The culms of both, not to mention their pretty flowers, reflect a pur ple tinge, and help to declare the ripeness of the year. Perhaps I have the more sympathy with them because they are despised by the farmer, and occupy sterile and neglected soil. They are high-colored, like ripe grapes, and express a maturity which the spring did not suggest. Only the August sun could have thus burnished these culms and leaves. The farmer has long since done his upland haying^ and he will not condescend to bring his scythe to where these slender wild grasses have a\ length flowered thinly; you often see spacer of bare sand amid them. But I walk encour-aged between the tufts of Purple Wood-Grass r , over the sandy fields, and along the edge ol the Shrub-Oaks, glad to recognize these sim ple contemporaries. With thoughts cutting a broad swathe I "get" them, with horse-rak ing thoughts I gather them into windrows. The fine-eared poet may hear the whetting of my scythe. These two were almost the first grasses that I learned to distinguish, for I had not known by how many friends I was surrounded,

— I had seen them simply as grasses standing. The purple of their culms also excites me like that of the Poke-Weed stems.

•Think what refuge there is for one, before August is over, from college commencements and society that isolates! I can skulk amid the tufts of Purple Wood-Grass on the bor ders of the " Great Fields." Wherever I walk these afternoons, the Purple - Fingered Grass also stands like a guide-board, and points my thoughts to more poetic paths than they have lately travelled.

A man shall perhaps rush by and trample down plants as high as his head, and cannot be said to know that they exist, though he may have cut many tons of them, littered his stables with them, and fed them to his cattle for years. Yet, if he ever favorably attends to them, he may be overcome by their beauty. Each humblest plant, or weed, as we call it, stands there to express some thought or mood of ours ; and yet how long it stands in vain! I had walked over those Great Fields so many Augusts, and never yet distinctly recognized these purple companions that I had there. I had brushed against them and trodden on them, forsooth ; and now, at last, they, as it were, rose up and blessed me. Beauty and true wealth are always thus cheap and despised. Heaven

15

might be defined as the place which men avoid. Who can doubt that these grasses, which the farmer says are of no account to him, find some compensation in your appreci ation of them ? I may say that I never saw them before, — though, when I came to look them face to face, there did come down to me a purple gleam from previous years; and now, wherever I go, I see hardly anything else. It is the reign and presidency of the Andropogons.

Almost the very sands confess the ripening influence of the August sun, and methinks, to gether with the slender grasses waving over them, reflect a purple tinge. The impurpled sands! Such is the consequence of all this sun shine absorbed into the pores of plants and of the earth. All sap or blood is now wine-col ored. At last we have not only the purple sea, but the purple land.

The Chestnut Beard-Grass, Indian-Grass, or Wood-Grass, growing here and there in waste places, but more rare than the former, (from two to four or five feet high,) is still handsomer and of more vivid colors than its congeners, and might well have caught the Indian's eye. It has a long, narrow, one-sided, and slightly nod ding panicle of bright purple and yellow flow ers, like a banner raised above its reedy leaves. These bright standards are now advanced on

the distant hill-sides, not in large armies, but in scattered troops or single file, like the red men. They stand thus fair and bright, repre sentative of the race which they are named af ter, but for the most part unobserved as they. The expression of this grass haunted me for a week, after I first passed and noticed it, like the glance of an eye. It stands like an Indian chief taking a last look at his favorite hunting-grounds.

THE RED MAPLE.

BY the twenty-fifth of September, the Red Ma ples generally are beginning to be ripe. Some large ones have been conspicuously changing for a week, and some single trees are now very brilliant. I notice a small one, half a mile off across a meadow, against the green wood-side there, a far brighter red than the blossoms of any tree in summer, and more conspicuous. I have observed this tree for several autumns in variably changing earlier than its fellows, just as one tree ripens its fruit earlier than another. It might serve to mark the season, perhaps. I should be sorry, if it were cut down. I know of two or three such trees in different parts of our town, which might, perhaps, be propagated from, as early ripencrs or September trees, and their seed be advertised in the market, as well

as that of radishes, if we cared as much about them.

At present these burning bushes stand chiefly along the edge of the meadows, or I distinguish them afar on the hillsides here and there. Some times you will see many small ones in a swamp turned quite crimson when all other trees around are still perfectly green, and the former appear so much the brighter for it. They take you by surprise, as you are going by on one side, across the fields, thus early in the season, as if it were some gay encampment of the red men, or other foresters, of whose arrival you had not heard.

Some single trees, wholly bright scarlet, seen against others of their kind still freshly green, or against evergreens, are more memorable than whole groves will be by-and-by. How beauti ful, when a whole tree is like one great scarlet fruit full of ripe juices, every leaf, from lowest limb to topmost spire, all aglow, especially if you look toward the sun! What more remark able object can there be in the landscape ? Vis ible for miles, too fair to be believed. If such a phenomenon occurred but once, it would be handed down by tradition to posterity, and get into the mythology at last.

The whole tree thus ripening in advance of its fellows attains a singular preeminence, and sometimes maintains it for a week or two. I

am thrilled at the sight of it, bearing aloft its scarlet standard for the regiment of green-clad foresters around, and I go half a mile out of my way to examine it. A single tree becomes thus the crowning beauty of some meadowy vale, and the expression of the whole surrounding forest is at once more spirited for it.

A small Red Maple has grown, perchance, far away at the head of some retired valley, a mile from any road, unobserved. It has faith fully discharged the duties of a Maple there, all winter and summer, neglected none of its econ omies, but added to its stature in the virtue which belongs to a Maple, by a steady growth for so many months, never having gone gadding abroad, and is nearer heaven than it was in the spring. It has faithfully husbanded its sap, and afforded a shelter to the wandering bird, has long since ripened its seeds and committed them to the winds, and has the satisfaction of know ing, perhaps, that a thousand little well-behaved Maples are already settled in life somewhere. It deserves well of Mapledom. Its leaves have been asking it from time to time, in a whisper, " When shall we redden ? " And now, in this month of September, this month of travelling, when men are hastening to the sea-side, or the mountains, or the lakes, this modest Maple, still without budging an inch, travels in its reputa-

tion, — runs up its scarlet flag on that hillside, which shows that it has finished its summer's work before all other trees, and withdraws from the contest. At the eleventh hour of the year, the tree which no scrutiny could have detected here when it was most industrious is thus, by the tint of its maturity, by its very blushes, re vealed at last to the careless and distant travel ler, and leads his thoughts away from the dusty road into those brave solitudes which it inhab its. It flashes out conspicuous with all the vir tue and beauty of a Maple, — Acer rubrum. We may now read its title, or rubric, clear. Its virtues, not its sins, are as scarlet.

Notwithstanding the Red Maple is the most intense scarlet of any of our trees, the Sugar-Maple has been the most celebrated, and Mi-chaux in his " Sylva" does not speak of the autumnal color of the former. About the sec ond of October, these trees, both large and small, are most brilliant, though many are still green. In " sprout-lands " they seem to vie with one another, and ever some particular one in the midst of the crowd will be of a peculiarly pure scarlet, and by its more intense color at tract our eye even at a distance, and carry off the palm. A large Red-Maple swamp, when at the height of its change, is the most obvi ously brilliant of all tangible things, where I

dwell, so abundant is this tree with us. It varies much both in form and color. A great many are merely yellow, more scarlet, others scarlet deepening into crimson, more red than common. Look at yonder swamp of Maples mixed with Pines, at the base of a Pine-clad hill, a quarter of a mile off, so that you get the full effect of the bright colors, without detecting the imperfections of the leaves, and see their yellow, scarlet, and crimson fires, of all tints, mingled and contrasted with the green. Some Maples are yet green, only yellow or crimson-tipped on the edges of their flakes, like the edges of a Hazel-Nut burr; some are wholly brilliant scarlet, raying out regularly and finely every way, bilaterally, like the veins of a leaf; others, of more irregular form, when I turn my head slightly, emptying out some of its earthiness and concealing the trunk of the tree, seem to rest heavily flake on flake, like yellow and scar let clouds, wreath upon wreath, or like snow drifts driving through the air, stratified by the wind. It adds greatly to the beauty of such a swamp at this season, that, even though there may be no other trees interspersed, it is not seen as a simple mass of color, but, different trees being of different colors and hues, the outline of each crescent tree-top is distinct, and where one laps on to another. Yet a painter would

hardly venture to make them thus distinct a quarter of a mile off.

As I go across a meadow directly toward a low rising ground this bright afternoon, I see, some fifty rods off toward the sun, the top of a Maple swamp just appearing over the sheeny russet edge of the hill, a stripe apparently twen ty rods long by ten feet deep, of the most in tensely brilliant scarlet, orange, and yellow, equal to any flowers or fruits, or any tints ever painted. As I advance, lowering the edge of the hill which makes the firm foreground or lower frame of the picture, the depth of the brilliant grove revealed steadily increases, sug gesting that the whole of the inclosed valley is filled with such color. One wonders that the tithing-men and fathers of the town are not out to see what the trees mean by their high colors and exuberance of spirits, fearing that some mischief is brewing. I do not see what the Puritans did at this season, when the Maples blaze out in scarlet. They certainly could not have worshipped in groves then. Perhaps that is what they built meeting-houses and fenced them round with horse-sheds for.

THE ELM.

Now, too, the first of October, or later, the Elms are at the height of their autumnal beauty,

great brownish-yellow masses, warm from their September oven, hanging over the highway Their leaves are perfectly ripe. I wonder if there is any answering ripeness in the lives of the men who live beneath them. As I look down our street, which is lined with them, they remind me both by their form and color of yel lowing sheaves of grain, as if the harvest had indeed come to the village itself, and we might expect to find some maturity and flavor in the thoughts of the villagers at last. Under those bright rustling yellow piles just ready to fall on the heads of the walkers, how can any crudity or greenness of thought or act prevail? When I stand where half a dozen large Elms droop over a house, it is as if I stood within a ripe pumpkin-rind, and I feel as mellow as if I were the pulp, though I may be somewhat stringy and seedy withal. What is the late greenness of the English Elm, like a cucumber out of season, which does not know when to have done, compared with the early and golden ma turity of the American tree ? The street is the scene of a great harvest-home. It would be worth the while to set out these trees, if only for their autumnal value. Think of these great yellow canopies or parasols held over our heads and houses by the mile together, making the vil lage all one and compact,— an ulmarium, which

is at the same time a nursery of men! And then how gently and unobserved they drop their burden and let in the sun when it is wanted, their leaves not heard when they fall on our roofs and in our streets ; and thus the village parasol is shut up and put away! I see the market-man driving into the village, and disap pearing under its canopy of Elm-tops, with his crop, as into a great granary or barn-yard. I am tempted to go thither as to a husking of thoughts, now dry and ripe, and ready to be separated from their integuments; but, alas ! I foresee that it will be chiefly husks and little thought, blasted pig-corn, fit only for cob-meal, — for, as you sow, so shall you reap.

FALLEN LEAVES.

BY the sixth of October the leaves generally begin to fall, in successive showers, after frost or rain ; but the principal leaf-harvest, the acme of the Fall) is commonly about the sixteenth. Some morning at that date there is perhaps a harder frost than we have seen, and ice formed under the pump, and now, when the morning wind rises, the leaves come down in denser showers than ever. They suddenly form thick beds or carpets on the ground, in this gentle air, or even without wind, just the size and form of the tree above. Some trees, as small Hickories,

appear to have dropped their leaves instantane ously, as a soldier grounds arms at a signal; and those of the Hickory, being bright yellow still, though withered, reflect a blaze of light from the ground where they lie. Down they have come on all sides, at the first earnest touch of au tumn's wand, making a sound like rain.

Or else it is after moist and rainy weather that we notice how great a fall of leaves there has been in the night, though it may not yet be the touch that loosens the Rock-Maple leaf. The streets are thickly strewn with the trophies, and fallen Elm-leaves make a dark brown pave ment under our feet. After some remarkably warm Indian-summer day or days, I perceive that it is the unusual heat which, more than anything, causes the leaves to fall, there having been, perhaps, no frost nor rain for some time. The intense heat suddenly ripens and wilts them, just as it softens and ripens peaches and other fruits, and causes them to drop.

The leaves of late Red Maples, still bright, strew the earth, often crimson-spotted on a yel low ground, like some wild apples, — though they preserve these bright colors on the ground but a day or two, especially if it rains. On causeways I go by trees here and there all bare and smoke-like, having lost their brilliant cloth ing ; but there it lies, nearly as bright as ever,

on the ground on one side, and making nearly as regular a figure as lately on the tree. I would rather say that I first observe the trees thus flat on the ground like a permanent colored shadow, and they suggest to look for the boughs that bore them. A queen might be proud to walk where these gallant trees have spread their bright cloaks in the mud. I see wagons roll over them as a shadow or a reflection, and the drivers heed them just as little as they did their shadows before.

Birds'-nests, in the Huckleberry and other shrubs, and in trees, are already being filled with the withered leaves. So many have fallen in the woods, that a squirrel cannot run after a falling nut without being heard. Boys are rak ing them in the streets, if only for the pleasure of dealing with such clean crisp substances. Some sweep the paths scrupulously neat, and then stand to see the next breath strew them with new trophies. The swamp-floor is thickly covered, and the Lycopodium lucidulum looks suddenly greener amid them. In dense woods they half-cover pools that are three or four rods long. The other day I could hardly find a well-known spring, and even suspected that it had dried up, for it was completely concealed by freshly fallen leaves; and when I swept them aside and revealed it, it was like striking the

earth, with Aaron's rod, for a new spring. Wet grounds about the edges of swamps look dry with them. At one swamp, where I was sur veying, thinking to step on a leafy shore from a rail, I got into the water more than a foot deep. When I go to the river the day after the prin cipal fall of leaves, the sixteenth, I find my boat all covered, bottom and seats, with the leaves of the Golden Willow under which it is moored, and I set sail with a cargo of them rustling under my feet. If I empty it, it will be full again to-morrow. I do not regard them as lit ter, to be swept out, but accept them as suit able straw or matting for the bottom of my car riage. When I turn up into the mouth of the Assabet, which is wooded, large fleets of leaves are floating on its surface, as it were getting out to sea, with room to tack; but next the shore, a little farther up, they are thicker than foam, quite concealing the water for a rod in width, under and amid the Alders, Button-Bushes, and Ma ples, still perfectly light and dry, with fibre un-relaxed ; and at a rocky bend where they are met and stopped by the morning wind, they sometimes form a broad and dense crescent quite across the river. When I turn my prow that way, and the wave which it makes strikes them, list what a pleasant rustling from these dry sub stances grating on one another! Often it is

their undulation only which reveals the water beneath them. Also every motion of the wood-turtle on the shore is betrayed by their rustling there. Or even in mid-channel, when the wind rises, I hear them blown with a rustling sound. Higher up they are slowly moving round and round in some great eddy which the river makes, as that at the " Leaning Hemlocks," where the water is deep, and the current is wearing into the bank.

Perchance, in the afternoon of such a day, when the water is perfectly calm and full of re flections, I paddle gently down the main stream, and, turning up the Assabet, reach a quiet cove, where I unexpectedly find myself surrounded by myriads of leaves, like fellow-voyagers, which seem to have the same purpose, or want of pur pose, with myself. See this great fleet of scat tered leaf-boats which we paddle amid, in this smooth river-bay, each one curled up on every side by the sun's skill, each nerve a stiff spruce-knee, — like boats of hide, and of all patterns, Charon's boat probably among the rest, and some with lofty prows and poops, like the stately vessels of the ancients, scarcely moving in the sluggish current, — like the great fleets, the dense Chinese cities of boats, with which you mingle on entering some great mart, some New York or Canton, which we are all steadily pp-

preaching together. How gently each has been deposited on the water ! No violence has been used towards them yet, though, perchance, pal pitating hearts were present at the launching. And painted ducks, too, the splendid wood-duck among the rest, often come to sail and float amid the painted leaves, — barks of a nobler model still!

What wholesome herb-drinks are to be had in the swamps now ! What strong medicinal, but rich, scents from the decaying leaves! The rain falling on the freshly dried herbs and leaves, and filling the pools and ditches into which they have dropped thus clean and rigid, will soon con vert them into tea, — green, black, brown, and yellow teas, of all degrees of strength, enough to set all Nature a gossiping. Whether we drink them or not, as yet, before their strength is drawn, these leaves, dried on great Nature's coppers, are of such various pure and delicate tints as might make the fame of Oriental teas.

How they are mixed up, of all species, Oak and Maple and Chestnut and Birch ! But Na ture is not cluttered with them ; she is a perfect husbandman; she stores them all. Consider what a vast crop is thus annually shed on the earth! This, more than any mere grain or seed, is the great harvest of the year. The trees are now repaying the earth with interest what they

have taken from it. They are discounting. They are about to add a leaf's thickness to the depth of the soil. This is the beautiful way in which Nature gets her muck, while I chaffer with this man and that, who talks to me about sulphur and the cost of carting. We are all the richer for their decay. I am more interested in this crop than in the English grass alone or in the corn. It prepares the virgin mould for future cornfields and forests, on which the earth fat tens. It keeps our homestead in good heart.

For beautiful variety no crop can be com pared with this. Here is not merely the plain yellow of the grains, but nearly all the colors that we know, the brightest blue not excepted: the early blushing Maple, the Poison-Sumach blazing its sins as scarlet, the mulberry Ash, the rich chrome-yellow of the Poplars, the brilliant red Huckleberry, with which the hills' backs are painted, like those of sheep. The frost touches them, and, with the slightest breath of returning day or jarring of earth's axle, see in what show ers they come floating down! The ground is all party-colored with them. But they still live in the soil, whose fertility and bulk they in crease, and in the forests that spring from it. They stoop to rise, to mount higher in coming years, by subtle chemistry, climbing by the sap in the trees, and the sapling's first fruits thus

shed, transmuted at last, may adorn its crown, when, in after-years, it has become the monarch of the forest.

It is pleasant to walk over the beds of these fresh, crisp, and rustling leaves. How beauti fully they go to their graves ! how gently lay themselves down and turn to mould! — painted of a thousand hues, and fit to make the beds of us living. So they troop to their last resting-place, light and frisky. They put on no weeds, but merrily they go scampering over the earth, selecting the spot, choosing a lot, ordering no iron fence, whispering all through the woods about it, — some choosing the spot where the bodies of men are mouldering beneath, and meeting them half-way. How many flutter-ings before they rest quietly in their graves! They that soared so loftily, how contentedly they return to dust again, and are laid low, re signed to lie and decay at the foot of the tree, and afford nourishment to new generations of their kind, as well as to flutter on high! They teach us how to die. One wonders if the time will ever come when men, with their boasted faith in immortality, will lie down as gracefully and as ripe, — with such an Indian-summer serenity will shed their bodies, as they do their hair and nails.

When the leaves fall, the whole earth is a

16

cemetery pleasant to walk in I love to wan der and muse over them in their graves. Here are no lying nor vain epitaphs. What though you own no lot at Mount Auburn ? Your lot is surely cast somewhere in this vast cemetery, which has been consecrated from of old. You need attend no auction to secure a place. There is room enough here. The Loose-strife shall bloom and the Huckleberry-bird sing over your bones. The woodman and hunter shall be your sextons, and the children shall tread upon the borders as much as they will. Let us walk in the cemetery of the leaves, — this is your true Greenwood Cemetery.

THE SUGAR-MAPLE.

BUT think not that the splendor of the year is over; for as one leaf does not make a sum mer, neither does one falling leaf make an au tumn. The smallest Sugar- Maples in our streets make a great show as early as the fifth of October, more than any other trees there. As I look up the Main Street, they appear like painted screens standing before the houses; yet many are green. But now, or generally by the seventeenth of October, when almost all Red Maples, and some White Maples, are bare, the large Sugar-Maples also are in their glory, glow-

ing with yellow and red, and show unexpectedly bright and delicate tints. They are remarkable for the contrast they often afford of deep blush ing red on one half and green on the other. They become at length dense masses of rich yellow with a deep scarlet blush, or more than blush, on the exposed surfaces. They are the brightest trees now in the street.

The large ones on our Common are particu larly beautiful. A delicate, but warmer than golden yellow is now the prevailing color, with scarlet cheeks. Yet, standing on the east side of the Common just before sundown, when the western light is transmitted through them, I see that their yellow even, compared with the pale lemon yellow of an Elm close by, amounts to a scarlet, without noticing the bright scarlet portions. Generally, they are great regular oval masses of yellow and scarlet. All the sunny warmth of the season, the Indian - summer, seems to be absorbed in their leaves. The lowest and inmost leaves next the bole are, as usual, of the most delicate yellow and green, like the complexion of young men brought up in the house. There is an auction on the Com mon to-day, but its red flag is hard to be dis cerned amid this blaze of color.

Little did the fathers of the town anticipate this brilliant success, when they caused to be im<

ported from farther in the country some straight poles with their tops cut off, which they called Sugar-Ma pies; and, as I remember, after they were set out, a neighboring merchant's clerk, by way of jest, planted beans about them. Those which were then jestingly called bean-poles are to-day far the most beautiful objects notice able in our streets. They are worth all and more than they have cost,—though one of the selectmen, while setting them out, took the cold which occasioned his death, — if only because they have filled the open eyes of children with their rich color unstintedly so many Octobers. We will not ask them to yield us sugar in the spring, while they afford us so fair a prospect in the autumn. Wealth in-doors may be the in heritance of few, but it is equally distributed on the Common. All children alike can revel in this golden harvest.

Surely trees should be set in our streets with a view to their October splendor; though I doubt whether this is ever considered by the " Tiee Society." Do you not think it will make some odds to these children that they w T ere brought up under the Maples ? Hundreds of eyes are steadily drinking in this color, and by these teachers even the truants are caught and educated the moment they step abroad. Indeed, neither the truant nor the studious is at present

taught color in the schools. These are instead of the bright colors in apothecaries' shops and city windows. It is a pity that we have no more Red Maples, and some Hickories, in our streets as well. Our paint-box is very imper fectly filled. Instead of, or beside, supplying such paint-boxes as we do, we might supply these natural colors to the young. Where else will they study color under greater advantages? What School of Design can vie with this ? Think how much the eyes of painters of all kinds, and of manufacturers of cloth and paper, and paper-stainers, and countless others, are to be educated by these autumnal colors. The sta tioner's envelopes may be of very various tints, yet, not so various as those of the leaves of a single tree. If you want a different shade or tint of a particular color, you have only to look farther within or without the tree or the wood. These leaves are not many dipped in one dye, as at the dye-house, but they are dyed in light of infinitely various degrees of strength, and left to set and dry there.

Shall the names of so many of our colors continue to be derived from those of obscure foreign localities, as Naples yellow, Prussian blue, raw Sienna, burnt Umber, Gamboge ? — (surely the Tyrian purple must have faded by this time), — or from comparatively trivial arti-cles of commerce, — chocolate, lemon, coffee, cinnamon, claret ? — (shall we compare our Hickory to a lemon, or a lemon to a Hick ory ?) — or from ores and oxides which few ever see ? Shall we so often, when describing to our neighbors the color of something we have seen, refer them, not to some natural object in our neighborhood, but perchance to a bit of earth fetched from the other side of the planet, which possibly they may find at the apothe cary's, but which probably neither they nor we ever saw ? Have we not an earth under our feet, — ay, and a sky over our heads ? Or is the last all ultramarine ? What do we know of sapphire, amethyst, emerald, ruby, amber, and the like, — most of us who take these names in vain ? Leave these precious words to cabinet-keepers, virtuosos, and maids-of-honor, — to the Nabobs, Begums, and Chobdars of Hindostan, or wherever else. I do not see why, since Amer ica and her autumn woods have been discovered, our leaves should not compete with the precious stones in giving names to colors; and, indeed, I believe that in course of time the names of some of our trees and shrubs, as well as flowers, will get into our popular chromatic nomenclature. But of much more importance than a knowl edge of the names and distinctions of color is the joy and exhilaration which these colored

leaves excite. Already these brilliant trees throughout the street, without any more variety, are at least equal to an annual festival and holi day, or a week of such. These are cheap and innocent gala-days, celebrated by one and all without the aid of committees or marshals, such a show as may safely be licensed, not attracting gamblers or rum-sellers, not requiring any special police to keep the peace. And poor indeed must be that New-England village's October which has not the Maple in its streets. This October festival costs no powder, nor ringing of bells, but every tree is a living liberty-pole on which a thousand bright flags are waving.

No wonder that we must have our annual Cattle-Show, and Fall Training, and perhaps Cornwallis, our September Courts, and the like. Nature herself holds her annual fair in October, not only in the streets, but in every hollow and on every hill-side. When lately we looked into that Red-Maple swamp all ablaze, where the trees were clothed in their vestures of most dazzling tints, did it not suggest a thousand gypsies beneath, — a race capable of wild delight, — or even the fabled fawns, satyrs, and wood-nymphs come back to earth ? Or was it only a congregation of wearied wood-choppers, or of proprietors come to inspect their lots, that we thought of ? Or, earlier still, when

we paddled on the river through that fine-grained September air, did there not appear to be some thing new going on under the sparkling surface of the stream, a shaking of props, at least, so that we made haste in order to be up in time ? Did not the rows of yellowing Willows and Button-Bushes on each side seem like rows of booths, under which, perhaps, some fluvia-tile egg-pop equally yellow was effervescing? Did not all these suggest that man's spirits should rise as high as Nature's,— should hang out their flag, and the routine of his life be in terrupted by an analogous expression of joy and hilarity ?

No annual training or muster of soldiery, no celebration with its scarfs and banners, could import into the town a hundredth part of the annual splendor of our October. We have only to set the trees, or let them stand, and Nature will find the colored drapery, — flags of all her nations, some of whose private signals hardly the botanist can read, — while we walk under the triumphal arches of the Elms. Leave it to Nature to appoint the days, whether the same as in neighboring States or not, and let the clergy read her proclamations, if they can un derstand them. Behold what a brilliant drap ery is her Woodbine flag ! What public-spir ited merchant, think you, has contributed this

part of the show ? There is no handsomer shingling and paint than this vine, at present covering a whole side of some houses. I do

O

not believe that the Ivy never sere is compara ble to it. No wonder it has been extensively introduced into London. Let us have a good many Maples and Hickories and Scarlet Oaks, then, I say. Blaze away ! Shall that dirty roll of bunting in the gun-house be all the colors a village can display ? A village is not com plete, unless it have these trees to mark the season in it. They are important, like the town-clock. A village that has them not will not be found to work well. It has a screw loose, an essential part is wanting. Let us have Willows for spring, Elms for summer, Maples and Walnuts and Tupeloes for au tumn, Evergreens for winter, and Oaks for all seasons. What is a gallery in a house to a gallery in the streets, which every market-man rides through, whether he will or not? Of course, there is not a picture-gallery in the country which would be worth so much to us as is the western view at sunset under the Elms of our main street. They are the frame to a picture which is daily painted behind them. An avenue of Elms as large as our largest and three miles long would seem to lead to some admirable place, though only C were at the end of it.

A village needs these innocent stimulants v/i bright and cheering prospects to keep off melan choly and superstition. Show me two villages, one embowered in trees and blazing with all the glories of October, the other a merely trivial and treeless waste, or with only a single tree or two for suicides, and I shall be sure that in the lat ter will be found the most starved and bigoted religionists and the most desperate drinker . Every washtub and milkcan and gravestone will be exposed. The inhabitants will disap pear abruptly behind their barns and houses, like desert Arabs amid their rocks, and I shall look to see spears in their hands. They will be ready to accept the most barren and forlorn doctrine, — as that the world is speedily com ing to an end, or has already got to it, or that they themselves are turned wrong side outward. They will perchance crack their dry joints at one another and call it a spiritual communi cation.

But to confine ourselves to the Maples. What if we were to take half as much pains in protecting them as we do in setting them out, — not stupidly tie our horses to our dahlia-stems ?

What meant the fathers by establishing this perfectly living institution before the church, — this institution which needs no repairing nor

repainting, which is continually enlarged and repaired by its growth ? Surely they

" Wrought in a sad sincerity ; Themselves from God they could not free: They planted better than they knew ; — The conscious trees to beauty grew."

Verily these Maples are cheap preachers, per-inanently settled, which preach their half-cen tury, and century, ay, and century-and-a-half sermons, with constantly increasing unction and influence, ministering to many generations of men; and the least we can do is to supply them with suitable colleagues as they grow infirm.

THE SCARLET OAK.

BELONGING to a genus which is remarkable for the beautiful form of its leaves, I suspect that some Scarlet-Oak leaves surpass those of all other Oaks in the rich and wild beauty of their outlines. I judge from an acquaintance with twelve species, and from drawings which I have seen of many others.

Stand under this tree and see how finely its leaves are cut against the sky, — as it were, only a few sharp points extending from a mid rib. They look like double, treble, or quadruple crosses They are far more ethereal than the

less deeply scolloped Oak-leaves. They have so little leafy terra firma that they appear melt ing away in the light, and scarcely obstruct our view. The leaves of very young plants are, like those of full-grown Oaks of other species, more entire, simple, and lumpish in their outlines; but these, raised high on old trees, have solved the leafy problem. Lifted higher and higher, and sublimated more and more, putting off some earthiness and cultivating more intimacy with the light each year, they have at length the least possible amount of earthy matter, and the greatest spread and grasp of skyey influences. There they dance, arm in arm with the light, — tripping it on fantastic points, fit partners in those aerial halls. So intimately mingled are they with it, that, what with their slenderness and their glossy surfaces, you can hardly tell at last what in the dance is leaf and what is light. And when no zephyr stirs, they are at most but a rich tracery to the forest-windows.

I am again struck with their beauty, when, a month later, they thickly strew the ground in the woods, piled one upon another under my feet. They are then brown above, but purple beneath. With their narrow lobes and their bold deep scollops reaching almost to the middle, they suggest that the material must be cheap, or else there has been a lavish expense

in their creation, as if so much had been cut out. Or else they seem to us the remnants of the stuff out of which leaves have been cut with a die. Indeed, when they lie thus one upon another, they remind me of a pile of scrap-tin.

Or bring one home, and study it closely at your leisure, by the fireside. It is a type, not from any Oxford font, not in the Basque nor the arrow-headed character, not found on the Rosetta Stone, but destined to be copied in sculpture one day, if they ever get to whit tling stone here. What a wild and pleasing outline, a combination of graceful curves and angles! The eye rests with equal delight on what is not leaf and on what is leaf, — on the broad, free, open sinuses, and on the long, sharp, bristle-pointed lobes. A simple oval out line would include it all, if you connected the points of the leaf; but how much richer is it than that, with its half-dozen deep scollops, in which the eye and thought of the beholder are embayed! If I were a drawing-master, I would set my pupils to copying these leaves, that they might learn to draw firmly and gracefully.

Regarded as water, it is like a pond with half a dozen broad rounded promontories extending nearly to its middle, half from each side, while its watery bays extend far inland, like sharp

friths, at each of whose heads several fine streams empty in, — almost a leafy archipel ago.

But it oftener suggests land, and, as Diony-sius and Pliny compared the form of the Morea to that of the leaf of the Oriental Plane-tree, so this leaf reminds me of some fair wild island in the ocean, whose extensive coast, alternate rounded bays with smooth strands, and sharp-pointed rocky capes, mark it as fitted for the habitation of man, and destined to become a centre of civilization at last. To the sailor's eye, it is a much-indented shore. Is it not, in fact, a shore to the aerial ocean, on which the windy surf beats ? At sight of this leaf we are all mariners, — if not vikings, buccaneers, and filibusters. Both our love of repose and our spirit of adventure are addressed. In our most casual glance, perchance, we think, that, if we succeed in doubling those sharp capes, we shall find deep, smooth, and secure havens in the ample bays. How different from the White-Oak leaf, with its rounded headlands, on which no lighthouse need be placed! That is an Eng land, with its long civil history, that may be read. This is some still unsettled New-found Island or Celebes. Shall we go and be rajahs there ?

By the twenty-sixth of October the large

Scarlet Oaks are in their prime, when other Oaks are usually withered. They have been kindling their fires for a week past, and now generally burst into a blaze. This alone of our indigenous deciduous trees (excepting the Dogwood, of which I do not know half a dozen, and they are but large bushes) is now in its glory. The two Aspens and the Sugar-Maple come nearest to it in date, but they have lost the greater part of their leaves. Of evergreens, only the Pitch-Pine is still com monly bright.

But it requires a particular alertness, if not devotion to these phenomena, to appreciate the wide-spread, but late and unexpected glory of the Scarlet Oaks. I do not speak here of the small trees and shrubs, which are commonly observed, and which are now withered, but of the large trees. Most go in and shut their doors, thinking that bleak and colorless November has already corne, when some of the most brilliant and memorable colors are not yet lit.

This very perfect and vigorous one, about forty feet high, standing in an open pasture, which was quite glossy green on the twelfth, is now, the twenty-sixth, completely changed to bright dark scarlet, — every leaf, between you and the sun, as if it had been dipped

into a scarlet dye. The whole tree is much like a heart in form, as well as color. Was not this worth waiting for? Little did you think, ten days ago, that that cold green tree would assume such color as this. Its leaves are still firmly attached, while those of other trees are falling around it. It seems to say, — "I am the last to blush, but I blush deeper than any of ye. I bring up the rear in my red coat. We Scarlet ones, alone of Oaks, have not given up the fight."

The sap is now, and even far into Novem ber, frequently flowing fast in these trees, as in Maples in the spring ; and apparently their bright tints, now that most other Oaks are withered, are connected with this phenomenon. They are full of life. It has a pleasantly astrin gent, acorn-like taste, this strong Oak-wine, as I find on tapping them with my knife.

Looking across this woodland valley, a quar ter of a mile wide, how rich those Scarlet Oaks, embosomed in Pines, their bright red branches intimately intermingled with them ! They have their full effect there. The Pine-boughs are the green calyx to their red petals. Or, as we go along a road in the woods, the sun striking end wise through it, and lighting up the red tents of the Oaks, which on each side are mingled with the liquid green of the Pines, makes a

very gorgeous scene. Indeed, without the ever greens for contrast, the autumnal tints would lose much of their effect.

The Scarlet Oak asks a clear sky and the brightness of late October days. These bring out its colors. If the sun goes into a cloud, they become comparatively indistinct. As I sit on a cliff in the southwest part of our town, the sun is now getting low, and the woods in Lin coln, south and east of me, are lit up by its more level rays; and in the Scarlet Oaks, scattered so equally over the forest, there is brought out a more brilliant redness than I had believed was in them. Every tree of this species which is visible in those directions, even to the horizon, now stands out distinctly red. Some great ones lift their red backs high above the woods, in the next town, like huge roses with a myriad of fine petals ; and some more slender ones, in a small grove of White Pines on Pine Hill in the east, on the very verge of the horizon, alternating with the Pines on the edge of the grove, and shoul dering them with their red coats, look like sol diers in red amid hunters in green. This time it is Lincoln green, too. Till the sun got low, I did not believe that there were so many red coats in the forest army. Theirs is an intense burning red, which would lose some of its strength, me-thinks, with every step you might take toward

17

them; for the shade that lurks amid their foli age does not report itself at this distance, and they are unanimously red. The focus of their reflected color is in the atmosphere far on this side. Every such tree becomes a nucleus of red, as it were, where, with the declining sun, that color grows and glows. It is partly bor rowed fire, gathering strength from the sun on its way to your eye. It has only some compar atively dull red leaves for a rallying-point, or kindling-stuff, to start it, and it becomes an intense scarlet or red mist, or fire, which finds fuel for itself in the very atmosphere. So viva cious is redness. The very rails reflect a rosy light at this hour and season. You see a redder tree than exists.

If you wish to count the Scarlet Oaks, do it now. In a clear day stand thus on a hill-top in the woods, when the sun is an hour high, and every one within range of your vision, excepting in the west, will be revealed. You might live to the age of Methuselah and never find a tithe of them, otherwise. Yet sometimes even in a dark day I have thought them as bright as I ever saw them. Looking westward, their colors are lost in a blaze of light; but in other directions the whole forest is a flower-garden, in which these late roses burn, alternating with green, while the so-called " gardeners," walking

here and there, perchance, beneath, with spade and water-pot, see only a few little asters amid withered leaves.

These are my China-asters, my late garden-flowers. It costs me nothing for a gardener. The falling leaves, all over the forest, are pro tecting the roots of my plants. Only look at what is to be seen, and you will have garden enough, without deepening the soil in your yard. We have only to elevate our view a little, to see the whole forest as a garden. The blossoming of the Scarlet Oak, — the forest-flower, sur passing all in splendor, (at least since the Ma ple) ! I do not know but they interest me more than the Maples, they are so widely and equally dispersed throughout the forest; they are so hardy, a nobler tree on the whole ; — our chief November flower, abiding the approach of winter with us, imparting warmth to early November prospects. It is remarkable that the latest bright color that is general should be this deep, dark scarlet and red, the intensest of colors. The ripest fruit of the year; like the cheek of a hard, glossy, red apple, from the cold Isle of Orleans, which will not be mellow for eating till next spring! When I rise to a hill top, a thousand of these great Oak roses, dis tributed on every side, as far as the horizon ! I admire them four or five miles off! This my

unfailing prospect for a fortnight past! This late forest-flower surpasses all that spring or summer could do. Their colors were but rare and dainty specks comparatively, (created for the near-sighted, who walk amid the humblest herbs and underwoods,) and made no impres sion on a distant eye. Now it is an extended forest or a mountain-side, through or along which we journey from day to day, that bursts into bloom. Comparatively, our gardening is on a petty scale, — the gardener still nursing a few asters amid dead weeds, ignorant of the gigantic asters and roses, which, as it were, overshadow him, and ask for none of his care. It is like a little red paint ground on a saucer, and held up against the sunset sky. Why not take more elevated and broader views, walk in the great garden, not skulk in a little " de bauched " nook of it ? consider the beauty of the forest, and not merely of a few impounded herbs ?

Let your walks now be a little more adven turous ; ascend the hills. If, about the last of October, you ascend any hill in the outskirts of our town, and probably of yours, and look

over the forest, you may see well, what I

have endeavored to describe. All this you surely will see, and much more, if you are pre pared to see it, — if you look for it. Otherwise,

regular and universal as this phenomenon is, whether you stand on the hill-top or in the hol low, you will think for threescore years and ten that all the wood is, at this season, sere and brown. Objects are concealed from our view, not so much because they are out of the course of our visual ray as because we do not bring our minds and eyes to bear on them ; for there is no power to see in the eye itself, any more than in any other jelly. We do not realize how far and widely, or how near and narrowly, we are to look. The greater part of the phenomena of Nature are for this reason concealed from us all our lives. The gardener sees only the gar dener's garden. Here, too, as in political econ omy, the supply answers to the demand. Nature does not cast pearls before swine. There is just as much beauty visible to us in the landscape as we are prepared to appreciate, — not a grain more. The actual objects which one man will see from a particular hiil-top are just as different from those which another will see as the behold ers are different. The Scarlet Oak must, in a sense, be in your eye when you go forth. We cannot see anything until we are possessed with the idea of it, take it into our heads, — and then we can hardly see anything else. In my botan ical rambles, I find, that, first, the idea, or image, of a plant occupies my thoughts, though it may

seem very foreign to this locality, — no nearer than Hudson's Bay, — and for some weeks or months I go thinking of it, and expecting it, unconsciously, and at length I surely see it, This is the history of my finding a score or more of rare plants, which I could name. A man sees only what concerns him. A botanist absorbed in the study of grasses does not distin guish the grandest Pasture Oaks. He, as it were, tramples down Oaks unwittingly in his walk, or at most sees only their shadows. I have found that it required a different inten tion of the eye, in the same locality, to see different plants, even when they were closely allied, as Juncaceos and Graminece : when I was looking for the former, I did not see the latter in the midst of them. How much more, then, it requires different intentions of the eye and of the mind to attend to different departments of knowledge! How differently the poet and the naturalist look at objects !

Take a New-England selectman, and set him on the highest of our hills, and tell him to look, — sharpening his sight to the utmost, and put ting on the glasses that suit him best, (ay, using a spy-glass, if he likes,) — and make a full report. What, probably, will he spy ? — what will he select to look at ? Of course, he will see a Brocken spectre of himself. He will see sev-eral meeting-houses, at least, and, perhaps, that somebody ought to be assessed higher than he is, since he has so handsome a wood-lot. Now take Julius Caesar, or Immanuel Swedenborg, or a Fegee-Islander, and set him up there. Or suppose all together, and let them com pare notes afterward. Will it appear that they have enjoyed the same prospect ? What they will see will be as different as Rome was from Heaven or Hell, or the last from the Fegee Islands. For aught we know, as strange a man as any of these is always at our elbow.

Why, it takes a sharp-shooter to bring down even such trivial game as snipes and wood cocks ; he must take very particular aim, and know what he is aiming at. He would stand a very small chance, if he fired at random into the sky, being told that snipes were flying there. And so is it with him that shoots at beauty ; though he wait till the sky falls, he will not bag any, if he does not already know its seasons and haunts, and the color of its wing, — if he has not dreamed of it, so that he can anticipate it; then, indeed, he flushes it at every step, shoots double and on the wing, with both bar rels, even in cornfields. The sportsman trains himself, dresses and watches unweariedly, and loads and primes for his particular game. He

prays for it, and offers sacrifices, and so he gets it. After due and long preparation, schooling his eye and hand, dreaming awake and asleep, with gun and paddle and boat he goes out after meadow-hens, which most of his townsmen never saw nor dreamed of, and paddles for miles against a head-wind, and wades in water up to his knees, being out all day without his dinner, and therefore he gets them. He had them half-way into his bag when he started, and has only to shove them down. The true sportsman can shoot you almost any of his game from his windows : what else has he windows or eyes for? It comes and perches at last on the barrel of his gun; but the rest of the world never see it with the feathers on. The geese fly exactly under his zenith, and honk when they get there, and he will keep himself supplied by firing up his chimney ; twenty musquash have the refusal of each one of his traps before it is empty. If he lives, and his game-spirit increases, heaven and earth shall fail him sooner than game; and when he dies, he will go to more extensive, and, perchance, happier hunting-grounds. The fisherman, too, dreams of fish, sees a bobbing cork in his dreams, till he can almost catch them in his sink-spout. I knew a girl who, being sent to pick huckleberries, picked wild gooseberries by the quart, where no one else knew that there were any, because she was accustomed to pick them up country where she came from. The astronomer knows where to go star-gathering, and sees one clearly in his mind before any have seen it with a glass. The hen scratches and finds her food right under where she stands ; but such is not the way with the hawk.

These bright leaves which I have mentioned are not the exception, but the rule; for I believe that all leaves, even grasses and mosses, acquire brighter colors just before their fall. When you come to observe faithfully the changes of each humblest plant, you find that each has, sooner or later, its peculiar autumnal tint; and if you undertake to make a complete list of the bright tints, it will be nearly as long as a catalogue of the plants in your vicinity.

WILD APPLES.

(1862.) THE HISTORY OF THE APPLE-TREE.

IT is remarkable how closely the history of the Apple-tree is connected with that of man. The geologist tells us that the order of the Rosacece, which includes the Apple, also the true Grasses, and the Labialae, or Mints, were introduced only a short time previous to the appearance of man on the globe.

It appears that apples made a part of the food of that unknown primitive people whose traces have lately been found at the bottom of the Swiss lakes, supposed to be older than the foundation of Home, so old that they had no metallic implements. An entire black and shrivelled Crab-Apple has been recovered from their stores.

Tacitus says of the ancient Germans, that they satisfied their hunger with wild apples (agrestia poma) among other things.

Niebuhr observes that " the words for a house,

a field, a plough, ploughing, wine, oil, milk, sheep, apples, and others relating to agricul ture and the gentler way of life, agree in Latin and Greek, while the Latin words for all objects pertaining to war or the chase are utterly alien from the Greek." Thus the ap ple-tree may be considered a symbol of peace no less than the olive.

The apple was early so important, and gener ally distributed, that its name traced to its root in many languages signifies fruit in general. M^Aov, in Greek, means an apple, also the fruit of other trees, also a sheep and any cattle, and finally riches in general.

The apple-tree has been celebrated by the Hebrews, Greeks, Romans, and Scandinavians. Some have thought that the first human pair were tempted by its fruit. Goddesses are fabled to have contended for it, dragons were set to watch it, and heroes were employed to pluck it.

The tree is mentioned in at least three places in the Old Testament, and its fruit in two or three more. Solomon sings, — " As the apple-tree among the trees of the wood, so is my beloved among the sons." And again, — " Stay me with flagons, comfort me with apples." The noblest part of man's noblest feature is named from this fruit, " the apple of the eye."

The apple-tree is also mentioned by Homer

and Herodotus. Ulysses saw in the glorious garden of Alcinoiis " pears and pomegranates, and apple-trees bearing beautiful fruit " (K al /M/Xcai dyXao/capTrot). And according to Homer, apples were among the fruits which Tantalus could not pluck, the wind ever blowing their boughs away from him. Theophrastus knew and described the apple-tree as a botanist.

According to the Prose Edda, " Iduna keeps in a box the apples which the gods, when they feel old age approaching, have only to taste of to become young again. It is in this manner that they will be kept in renovated youth until Ragnarok" (or the destruction of the gods).

I learn from Loudon that " the ancient Welsh bards were rewarded for excelling in song by the token of the apple-spray;" and "in the High lands of Scotland the apple-tree is the badge of the clan Lamont."

The apple-tree (Pyrus mains) belongs chiefly to the northern temperate zone. Loudon says, that " it grows spontaneously in every part of Europe except the frigid zone, and throughout Western Asia, China, and Japan." We have also two or three varieties of the apple in digenous in North America. The cultivated apple-tree was first introduced into this coun try by the earliest settlers, and is thought to do as well or better here than anywhere else.

Probably some of the varieties which are now cultivated were first introduced into Britain by the Romans.

Pliny, adopting the distinction of Theophras-tus, says,— " Of trees there are some which are altogether wild (sylvestres), some more civilized (urbaniores)." Theophrastus includes the apple among the last; and, indeed, it is in this sense the most civilized of all trees. It is as harmless as a dove, as beautiful as a rose, and as valu able as flocks and herds. It has been longer cultivated than any other, and so is more hu manized ; and who knows but, like the dog, it will at length be no longer traceable to its wild original ? It migrates with man, like the dog and horse and cow : first, perchance, from Greece to Italy, thence to England, thence to America; and our Western emigrant is still marching steadily toward the setting sun with the seeds of the apple in his pocket, or perhaps a few young trees strapped to his load. At least a million apple-trees are thus set farther westward this year than any cultivated ones grew last year. Consider how the Blossom-Week, like the Sabbath, is thus annually spreading over the prairies; for when man migrates, he carries with him not only his birds, quadrupeds, insects, vegetables, and his very sward, but his orchard also.

The leaves and tender twigs are an agree able food to many domestic animals, as the cow, horse, sheep, and goat ; and the fruit is sought after by the first, as well as by the hog. Thus there appears to have existed a natural alliance between these animals and this tree from the first. " The fruit of the Crab in the forests of France" is said to be " a great resource for the wild-boar."

Not only the Indian, but many indigenous insects, birds, and quadrupeds, welcomed the apple-tree to these shores. The tent-caterpil lar saddled her eggs on the very first twig that was formed, and it has since shared her affections with the wild cherry ; and the can ker-worm also in a measure abandoned the elm to feed on it. As it grew apace, the blue bird, robin, cherry-bird, king-bird, and many more, came with haste and built their nests and warbled in its boughs, and so became orchard-birds, and multiplied more than ever. It was an era in the history of their race. The downy woodpecker found such a savory morsel under its bark, that he perforated it in a ring quite round the tree, before he left it, — a thing which he had never done before, to my knowledge. It did not take the partridge long to find out how sweet its buds were, and every winter eve she flew, and still flies, from the

wood, to pluck them, much to the farmer's sor row. The rabbit, too, was not slow to learn the taste of its twigs and bark ; and when the fruit was ripe, the squirrel half-rolled, half-carried it to his hole; and even the musquash crept up the bank from the brook at evening, and greed ily devoured it, until he had worn a path in the grass there; and when it was frozen and thaw ed, the crow and the jay were glad to taste it occasionally. The owl crept into the first ap ple-tree that became hollow, and fairly hooted with delight, finding it just the place for him; so, settling down into it, he has remained there ever since.

My theme being the Wild Apple, I will merely glance at some of the seasons in the annual growth of the cultivated apple, and pass on to my special province.

The flowers of the apple are perhaps the most beautiful of any tree's, so copious and so delicious to both sight and scent. The walker is fre quently tempted to turn and linger near some more than usually handsome one, whose blos soms are two thirds expanded. How superior it is in these respects to the pear, whose blossoms are neither colored nor fragrant!

By the middle of July, green apples are so large as to remind us of coddling, and of the au tumn. The sward is commonly strewed with

little ones which fall still-born, as it were, — Na ture thus thinning them for us. The Roman writer Palladius said, — " If apples are inclined to fall before their time, a stone placed in a split root will retain them." Some such notion, still surviving, may account for some of the stones which we see placed to be overgrown in the forks of trees. They have a saying in Suffolk, England, —

" At Michaelmas time, or a little before, Half an apple goes to the core."

Early apples begin to be ripe about the first of August; but I think that none of them are so good to eat as some to smell. One is worth more to scent your handkerchief with than any perfume which they sell in the shops. The fra grance of some fruits is not to be forgotten, along with that of flowers. Some gnarly apple which I pick up in the road reminds me by its fragrance of all the wealth of Pomona, — car rying me forward to those days when they will be collected in golden and ruddy heaps in the orchards and about the cider-mills.

A week or two later, as you are going by or chards or gardens, especially in the evenings, you pass through a little region possessed by the fragrance of ripe apples, and thus enjoy them without price, and without robbing anybody.

There is thus about all natural products a cer tain volatile and ethereal quality which represents their highest value, and which cannot be vulgar ized, or bought and sold. No mortal has ever en-

t o

joyed the perfect flavor of any fruit, and only the godlike among men begin to taste its ambrosial qualities. For nectar and ambrosia are only those fine flavors of every earthly fruit which our coarse palates fail to perceive, —just as we oc cupy the heaven of the gods without knowing it. When I see a particularly mean man carrying a load of fair and fragrant early apples to market, I seem to see a contest going on between him and his horse, on the one side, and the apples on the other, and, to my mind, the apples always gain it. Pliny says that apples are the heaviest of all things, and that the oxen begin to sweat at the mere sight of a load of them. Our driver begins to lose his load the moment he tries to transport them to where they do not belong, that is, to any but the most beautiful. Though he gets out from time to time, and feels of them, and thinks they are all there, I see the stream of their evanescent and celestial qualities going to heaven from his cart, while the pulp and skin and core only are going to market. They are not apples, but pomace. Are not these still Iduna's apples, the taste of which keeps the gods forever young? and think you that they will let 18

Loki or Thjassi carry them off to Jotunheim, while they grow wrinkled and gray ? No, for Ragnarok, or the destruction of the gods, is not yet.

There is another thinning of the fruit, com monly n^ar the end of August or in September, when tb« ground is strewn with windfalls; and this happens especially when high winds occur after rain. In some orchards you may see fully three quarters of the whole crop on the ground, lying m a circular form beneath the trees, yet hard «vnd green, — or, if it is a hill-side, rolled far down the hill. However, it is an ill wind that blown nobody any good. All the country over, people are busy picking up the windfalls, and this will make them cheap for early apple-pies.

In October, the leaves falling, the apples are more distinct on the trees. I saw one year in a neighboring town some trees fuller of fruit than I remember to have ever seen before, small yel low apples hanging over the road. The branches were gracefully drooping with their weight, like a bai?>erry-bush, so that the whole tree acquired a new character. Even the topmost branches, instead of standing erect, spread and drooped in all directions ; and there were so many poles sup porting the lower ones, that they looked like pic tures of banian-trees. As an old English manu script says, " The mo appelen the tree bereth, the more sche boweth to the folk."

Surely the apple is the noblest of fruits. Let the most beautiful or the swiftest have it. That should be the " going " price of apples.

Between the fifth and twentieth of October I see the barrels lie under the trees. And perhaps I talk with one who is selecting some choice bar rels to fulfil an order. He turns a specked one over many times before he leaves it out. If I were to tell what is passing in my mind, I should say that every one was specked which he had handled ; for he rubs off all the bloom, and those fugacious ethereal qualities leave it. Cool eve-ings prompt the farmers to make haste, and at length I see only the ladders here and there left leaning against the trees.

It would be well, if we accepted these gifts with more joy and gratitude, and did not think it enough simply to put a fresh load of compost about the tree. Some old English customs are suggestive at least. I find them described chiefly in Brand's " Popular Antiquities." It appears that " on Christmas eve the farmers and their men in Devonshire take a large bowl of cider, with a toast in it, and carrying it in state to the orchard, they salute the apple-trees with much ceremony, in order to make them bear well the next season." This salutation consists in " throwing some of the cider about the roots of the tree, placing bits of the toast on the

branches," and then, " encircling one of the best bearing trees in the orchard, they drink the fol lowing toast three several times : —

* Here's to thee, old apple-tree,

Whence thou mayst bud, and whence thou mayst blow, And whence thou mayst bear apples enow !

Hats-full! caps-full!

Bushel, bushel, sacks-full!

And my pockets full, too ! Hurra !'"

Also what was called " apple-howling " used to be practised in various counties of England on New-Year's eve. A troop of boys visited the different orchards, and, encircling the apple-trees, repeated the following words : —

" Stand fast, root! bear well, top ! Pray God send us a good howling crop : Every twig, apples big ; Every bow, apples enow ! "

" They then shout in chorus, one of the boys ac companying them on a cow's horn. During this ceremony they rap the trees with their sticks." This is called " wassailing" the trees, and is thought by some to be " a relic of the heathen sacrifice to Pomona." Herrick sings, —

" Wassaile the trees that they may beare You many a plum and many a peare ; For more or less fruits they will bring As you so give them wassailing/'

Our poets have as yet a better right to sing of cider than of wine ; but it behooves them to sing better than English Phillips did, else they will do no credit to their Muse.

THE WILD APPLE.

So much for the more civilized apple-trees (urbanioresj as Pliny calls them). I love bet ter to go through the old orchards of ungrafted apple-trees, at whatever season of the year,— so irregularly planted : sometimes two trees standing close together; and the rows so de vious that you would think that they not only had grown while the owner was sleeping, but had been set out by him in a somnambulic state. The rows of grafted fruit will never tempt me to wander amid them like these. But I now, alas, speak rather from memory than from any recent experience, such ravages have been made!

Some soils, like a rocky tract called the Easterbrooks Country in my neighborhood, are so suited to the apple, that it will grow faster in them without any care, or if only the ground is broken up once a year, than it will in many places with any amount of care. The owners of this tract allow that the soil is excellent for fruit, but they say that it is so rocky that they

have not patience to plough it, and that, to gether with the distance, is the reason why it is not cultivated. There are, or were recently, ex tensive orchards there standing without order. Nay, they spring up wild and bear well there in the midst of pines, birches, maples, and oaks. I am often surprised to see rising amid these trees the rounded tops of apple-trees glowing with red or yellow fruit, in harmony with the autumnal tints of the forest.

Going up the side of a cliff about the first of November, I saw a vigorous young apple-tree, which, planted by birds or cows, had shot up amid the rocks and open woods there, and had now much fruit on it, uninjured by the frosts, when all cultivated apples were gathered. It was a rank wild growth, with many green leaves on it still, and made an impression of thorniness. The fruit was hard and green, but looked as if it would be palatable in the winter. Some was dangling on the twigs, but more half-buried in the wet leaves under the tree, or rolled far down the hill amid the rocks. The owner knows nothing of it. The day was not observed when it first blossomed, nor when it first bore fruit, unless by the chickadee. There was no dancing on the green beneath it in its honor, smd now there is no hand to pluck its fruit, — which is only gnawed by squirrels, as I per-

ceive. It has done double duty, — not only borne this crop, but each twig has grown a foot into the air. And this is such fruit! bigger than many berries, we must admit, and carried home will be sound and palatable next spring. What care I for Iduna's apples so long as I can get these ?

When I go by this shrub thus late and hardy, and see its dangling fruit, I respect the tree, and I am grateful for Nature's bounty, even though I cannot eat it. Here on this rugged and woody hill-side has grown an apple-tree, not planted by man, no relic of a former orchard, but a natural growth, like the pines and oaks. Most fruits which we prize and use depend entirely on our care. Corn and grain, potatoes, peaches, melons, etc., depend altogether on our planting; but the apple emulates man's independence and enter prise. It is not simply carried, as I have said, but, like him, to some extent, it has migrated to this New World, and is even, here and there, making its way amid the aboriginal trees; just as the ox and dog and horse sometimes run wild and maintain themselves.

Even the sourest and crabbedest apple, grow ing in the most unfavorable position, suggests such thoughts as these, it is so noble a fruit.

THE CRAB.

Nevertheless, our wild apple is wild only like myself, perchance, who belong not to the abo riginal race here, but have strayed into the woods from the cultivated stock. Wilder still, as I have said, there grows elsewhere in this country a native and aboriginal Crab-Apple, Malus coronaria, " whose nature has not yet been modified by cultivation." It is found from Western New-York to Minnesota, and southward. Michaux says that its ordinary height "is fifteen or eighteen feet, but it is sometimes found twenty-five or thirty feet high," and that the large ones " exactly resem ble the common apple-tree." " The flowers are white mingled with rose - color, and are col lected in corymbs." They are remarkable for their delicious odor. The fruit, according to him, is about an inch and a half in diameter, and is intensely acid. Yet they make fine sweetmeats, and also cider of them. He con cludes, that " if, on being cultivated, it does not yield new and palatable varieties, it will at least be celebrated for the beauty of its flowers, and for the sweetness of its perfume."

I never saw the Crab-Apple till May, 1861. I had heard of it through Michaux, but more modern botanists, so far as I know, have not

treated it as of any peculiar importance. Thus it was a half-fabulous tree to me. I contem plated a pilgrimage to the " Glades," a por tion of Pennsylvania where it was said to grow to perfection. I thought of sending to a nursery for it, but doubted if they had it, or would distinguish it from European varieties. At last I had occasion to go to Minnesota, and on entering Michigan I began to notice from the cars a tree with handsome rose-col ored flowers. At first I thought it some va riety of thorn; but it was not long before the truth flashed on me, that this was my long-sought Crab-Apple. It was the prevailing flow ering shrub or tree to be seen from the cars at that season of the year, — about the middle of May. But the cars never stopped before one, and so I was launched on the bosom of the Mississippi without having touched one, ex periencing the fate of Tantalus. On arriving at St. Anthony's Falls, I was sorry to be told that I was too far north for the Crab-Apple. Nevertheless I succeeded in finding it about eight miles west of the Falls; touched it and smelled it, and secured a lingering corymb of flowers for my herbarium. This must have been near its northern limit.

HOW THE WILD APPLE GROWS.

But though these are indigenous, like the Indians, I doubt whether they are any hardier than those backwoodsmen among the apple-trees, which, though descended from cultivated stocks, plant themselves in distant fields and forests, where the soil is favorable to them. I know of no trees which have more difficulties to contend with, and which more sturdily resist their foes. These are the ones whose story we have to tell. It oftentimes reads thus : —

Near the beginning of May, we notice little thickets of apple-trees just springing up in the pastures where cattle have been, — as the rocky ones of our Easterbrooks Country, or the top of Nobscot Hill, in Sudbury. One or two of these perhaps survive the drought and other ac cidents, — their very birthplace defending them against the encroaching grass and some other dangers, at first.

In two years' time 't had thus Reached the level of the rocks,
Admired the stretching world, Nor feared the wandering flocks.
But at this tender age
Its sufferings began : There came a browsing ox
And cut it down a span.

This time, perhaps, the ox does not notice it amid the grass; but the next year, when it has grown more stout, he recognizes it for a fellow-emigrant from the old country, the flavor of whose leaves and twigs he well knows; and though at first he pauses to welcome it, and express his surprise, and gets for answer, " The same cause that brought you here brought me," he nevertheless browses it again, reflecting, it may be, that he has some title to it.

Thus cut down annually, it does not despair; but, putting forth two short twigs for every one cut off, it spreads out low along the ground in the hollows or between the rocks, growing more stout and scrubby, until it forms, not a tree as yet, but a little pyramidal, stiff, twiggy mass, almost as solid and impenetrable as a rock. Some of the densest and most impenetrable clumps of bushes that I have ever seen, as well on account of the closeness and stub bornness of their branches as of their thorns, have been these wild-apple scrubs. They are more like the scrubby fir and black spruce on which you stand, and sometimes walk, on the tops of mountains, where cold is the demon they contend with, than anything else. No wonder they are prompted to grow thorns at last, to defend themselves against such foes. In their thorniness, however, there is no malice, only some malic acid.

The rocky pastures of the tract I have referred to, — for they maintain their ground best in a rocky field, — are thickly sprinkled with these little tufts, reminding you often of some rigid gray mosses or lichens, and you see thousands of little trees just springing up between them, with the seed still attached to them.

Being regularly clipped all around each year by the cows, as a hedge with shears, they are often of a perfect conical or pyramidal form, from one to four feet high, and more or less sharp, as if trimmed by the gardener's art. In the pastures on Nobscot Hill and its spurs, they make fine dark shadows when the sun is low. They are also an excellent covert from hawks for many small birds that roost and build in them. Whole flocks perch in them at night, and I have seen three robins' nests in one which was six feet in diameter.

No doubt many of these are already old trees, if you reckon from the day they were planted, but infants still when you consider their devel opment and the long life before them. I counted the annual rings of some which were just one foot high, and as wide as high, and found that they were about twelve years old, but quite sound a«d thrifty! They were so low that they were unnoticed by the walker, while many of their contemporaries from the nurseries were already bearing considerable crops. But what you gain in time is perhaps in this case, too, lost in power, — that is, in the vigor of the tree. This is their pyramidal state.

The cows continue to browse them thus for twenty years or more, keeping them down and compelling them to spread, until at last they are so broad that they become their own fence, when some interior shoot, which their foes cannot reach, darts upward with joy : for it has not for gotten its high calling, and bears its own pecul iar fruit in triumph.

Such are the tactics by which it finally defeats its bovine foes. Now, if you have watched the progress of a particular shrub, you will see that it is no longer a simple pyramid or cone, but that out of its apex there rises a sprig or two, growing more lustily perchance than an orchard-tree, since the plant now devotes the whole of its repressed energy to these upright parts. In a short time these become a small tree, an inverted pyramid resting on the apex of the other, so that the whole has now the form of a vast hour-glass. The spreading bottom, having served its pur pose, finally disappears, and the generous tree permits the now harmless cows to come in and stand in its shade, and rub against and redden its trunk, which has grown in spite of them, and even to taste a part of its fruit, and so disperse the seed.

Thus the cows create their own shade and food; and the tree, its hour-glass being inverted, lives a second life, as it were.

It is an important question with some nowa days, whether you should trim young apple-trees as high as your nose or as high as your eyes. The ox trims them up as high as he can reach, and that is about the right height, I think.

In spite of wandering kine, and other adverse circumstances, that despised shrub, valued only by small birds as a covert and shelter from hawks, has its blossom-week at last, and in course of time its harvest, sincere, though small.

By the end of some October, when its leaves have fallen, I frequently see such a central sprig, whose progress I have watched, when I thought it had forgotten its destiny, as I had, bearing its first crop of small green or yellow or rosy fruit, which the cows cannot get at over the bushy and thorny hedge which surrounds it, and I make haste to taste the new and undescribed variety. We have all heard of the numerous varieties of fruit invented by Van Mons and Knight. This is the system of Van Cow, and she has invented far more and more memorable varieties than both of them.

Through what hardships it may attain to bear a sweet fruit! Though somewhat small, it may prove equal, if not superior, in flavor to that

which has grown in a garden, — will perchance be all the sweeter and more palatable for the very difficulties it has had to contend with. Who knows but this chance wild fruit, planted by a cow or a bird on some remote and rocky hill side, where it is as yet unobserved by man, may be the choicest of all its kind, and foreign poten tates shall hear of it, and royal societies seek to propagate it, though the virtues of the perhaps truly crabbed owner of the soil may never be heard of,— at least, beyond the limits of his vil lage ? It was thus the Porter and the Baldwin grew.

Every wild-apple shrub excites our expectation thus, somewhat as every wild child. It is, per haps, a prince in disguise. What a lesson to man! So are human beings, referred to the highest standard, the celestial fruit which they suggest and aspire to bear, browsed on by fate; and only the most persistent and strongest gen ius defends itself and prevails, sends a tender scion upward at last, and drops its perfect fruit on the ungrateful earth. Poets arid philosophers and statesmen thus spring up in the country pastures, and outlast the hosts of unoriginal men.

Such is always the pursuit of knowledge. The celestial fruits, the golden apples of the Hesperides, are ever guarded by a hundred-

headed dragon which never sleeps, so that it is an Herculean labor to pluck them.

This is one, and the most remarkable way, in which the wild apple is propagated; but com monly it springs up at wide intervals in woods and swamps, and by the sides of roads, as the soil may suit it, and grows with comparative rapidity. Those which grow in dense woods are very tall and slender. I frequently pluck from these trees a perfectly mild and tamed fruit. As Palladius says, " Et injussu consterni-tur ubere mail ": And the ground is strewn with the fruit of an unbidden apple-tree.

It is an old notion, that, if these wild trees do not bear a valuable fruit of their own, they are the best stocks by which to transmit to posterity the most highly prized qualities of others. How ever, I am not in search of stocks, but the wild fruit itself, whose fierce gust has suffered no " inteneration." It is not my

" highest plot To plant the Bergamot."

THE FRUIT, AND ITS FLAVOR.

The time for wild apples is the last of Oc tober and the first of November. They then get to be palatable, for they ripen late, and they are still perhaps as beautiful as ever. I make a

great account of these fruits, which the farmers do not think it worth the while to gather,— wild flavors of the Muse, vivacious and inspiriting. The farmer thinks that he has better in his bar rels, but he is mistaken, unless he has a walker's appetite and imagination, neither of which can he have.

Such as grow quite wild, and are left out till the first of November, I presume that the owner does not mean to gather. They belong to chil dren as wild as themselves, — to certain active boys that I know, — to the wild-eyed woman of the fields, to whom nothing comes amiss, who gleans after all the world, — and, moreover, to us walkers. We have met with them, and they are ours. These rights, long enough insisted upon, have come to be an institution in some old countries, where they have learned how to live. I hear that " the custom of grippling, which may be called apple-gleaning, is, or was formerly, practised in Herefordshire. It consists in leaving a few apples, which are called the gripples, on every tree, after the general gather ing, for the boys, who go with climbing-poles and bags to collect them."

As for those I speak of, I pluck them as a
wild fruit, native to this quarter of the earth,—
fruit of old trees that have been dying ever since
I was a boy and are not yet dead, frequented
19
only by the woodpecker and the squirrel, deserted now by the owner, who has not faith enough to look under their boughs. From the appearance of the tree-top, at a little distance, you would expect nothing but lichens to drop from it, but your faith is rewarded by finding the ground strewn with spirited fruit, — some of it, perhaps, collected at squirrel-holes, with the marks of their teeth by which they carried them, — some containing a cricket or two silently feeding within, and some, especially in damp days, a shelless snail. The very sticks and stones lodged in the tree-top might have convinced you of the savoriness of the fruit which has been so eagerly sought after in past years.

I have seen no account of these among the " Fruits and Fruit-Trees of America," though they are more memorable to my taste than the grafted kinds; more racy and wild American flavors do they possess, when October and No vember, when December and January, and per haps February and March even, have assuaged them somewhat. An old farmer in my neigh borhood, who always selects the right word, says that " they have a kind of bow-arrow tang."

Apples for grafting appear to have been se lected commonly, not so much for their spirited flavor, as for their mildness, their size, and bear-
ing qualities, — not so much for their beauty, as for their fairness and soundness. Indeed, I have no faith in the selected lists of pomological gen tlemen. Their " Favorites " and " None-suches " and " Seek-no-farthers," when I have fruited them, commonly turn out very tame and forget-able. They are eaten with comparatively little zest, and have no real tang nor smack to them.

What if some of these wildings are acrid and puckery, genuine verjuice, do they not still be long to the Pomacece, which are uniformly inno cent and kind to our race ? I still begrudge them to the cider-mill. Perhaps they are not fairly ripe yet.

No wonder that these small and high-colored apples are thought to make the best cider. Lou-don quotes from the " Herefordshire Report," that " apples of a small size are always, if equal in quality, to be preferred to those of a larger size, in order that the rind and kernel may bear the greatest proportion to the pulp, which affords the weakest and most watery juice." And he says, that, " to prove this, Dr. Symonds, of Here ford, about the year 1800, made one hogshead of cider entirely from the rinds and cores of ap ples, and another from the pulp only, when the first was found of extraordinary strength and flavor, while the latter was sweet and insipid."

Evelyn says that the " Red-strake " was the
favorite cider-apple in his day; and he quotes one Dr. Newburg as saying, " In Jersey 't is a general observation, as I hear, that the more of red any apple has in its rind, the more proper it is for this use. Pale-faced apples they exclude as much as may be from their cider-vat." This opinion still prevails.

All apples are good in November. Those which the farmer leaves out as unsalable, and unpalatable to those who frequent the markets, are choicest fruit to the walker. But it is re-markable that the wild apple, which I praise as so spirited and racy when eaten in the fields or woods, being brought into the house, has fre quently a harsh and crabbed taste. The Saun-terer's Apple not even the saunterer can eat in the house. The palate rejects it there, as it does haws and acorns, and demands a tamed one; for there you miss the November air, which is the sauce it is to be eaten with. Accordingly, when Tityrus, seeing the lengthening shadows, invites Melibceus to go home and pass the night with him, he promises him mild apples and soft chest nuts,— mitia poma, castanece molles. I fre quently pluck wild apples of so rich and spicy a flavor that I wonder all orchardists do not get a scion from that tree, and I fail not to bring home my pockets full. But perchance, when I take one out of my desk and taste it in my chamber,

I find it unexpectedly crude, — sour enough to set a squirrel's teeth on edge and make a jay scream.

These apples have hung in the wind and frost and rain till they have absorbed the qualities of the weather or season, and thus are highly sea soned, and they pierce and sting and permeate us with their spirit. They must be eaten in season^ accordingly, — that is, out-of-doors.

To appreciate the wild and sharp flavors oi these October fruits, it is necessary that you be breathing the sharp October or November air. The out-door air and exercise which the walker gets give a different tone to his palate, and he craves a fruit which the sedentary would call harsh and crabbed. They must be eaten in the fields, when your system is all aglow with exer cise, when the frosty weather nips your fingers, the wind rattles the bare boughs or rustles the few remaining leaves, and the jay is heard screaming around. What is sour in the house a bracing walk makes sweet. Some of these apples might be labelled, " To be eaten in the wind."

Of course no flavors are thrown away; they are intended for the taste that is up to them. Some apples have two distinct flavors, and per haps one-half of them must be eaten in the house, the other out-doors. One Peter Whitney

wrote from Northborough in 1782, for the Pro ceedings of the Boston Academy, describing an apple-tree in that town " producing fruit of op posite qualities, part of the same apple being frequently sour and the other sweet;" also some all sour, and others all sweet, and this diversity on all parts of the tree.

There is a wild apple on Nawshawtuck Hill in my town which has to me a peculiarly pleasant bitter tang, not perceived till it is three-quarters tasted. It remains on the tongue. As you eat it, it smells exactly like a squash-bug. It is a sort of triumph to eat and relish it.

I hear that the fruit of a kind of plum-tree in Provence is " called Prunes sibarelles^ because it is impossible to whistle after having eaten them, from their sourness." But perhaps they were only eaten in the house and in summer, and if tried out-of-doors in a stinging atmosphere, who knows but you could whistle an octave higher and clearer ?

In the fields only are the sours and bitters of Nature appreciated; just as the wood-chopper eats his meal in a sunny glade, in the middle of a winter day, with content, basks in a sunny ray there and dreams of summer in a degree of cold which, experienced in a chamber, would make a student miserable. They who are at work abroad are not cold, but rather it is they who sit

shivering in houses. As with temperatures, so with flavors; as with cold and heat, so with sour and sweet. This natural raciness, the sours and bitters which the diseased palate refuses, are the true condiments.

Let your condiments be in the condition of your senses. To appreciate the flavor of these wild apples requires vigorous and healthy senses, papillce firm and erect on the tongue and palate, not easily flattened and tamed.

From my experience with wild apples, I can understand that there may be reason for a sav age's preferring many kinds of food which the civilized man rejects. The former has the palate of an out-door man. It takes a savage or wild taste to appreciate a wild fruit.

What a healthy out-of-door appetite it takes to relish the apple of life, the apple of the world, then !

" Nor is it every apple I desire,

Nor that which pleases every palate best; 'T is not the lasting Deuxan I require,

Nor yet the red-cheeked Greening I request, Nor that which first beshrewed the name of wife, Nor that whose beauty caused the golden strife : No, no! bring me an apple from the tree of life."

So there is one thought for the field, another for the house. I would have my thoughts, like wild apples, to be food for walkers, and will not war rant them to be palatable, if tasted in the house.

THEIR BEAUTY.

Almost all wild apples are handsome. They cannot be too gnarly and crabbed and rusty to look at. The gnarliest will have some redeem ing traits even to the eye. You will discover some evening redness dashed or sprinkled on some protuberance or in some cavity. It is rare that the summer lets an apple go without streak ing or spotting it on some part of its sphere. It will have some red stains, commemorating the mornings and evenings it has witnessed; some dark and rusty blotches, in memory of the clouds and foggy, mildewy days that have passed over it; and a spacious field of green reflecting the general face of Nature, — green even as the fields; or a yellow ground, which implies a milder flavor, — yellow as the harvest, or russet as the hills.

Apples, these I mean, unspeakably fair, — ap ples not of Discord, but of Concord! Yet not so rare but that the homeliest may have a share. Painted by the frosts, some a uniform clear bright yellow, or red, or crimson, as if their spheres had regularly revolved, and enjoyed the influence of the sun on all sides alike, — some with the faintest pink blush imaginable, — some brindled with deep red streaks like a cow, or with hundreds of fine blood-red rays running regularly from the stem-dimple to the blossom-

end, like meridional lines, on a straw-colored ground, — some touched with a greenish rust, like a fine lichen, here and there, with crimson blotches or eyes more or less confluent and fiery when wet, — and others gnarly, and freckled or peppered all over on the stem side with fine crimson spots on a white ground, as if accident ally sprinkled from the brush of Him who paints the autumn leaves. Others, again, are some times red inside, perfused with a beautiful blush, fairy food, too beautiful to eat, — apple of the Hesperides, apple of the evening sky! But like shells and pebbles on the sea-shore, they must be seen as they sparkle amid the withering leaves in some dell in the woods, in the autum nal air, or as they lie in the wet grass, and not when they have wilted and faded in the house.

THE NAMING OF THEM.

It would be a pleasant pastime to find suit able names for the hundred varieties which go to a single heap at the cider-mill. Would it not tax a man's invention, — no one to be named after a man, and all in the lingua vernacula? Who shall stand godfather at the christening of the wild apples ? It would exhaust the Latin and Greek languages, if they were used, and make the lingua vernacula flag. We should

have to call in the sunrise and the sunset, the rainbow and the autumn woods and the wild flowers, and the woodpecker and the purple finch and the squirrel and the jay and the but terfly, the November traveller and the truant boy, to our aid.

In 1836 there were in the garden of the Lon don Horticultural Society more than fourteen hundred distinct sorts. But here are species which they have not in their catalogue, not to mention the varieties which our Crab might yield to cultivation.

Let us enumerate a few of these. I find my self compelled, after all, to give the Latin names of some for the benefit of those who live where English is not spoken, — for they are likely to have a world-wide reputation.

There is, first of all, the Wood-Apple (Mains sylvatica) ; the Blue-Jay Apple; the Apple which grows in Dells in the Woods, (sylveslrivallis ,) also in Hollows in Pastures (campestrivallis) ; the Apple that grows in an old Cellar-Hole (Mains cellaris)\'7d the Meadow-Apple; the Par tridge-Apple ; the Truant's Apple, (Cessatoris,) which no boy will ever go by without knocking off some, however late it may be; the Saun-terer's Apple, — you must lose yourself before you can find the way to that; the Beauty of the Air (Decus Aeris) ; December-Eating; the

Frozen-Thawed (gelato-soluta)) good only in that state; the Concord Apple, possibly the same with the Masketaquidensis; the Assabet Apple; the Brindled Apple ; Wine of New England ; the Chickaree Apple ; the Green Apple (Malus viridis) ; — this has many synonymes ; in an imperfect state, it is the Cholera morbifera aut dysenteriferci) puendis dilectissima ; — the Apple which Atalanta stopped to pick up; the Hedge-Apple (Malus Sepiitm) ; the Slug-Apple (lima-cea) ; the Railroad-Apple, which perhaps came from a core thrown out of the cars; the Apple whose Fruit we tasted in our Youth ; our Par ticular Apple, not to be found in any catalogue, — Pedestrium Solatium; also the Apple where hangs the Forgotten Scythe ; Id ana's Apples, and the Apples which Loki found in the Wood; and a great many more I have on my list, too numerous to mention, — all of them good. As Bodaeus exclaims, referring to the cultivated kinds, and adapting Virgil to his case, so I, adapting Bodceus,—

" Not if I had a hundred tongues, a hundred mouths, An iron voice, could I describe all the forms And reckon up all the names of these wild apples."

THE LAST GLEANING.

By the middle of November the wild apples have lost some of their brilliancy, and have chiefly fallen. A great part are decayed on the

ground, and the sound ones are more palatable than before. The note of the chickadee sounds now more distinct, as you wander amid the old trees, and the autumnal dandelion is half-closed and tearful. But still, if you are a skilful gleaner, you may get many a pocket-full even of grafted fruit, long after apples are supposed to be gone out-of-doors. I know a Blue-Pear-main tree, growing within the edge of a swamp, almost as good as wild. You would not sup pose that there was any fruit left there, on the first survey, but you must look according to sys tem. Those which lie exposed are quite brown and rotten now, or perchance a few still show one blooming cheek here and there amid the wet leaves. Nevertheless, with experienced eyes, I explore amid the bare alders and the huckle berry-bushes and the withered sedge, and in the crevices of the rocks, which are full of leaves, and pry under the fallen and decaying ferns, which, with apple and alder leaves, thickly strew the ground. For I know that they lie concealed, fallen into hollows long since and covered up by the leaves of the tree itself, — a proper kind of packing. From these lurking-places, anywhere within the circumference of the tree, I draw forth the fruit, all wet and glossy, maybe nibbled by rabbits and hollowed out by crickets and per haps with a leaf or two cemented to it (as Curzon an old manuscript from a monastery's

mouldy cellar), but still with a rich bloom on it, and at least as ripe and well kept, if not better than those in barrels, more crisp and lively than they. If these resources fail to yield anything, I have learned to look between the bases of the suckers which spring thickly from some horizon tal limb, for now and then one lodges there, or in the very midst of an alder-clump, where they are covered by leaves, safe from cows which may have smelled them out. If I am sharp-set, for I do not refuse the Blue-Pearmain, I fill my pockets on each side; and as I retrace my steps in the frosty eve, being perhaps four or five miles from home, I eat one first from this side, and then from that, to keep my balance.

I learn from Topscll's Gesner, whose authority appears to be Albertus, that the following is the way in which the hedgehog collects and carries home his apples. He says, — " His meat is apples, worms, or grapes: when he findeth ap ples or grapes on the earth, he rolleth himself upon them, until he have filled all his prickles, and then carrieth them home to his den, never bearing above one in his mouth; and if it for tune that one of them fall off by the way, he likewise shaketh off all the residue, and wallow-eth upon them afresh, until they be all settled upon his back again. So, forth he goeth, making a noise like a cart-wheel; and if he have any young ones in his nest, they pull off his load wherewithal he is loaded, eating thereof what they please, and laying up the residue for the time to come."

THE " FROZEN-THAWED " APPLE.

Toward the end of November, though some of the sound ones are yet more mellow and perhaps more edible, they have generally, like the leaves, lost their beauty, and are beginning to freeze. It is finger-cold, and prudent farmers get in their barrelled apples, and bring you the apples and cider which they have engaged; for it is time to put them into the cellar. Perhaps a few on the ground show their red cheeks above the early snow, and occasionally some even preserve their color and soundness under the snow throughout the winter. But generally at the beginning of the winter they freeze hard, and soon, though undecayed, acquire the color of a baked apple.

Before the end of December, generally, they experience their first thawing. Those which a month ago were sour, crabbed, and quite un palatable to the civilized taste, such at least as were frozen while sound, let a warmer sun come to thaw them, for they are extremely sensitive to its rays, are found to be filled with a rich, sweet cider, better than any bottled cider that I know of, and with which I am better ac quainted than with wine. All apples are good in this state, and your jaws are the cider-press. Others, which have more substance, are a sweet and luscious food, — in my opinion of more worth than the pine-apples which are imported from the West Indies. Those which lately even I tasted only to repent of it, — for I am semi-civilized, — which the farmer willingly left on the tree, I am now glad to find have the prop erty of hanging on like the leaves of the young oaks. It is a way to keep cider sweet without boiling. Let the frost come to freeze them first, solid as stones, and then the rain or a warm winter day to thaw them, and they will seem to have borrowed a flavor from heaven through the medium of the air in which they hang. Or perchance you find, when you get home, that those which rattled in your pocket have thawed, and the ice is turned to cider. But after the third or fourth freezing and thawing they will not be found so good.

What are the imported half-ripe fruits of the torrid South, to this fruit matured by the cold of the frigid North ? These are those crabbed apples with which I cheated my companion, and kept a smooth face that I might tempt him to eat. Now we both greedily fill our pockets with them, — bending to drink the cup and save our lappets from the overflowing juice, — and grow more social with their wine. Was there one that hung so high and sheltered by the tangled branches that our sticks could not dis lodge it?

It is a fruit never carried to market, that I am aware of, — quite distinct from the apple of the markets, as from dried apple and cider, — and it is not every winter that produces it in perfection.

The era of the Wild Apple will soon be past. It is a fruit which will probably become extinct in New England. You may still wander through old orchards of native fruit of great extent, which for the most part went to the cider-mill, now all gone to decay. I have heard of an orchard in a distant town, on the side of a hill, where the apples rolled down and lay four feet deep against a wall on the lower side, and this the owner cut down for fear they should be made into cider. Since the temperance reform and the general introduction of grafted fruit, no native apple-trees, such as I see everywhere in deserted pastures, and where the woods have grown up around them, are set out. I fear that he who walks over these fields a century hence will not know the pleasure of knocking off

wild apples. Ah, poor man, there are many pleasures which he will not know! Notwith standing the prevalence of the Baldwin and the Porter, I doubt if so extensive orchards are set out to-day in my town as there were a century ago, when those vast straggling cider-orchards were planted, when men both ate and drank apples, when the pomace-heap was the only nursery, and trees cost nothing but the trouble of setting them out. Men could afford then to stick a tree by every wall-side and let it take its chance. I see nobody planting trees to-day in such out-of-the-way places, along the lonely roads and lanes, and at the bottom of dells in the wood. Now that they have grafted trees, and pay a price for them, they collect them into a plat by their houses, and fence them in, — and the end of it all will be that we shall be compelled to look for our apples in a barrel.

This is " The word of the Lord that came to Joel the son of Pethuel.

" Hear this, ye old men, and give ear, all ye inhabitants of the land! Hath this been in your days, or even in the days of your fathers ? . . . .

" That which the palmer-worm hath left hath the locust eaten ; and that which the locust hath left hath the canker-worm eaten; and that which

the canker-worm hath left hath the caterpillar eaten.

" Awake, ye drunkards, and weep! and howl, all ye drinkers of wine, because of the new wine ! for it is cut off from your mouth.

" For a nation is come up upon my land, strong, and without number, whose teeth are the teeth of a lion, and he hath the cheek-teeth of a great lion.

" He hath laid my vine waste, and barked my fig-tree; he hath made it clean bare, and cast it away; the branches thereof are made white

" Be ye ashamed, O ye husbandmen ! howl, O ye vine-dressers! . . . .

" The vine is dried up, and the fig-tree lan-guisheth ; the pomegranate-tree, the palm-tree also, and the apple-tree, even all the trees of the field, are withered : because joy is withered away from the sons of men."

NIGHT AND MOONLIGHT.

CHANCING to take a memorable walk by moon light some years ago, I resolved to take more such walks, and make acquaintance with an other side of nature : I have done so.

According to Pliny, there is a stone in Arabia called Selenites, " wherein is a white, which in creases and decreases with the moon." My journal for the last year or two, has been selen itic in this sense.

Is not the midnight like Central Africa to most of us ? Are we not tempted to explore it, — to penetrate to the shores of its lake Tchad, and discover the source of its Nile, perchance the Mountains of the Moon? Who knows what fertility and beauty, moral and natural, are there to be found? In the Mountains of the Moon, in the Central Africa of the night, there is where all Niles have their hidden heads. The expeditions up the Nile as yet extend but to the Cataracts, or perchance to the mouth of the White Nile; but it is the Black Nile that con cerns us.

I shall be a benefactor if I conquer some realms from the night, if I report to the gazettes anything transpiring about us at that season worthy of their attention,—if I can show men that there is some beauty awake while they are asleep, — if I add to the domains of poetry.

Night is certainly more novel and less profane than day. I soon discovered that I was ac quainted only with its complexion, and as for the moon, I had seen her only as it were through a crevice in a shutter, occasionally. Why not walk a little way in her light ?

Suppose you attend to the suggestions which the moon makes for one month, commonly in vain, will it not be very different from anything in literature or religion? But why not study this Sanscrit ? What if one moon has come and gone with its world of poetry, its weird teach ings, its oracular suggestions, — so divine a crea ture freighted with hints for me, and I have not used her ? One moon gone by unnoticed ?

I think it was Dr. Chalmers who said, criticis ing Coleridge, that for his part he wanted ideas which he could see all round, and not such as he must look at away up in the heavens. Such a man, one would say, would never look at the moon, because she never turns her other side to us. The light which comes from ideas which have their orbit as distant from the earth, and which is no less cheering and enlightening to the be-

nighted traveller than that of the moon and stars, is naturally reproached or nicknamed as moonshine by such. They are moonshine, are they ? Well, then do your night-travelling when there is no moon to light you; but I will be thankful for the light that reaches me from the star of least magnitude. Stars are lesser or greater only as they appear to us so. I will be thankful that I see so much as one side of a celestial idea, — one side of the rainbow, — and the sunset sky.

Men talk glibly enough about moonshine, as if they knew its qualities very well, and despised them; as owls might talk of sunshine. None of your sunshine, — but this word commonly means merely something which they do not un derstand,— which they are abed and asleep to, however much it may be worth their \vhile to be up and awake to it.

It must be allowed that the light of the moon, sufficient though it is for the pensive walker, and not disproportionate to the inner light we have, is very inferior in quality and intensity to that of the sun. But the moon is not to be judged alone by the quantity of light she sends to us, but also by her influence on the earth and its inhabitants. " The moon gravitates toward the earth, and the earth reciprocally toward the moon." The poet who walks by moonlight is

conscious of a tide in his thought which is to be referred to lunar influence. I will endeavor to separate the tide in my thoughts from the cur rent distractions of the day. I would warn my hearers that they must not try my thoughts by a daylight standard, but endeavor to realize that I speak out of the night, All depends on your point of view. In Drake's " Collection of Voy ages," Wafer says of some Albinoes among the Indians of Darien, u They are quite white, but their whiteness is like that of a horse, quite dif ferent from the fair or pale European, as they have not the least tincture of a blush or sanguine complexion. * * Their eyebrows are milk-white, as is likewise the hair of their heads, which is very fine. * * * They seldom go abroad in the daytime, the sun being disagree able to them, and causing their eyes, which are weak and poring, to water, especially if it shines towards them, yet they see very well by moon light, from which we call them moon-eyed."

Neither in our thoughts in these moonlight walks, methinks, is there " the least tincture of a blush or sanguine complexion," but we are in tellectually and morally Albinoes, — children of

Endymion,— such is the effect of conversing much with the moon.

I complain of Arctic voyagers that they do not enough remind us of the constant peculiar dreariness of the scenery, and the perpetual twi light of the Arctic night. So he whose theme is moonlight, though he may find it difficult, must, as it were, illustrate it with the light of the rnoon alone.

Many men walk by day; few walk by night. It is a very different season. Take a July night, for instance. About ten o'clock, — when man is asleep, and day fairly forgotten, — the beauty of moonlight is seen over lonely pastures where cattle are silently feeding. On all sides novel ties present themselves. Instead of the sun there are the moon and stars, instead of the wood-thrush there is the whip-poor-will, — in stead of butterflies in the meadows, fire-flies, winged sparks of fire! who would have believed it? What kind of cool deliberate life dwells in those dewy abodes associated with a spark of fire ? So man has fire in his eyes, or blood, or brain. Instead of singing birds, the half-throt tled note of a cuckoo flying over, the croaking of frogs, and the intenser dream of crickets. But above all, the wonderful trump of the bull-frog, ringing from Maine to Georgia. The potato-vines stand upright, the corn grows apace, the bushes loom, the grain-fields are boundless. On our open river terraces once cultivated by the Indian, they appear to occupy the ground like an army, — their heads nodding in the breeze.

Small trees and shrubs are seen in the midst, overwhelmed as by an inundation. The shadows of rocks and trees, and shrubs and hills, are more conspicuous than the objects themselves. The slightest irregularities in the ground are revealed by the shadows, and what the feet find com paratively smooth, appears rough and diversified in consequence. For the same reason the whole landscape is more variegated and picturesque than by day. The smallest recesses in the rocks are dim and cavernous; the ferns in the wood appear of tropical size. The sweet fern and in digo in overgrown wood-paths wet you with dew up to your middle. The leaves of the shrub-oak are shining as if a liquid were flowing over them. The pools seen through the trees are as full of light as the sky. " The light of the day takes refuge in their bosoms," as the Purana says of the ocean. All white objects are more remark able than by day. A distant cliff looks like a phosphorescent space on a hillside. The woods are heavy and dark. Nature slumbers. You see the moonlight reflected from particular stumps in the recesses of the forest, as if she se lected what to shine on. These small fractions of her light remind one of the plant called moon-seed,— as if the moon were sowing it in such places.

In the night the eyes are partly closed or retire into the head. Other senses take the lead. The walker is guided as well by the sense of smell. Every plant and field and forest emits its odor now, swamp-pink in the meadow and tansy in the road; and there is the peculiar dry scent of corn which has begun to show its tassels. The senses both of hearing and smelling are more alert. We hear the tinkling of rills which we never detected before. From time to time, high up on the sides of hills, you pass through a stratum of warm air. A blast which has come up from the sultry plains of noon. It tells of the day, of sunny noon-tide hours and banks, of the laborer wiping his brow and the bee hum ming amid flowers. It is an air in which work has been done, — which men have breathed. It circulates about from wood-side to hill-side like a dog that has lost its master, now that the sun is gone. The rocks retain all night the warmth of the sun which they have absorbed. And so does the sand. If you dig a few inches into it you find a warm bed. You lie on your back on a rock in a pasture on the top of some bare hill at midnight, and speculate on the height of the starry canopy. The stars are the jewels of the night, and perchance surpass anything which day has to show. A companion with whom I was sailing one very windy but bright moon light night, when the stars were few and faint,

thought that a man could get along with them, — though he was considerably reduced in his circumstances, — that they were a kind of bread and cheese that never failed.

No wonder that there have been astrologers, that some have conceived that they were personally related to particular stars. Dubartas, as translated by Sylvester, says he'll

" not believe that the great architect With all these fires the heavenly arches decked Only for show, and with these glistering shields, T" awake poor shepherds, watching in the fields." He'll " not believe that the least flower which pranks Our garden borders, or our common banks, And the least stone, that in her warming lap Our mother earth doth covetously wrap, Hath some peculiar virtue of its own, And that the glorious stars of heav'n have none."

And Sir Walter Raleigh well says, " the stars are instruments of far greater use, than to give an obscure light, and for men to gaze on after sunset;" and he quotes Plotinus as affirming that they " are significant, but not efficient;" and also Augustine as saying, " Deus regit in-feriora corpora per superiora: " God rules the bodies below by those above. But best of all is this which another writer has expressed: " Sa piens adjuvabit opus astrorum quemadmodum ag~ ricola terrce naturam: " a wise man assisteth

the work of the stars as the husbandman help-eth the nature of the soil.

It does not concern men who are asleep in their beds, but it is very important to the traveller, whether the moon shines brightly or is obscured. It is not easy to realize the serene joy of all the earth, when she commences to shine unobstructedly, unless you have often been abroad alone in moonlight nights. She seems to be waging continual war with the clouds in your behalf. Yet we fancy the clouds to be her foes also. She comes on magnifying her dan gers by her light, revealing, displaying them in all their hugeness and blackness, then suddenly casts them behind into the light concealed, and goes her way triumphant through a small space of clear sky.

In short, the moon traversing, or appearing to traverse, the small clouds which lie in her way, now obscured by them, now easily dissipating and shining through them, makes the drama of the moonlight night to all watchers and night-travellers. Sailors speak of it as the moon eat ing up the clouds. The traveller all alone, the moon all alone, except for his sympathy, over coming with incessant victory whole squadrons of clouds above the forests and lakes and hills. When she is obscured he so sympathizes with her that he could whip a dog for her relief, as

Indians do. When she enters on a clear field of great extent in the heavens, and shines unob-structedly, he is glad. And when she has fought her way through all the squadron of her foes, and rides majestic in a clear sky unscathed, and there are no more any obstructions in her path, he cheerfully and confidently pursues his way, and rejoices in his heart, and the cricket also seems to express joy in its song.

How insupportable would be the days, if the night with its dews and darkness did not come to restore the drooping world. As the shades begin to gather around us, our primeval instincts are aroused, and we steal forth from our lairs, like the inhabitants of the jungle, in search of those silent and brooding thoughts which are the natural prey of the intellect.

Richter says that " The earth is every day overspread with the veil of night for the same reason as the cages of birds are darkened, viz: that we may the more readily apprehend the higher harmonies of thought in the hush and quiet of darkness. Thoughts which day turns into smoke and mist, stand about us in the night as light and flames; even as the column which fluctuates above the crater of Vesuvius, in the daytime appears a pillar of cloud, but by night a pillar of fire."

There are nights in this climate of such serene and majestic beauty, so medicinal and fer tilizing to the spirit, that methinks a sensitive nature would not devote them to oblivion, and perhaps there is no man but would be better and wiser for spending them out of doors, though he should sleep all the next day to pay for it; should sleep an Endymion sleep, as the ancients expressed it, — nights which warrant the Grecian epithet ambrosial, when, as in the land of Beu-lah, the atmosphere is charged with dewy fra grance, and with music, and we take our repose and have our dreams awake, — when the moon, not secondary to the sun,

"gives us bis blaze again, Void of its flame, and sheds a softer day. Now through the passing cloud she seems to stoop, Now up the pure cerulean rides sublime."

Diana still hunts in the New England sky.

" In Heaven queen she is among the spheres.

She, mistress-like, makes all things to be pure. Eternity in her oft change she bears; She Beauty is; by her the fair endure.

Time wears her not; she doth his chariot guide;

Mortality below her orb is placed ; By her the virtues of the stars down slide;

By her is Virtue's perfect image cast."

The Hindoos compare the moon to a saintly being who has reached the last stage of bodily existence.

Great restorer of antiquity, great enchanter. In a mild night, when the harvest or hunter's moon shines unobstructedly, the houses in our village, whatever architect they may have had by day, acknowledge only a master. The village street is then as wild as the forest. New and old things are confounded. I know not whether I am sitting on the ruins of a wall, or on the ma terial which is to compose a new one. Nature is an instructed and impartial teacher, spreading no crude opinions, and flattering none ; she will be neither radical nor conservative. Consider the moonlight, so civil, yet so savage!

The light is more proportionate to our knowl edge than that of day. It is no more dusky in ordinary nights, than our mind's habitual atmos phere, and the moonlight is as bright as our most illuminated moments are.

" In such a night let me abroad remain Till morning breaks, and all's confused again."

Of what significance the light of day, if it is not the reflection of an inward dawn? —to what purpose is the veil of night withdrawn, if the morning reveals nothing to the soul ? It is merely garish and glaring.

When Ossian in his address to the sun ex claims,

" Where has darkness its dwelling ? Where is the cavernous home of the stars,

When thou quickly followest their steps, Pursuing them like a hunter in the sky, — Thou climbing the lofty hills, They descending on barren mountains ? "

who does not in his thought accompany the stars to their " cavernous home," " descending " with them " on barren mountains ? "

Nevertheless, even by night the sky is blue and not black, for we see through the shadow of the earth into the distant atmosphere of day, where the sunbeams are revelling.

THE END.

Printed in Dunstable, United Kingdom